A long-hidden force stirs in the heart of the Utah desert, and a killer sets out on a path to power and vengeance, leaving a trail of bodies in their wake.

Gene Bradshaw and Jack Cartwright, newly partnered detectives, are called to a gruesome murder scene, and neither knows what to make of it. The mutilated body is so unidentifiable it'd be easy to call it an animal attack, but neither detective buys such a simple explanation. While Gene relies on his gut that something more sinister is afoot, Jack knows the killer isn't an animal, and it's certainly not a human.

To catch the murderer, Jack and Gene must set their differences aside and learn to work together. But the closer they become, the more the lines blur between personal and professional. When the case takes an unexpected turn, Gene learns there's more to his partner's world than he ever imagined, and he has to dive headfirst into it, whether he's ready or not.

Set against the deep, desolate canyons and the endless landscape of Southern Utah, *Through Smoke and Shadows* weaves a twisting tale of the evil that lurks down dark alleys, in our closets, and even in plain sight.

THROUGH SMOKE

AND SHADOWS

Beyond a Shadow, Book One

L. Alyse Amidon

A NineStar Press Publication
www.ninestarpress.com

Through Smoke and Shadows

First Edition, April 2025

ISBN: 978-1-64890-858-3

Also available in eBook, ISBN: 978-1-64890-857-6

CONTENT WARNING:

This book contains graphic depiction of a human autopsy, beheading, eye gouging, a gun and knife fight, graphic violence/gore in an epic on-page battle, use of guns/gun violence, murder, smoking, strong language, torture. Warnings also for depiction of: a cult, death, death of a family member (minor character), transphobia (mention or/allusion to).

For Jacob, my best friend and the best big brother a girl could have.

Prologue

LITTLE COTTONWOOD CANYON
About six miles west of Solitude Mountain Resort

"Y‍ou got demons inside you, *girl.*" His sweet, sickly Southern drawl made my skin itch.

Real original, I thought, turning my head to spit blood on the floor.

"Someone ought to help you with that."

The man was older than others I'd met, maybe forty-five and tall, with a somewhat portly build to him. It was embarrassing to admit, but I'd dismissed him earlier, thought him harmless. Now, chained to a chair, beaten and torn, I was paying for that mistake. But I wasn't too worried.

He walked over to the far corner of the...barn? Was that where we were? It had to be something akin to a barn, with its high ceilings, unfinished floors, and walls made of wood. It didn't smell like animals, though, so perhaps it was an outbuilding.

"Been tracking you for a while," he said as he pulled out a knife, the blade catching the small bit of moonlight seeping in through the cracks in the roof. "Never thought I'd catch you."

"First mistake was underestimating yourself."

The man's eyes narrowed as he approached. "More like I was *over-estimating* you."

He smiled a cruel smile before sticking the blade into my stomach. I'd be lying if I said it didn't hurt, but it wasn't *that* bad. I'd probably had worse menstrual pains if I were being honest.

The coppery taste of blood filled my mouth yet again, and I returned his smile with my own. I squirmed forward as best I could, considering my bindings, and pulled the blade further into my gut.

"You really think I got *demons inside me*?" I asked. "You think a *knife's* gonna do anything?" I laughed.

The man's face turned from haughty to frustrated in an instant, and he twisted the knife, causing blood to rise in my throat. I didn't stop laughing, though, and it sounded as if I was gurgling mouthwash. Blood dribbled down my chin.

With a huff, the man pulled the blade out abruptly and stalked over to his corner, where he rifled through his bag of toys. I went limp and opened my mouth, letting gravity pull the blood from it, watching as it ebbed out of me ever so slowly. I wasn't sure how long the man stayed in his corner, but sooner than I would have liked, his shoes came into view before the pool of blood.

The hilt of a different knife, a larger one, pushed my chin up so that I was forced to meet his gaze, and I noticed he was older than I thought. His *eyes*...they held so much more light than I realized.

"You think you're so clever, don't you? You think you can go around doing whatever you want, huh? You can't."

The edge of my mouth quirked up on instinct. "I beg to differ."

A hint of challenge gleamed in his eyes.

In the next instant, his free hand gripped my hair in a tight hold while the other flipped the knife around and used it to slice my throat from end to end.

Now, that one? That one hurt. A lot. And a considerable amount of blood was added to the little pool I had going.

For a beat, neither of us breathed.

When he released his hold, I let my head and body fall limp. He stumbled back, his breathing labored—the sounds of a man who had completed some long-awaited task. I gave him time to get a hold of himself. When he started cleaning up his mess, I made my move. He came over to unchain my body, and I snapped the chains around my wrists, lifting my gaze to meet his.

Fear filled his eyes as I took hold of his lapels. I pulled him in close.

"I told you the knife wasn't going to work."

I shoved him to the ground, and he grunted on impact, rolling over to his front and then trying to push himself up.

I stood, and the rest of the chains slid down my body. I picked up a broken piece, wrapped it around his neck, and pulled him upright. His hands shot to his throat, desperately clawing at it to pull the chain away from his skin.

"What? You thought that's all it would take?" I *tsk*ed. "You should have known better."

He elbowed me in the ribs, but I just tightened my grip. His mouth agape, he tried to suck air into his lungs, though his efforts were futile. As his face drained of color and his eyes rolled up into his head, I released him, shoving him away.

He gasped for breath on all fours. I kicked him over onto his back, and he stared up at me in fear. I stood over him and imagined how I must appear to him. A tall, pale woman with bruises he'd inflicted littering her skin, fresh knife wounds on her neck and stomach. Blood draining out of her. I gave him a wicked smile.

"For the record, there are no demons inside me."

His eyes grew wide as I lunged for his throat.

Chapter One

Jack Cartwright sighed as he attempted to light a cigarette. The harsh wind nipped at his bare fingers. If this took much longer, he'd lose them to frostbite. If he could just get the *damn* lighter to—

"Whoa, whoa, what are you doing? You can't smoke here!"

Jack remained focused on the task at hand. "We're outside, aren't we?" he asked around the cigarette in his mouth.

"It's a *crime scene*. Come on, man."

Jack huffed and finally gave up on the lighter, shoving both it and the cigarette into his pocket. "Fine. What do we got?"

His partner, Gene, turned to face the scene before them. *He* was more prepared for the cold weather this morning in his gray wool coat, his broad shoulders stretching it taut across his shoulders. "Looks like… Honestly, I'm not sure what the hell it looks like. Probably a male victim, but it's hard to tell…"

Jack studied the scene. It certainly wasn't pretty—a pair of hands, legs from about the knee down, and what little else of the body remained appeared as if it had gone through a meat grinder. The hands and legs, completely dried out, seemed almost mummified, with no flesh beneath the skin.

"Signs of a struggle over there." Gene gestured to a patch of dirt a few feet away from the body.

To Jack, that was all it was: dirt. "Again, not much that's particularly telling of what happened though."

"Animal attack?"

"Possibly. But we haven't recovered any hair or found any evidence of bite marks on the body, so…" Gene shook his head. "I got the forensics guys going over everything, and we're setting up a grid search of the area to see if we can find something."

Jack grunted an affirmative as he walked around the body. It was hard to tell if it was a man or a woman. There were no remnants of clothes or jewelry or anything. He squatted low next to the body to examine it more closely, but it wasn't helpful.

Grimacing, Jack stood and circled around to Gene. "All right, then. I'm gonna head to the office." He clapped Gene on the shoulder.

"You're leaving?"

"Is there a reason for me to stay? We caught a body in the middle of nowhere, probably an animal attack. We got no ID, no evidence, nothing. This is the forensics guys' playground, and supervising them is a one-man job, last I checked." He pulled the cigarette out of his pocket and put it between his lips. "Holler if you need me." With that, he was gone.

Gene called out, as he crossed the yellow tape, "You should quit smoking. Might make you less of an asshole." The last bit was quieter, muttered, but Jack caught it and smiled.

*

The dark house seemed empty. Jack peered in through the windows. No sign of life. He tried the handle at the front door—no luck, so he retraced his steps, rounded the corner of the house, and went through the fence to the backyard. Across the way, another gate stood ajar, his sister just beyond it. She turned at the sound of his gate creaking open. Her pale green eyes—identical to Jack's—met his, and a frown dotted her brow.

As he crossed the yard, her dog, a black-and-white Pit-lab mix, bounded up to him, tail wagging. He bent to greet her and was immediately attacked with a slobbery tongue. He couldn't help but laugh.

"What are you doing here?" Maggie said above them.

Jack gave the dog another pat on the head and straightened up. "Front door was locked."

The dog ran toward the deck, and Maggie silently followed her.

Jack tagged after them. The door led into the kitchen on his right and the living room on his left. The house seemed well-lived in. Mail littered the bar, clean and dirty dishes sat on the counters, books lay scattered on the coffee table, and used blankets covered the couch.

Maggie busied herself, removing her coat and giving the dog water and a treat.

"Want something to drink?" she asked. "Eat? Anything?"

"I'm good."

Maggie finally settled, placing one hand on the corner of the counter and the other on her hip, her gaze wide and piercing. "Why are you here?"

"I can't come for a visit?"

"Is that why you're here?"

Jack stayed silent.

Maggie crossed her arms, standing a little straighter. "Exactly. So let's cut through the bullshit and get right to it. Why are you here?"

"I need your help."

"This about the body they found down in Moab?"

"You heard about that?"

She eyed him as if to say, *Of course.* "Sorry, but I can't help you. I'm out of the business. Have been for a while."

Jack scoffed.

"It's true. Look around, Jack!" She gestured around her. "I have a house and a husband...somewhere. He's on a business trip. Point is—*I'm out.* Completely. I don't want anything to do with that world any more. I want to live my nice, boring, *simple* life and enjoy it. So if that's the only reason you came by, honestly, you should go."

"Oh, come on, Mags. You're not the least bit curious? You wouldn't *believe*—"

"No, don't." She held up a hand. "I don't want anything to do with it. Please."

Jack deflated. "Fine. Can I at least have some of your contacts? You know I've been...out of touch for a while."

This time, it was she who scoffed. "That's what you get for going behind the blue line."

Despite her words, she walked to another corner of the house, leading him into a spare room with a small desk. She rifled through the drawers, searching for something. "I can give you some names, but I don't think they'll talk to you."

"Maybe you could call them and let them know they can trust me?"

Keeping her eyes down, she said deadpan, "Not sure I *can* say that."

"Mags, I'm begging you. Please. This body—it was like nothing I've ever seen—like *ground meat*. No evidence of hair or saliva or *anything*. It's—" He took a breath. "—unbelievable."

Maggie paused, and he knew he'd gotten her interest. He thought she'd ask a question, try to learn more, but she seemed to snap herself out of it and refocused on the desk.

Finally, she pulled out a small, beat-up journal. "Ah. Here it is."

She flipped it open and swiped a sticky note from the desk to scribble down a few names and numbers. When she finished, she held it out to him.

"Here. Dana *may* return your call. They at least knew you before you...you know."

Jack accepted the note. "You have to admit becoming a cop made things *a lot* easier on us, and—"

"Yeah, it seems great. And I'm sure your partner is *loads* of help on these types of cases. That's why you're here, right?"

"Come on, that's not fair."

Maggie held up her hands. "I don't want to have this fight again. Take the names and go."

Jack swallowed the rest of his argument and turned to leave—out the front door this time—then paused and faced her again. "I'm surprised you got out. I know in recent years, you and I had different ways of going about this, but I thought we shared the same *reason* for doing it."

"Right, and what is that?"

"Remember all those hours we spent pouring over the family journals? Basically, sacrificing any semblance of a normal life because…well, we had to know more."

He took a step closer to her. "Remember our first hunt? We were, what, fourteen? We snuck out and stole the car, drove it all the way down to Provo Canyon. Mom 'bout killed us, but it was worth it, wasn't it? We had to know—to see it through ourselves for once. It's that *thirst* for knowledge, for finding out the truth, even if it lies outside of what so many think to be reality. What we do, it's bigger than us. It's important."

She was quiet, obviously thinking up some response, her eyes showing her working through some invisible speech inside her head. When she'd sorted through it, they gleamed with a sense of loftiness.

"The truth isn't always worth sacrificing yourself for. No matter how intriguing it is." She gave him a small smile and gestured to the door, gently ushering him out. "Take it from your elder."

"You're, like, *twenty minutes* older than me."

"Only word I heard was *older.*"

Jack laughed as he pulled the front door open. "Whatever. I'll see you later."

"See ya."

He stood at the top of the front steps after the door closed, smiling and shaking his head, before jogging down them and heading to the office.

Chapter Two

Gene Bradshaw was not amused. He'd only been partnered with Jack for six months, and he did not like that this behavior was becoming typical of him. Jack was a good detective, but he wasn't necessarily a good cop. He didn't seem dirty or anything, but Gene had heard stories: Jack skipping out on work early, going solo on cases, being a pain in the ass for a partner...

And as Gene stood outside in the freezing cold, "supervising" the forensics team, he genuinely hated his partner. He was the only one who would work with Jack, though, and that only made Gene feel sorry for him. In truth, it wasn't as if the captain had forced Jack onto Gene. Quite the opposite. Gene had specifically requested him.

He remembered the first time he'd met Jack and seen him in action. The Major Crimes teams had been called to a double homicide in West Valley, and while Daniels, Jack's then partner, bickered with the local police, Jack had found the murder weapon stashed in a pet waste disposal bin. Gene had walked up to the scene, where Jack was shoulder-deep in literal shit, and felt sorry for Daniels. However, minutes later, Jack had emerged with a 9 mm Glock 17 that matched the casings nearby, his green eyes glinting with satisfaction, and Gene knew he'd misjudged him. He'd also thought Daniels had been exaggerating about him as he tended to do. Now, he wasn't so sure.

"Hey!" Gene yelled at a rookie about to kick an evidence marker. "Watch where you step!"

The rookie's face reddened. "Sorry, Sergeant."

"You should be out on the grid search, not fucking up my crime scene. Get."

The rookie didn't need to be told twice and scurried away to join the search of the surrounding area.

Gene refocused on the scene before him. He wasn't very confident the search would find anything. It was pretty likely this would turn out to be an animal attack, all things considered. If he were honest with himself, though, his instincts told him this wasn't an animal. Which made his head spin. The idea that a *person* could do this…didn't sit right with him.

He pulled out his notebook and circled the remains for what felt like the millionth time that day, scribbling down anything and everything that might be a clue. He was nothing if not thorough. *Body has faint scent around it, maybe lavender? (a perfume? deodorant?). Fingers mostly intact, finger pads gone—purposeful? (ask ME). Where is the head? Why are legs mostly intact? Interrupted?*

"Sarge?"

Gene tore his eyes away and lifted his gaze to the detective leading the grid search.

"We found something."

*

Gene finally made it to the office in Salt Lake as the sun tucked itself behind the mountains. As he trudged to his desk, most of the other detectives were heading home. Jack's desk sat empty.

"Hey," Gene said, stopping one of his colleagues, "you seen Cartwright?"

"Uh, no, haven't seen him all day."

Gene cursed under his breath. *Dammit, Cartwright.* He waved his colleague on and plopped into his chair. He opened the case file and started going over everything they had so far. It wasn't much, but anything would be good enough to distract him from his growing annoyance with his partner.

They'd found an abandoned vehicle in a ditch about eight miles west of the crime scene—a 2007 Dodge Ram. It didn't seem as if it had been there long, but it had no plates, and the inside had been wiped down. There was nothing explicitly tying it to the body they found, but they made note of it all the same. *And who knows, maybe it'll break the case.* Trying to lean into his optimism, Gene started sifting through reports of stolen cars.

About an hour passed, and Gene's neck had grown stiff. He stretched his hands up, interlocking his fingers and reaching. He tilted his head side to side, cracked his neck, then dropped his arms and rolled his shoulders. In this momentary pause, he heard laughter from the breakroom. He glanced over his shoulder at none other than Jack fucking Cartwright cutting it up with another detective. Gene pushed himself out of his chair and charged up to him.

"Hey, what the hell?"

Jack leaned against the counter, his hands on either side of his lean hips, a lazy, devil-may-care smile on his face. Gene tried not to let it affect him. No matter how good the smile looked on him, he still wanted to punch him.

"It took me four hours to drive from Moab to Salt Lake, and I got here—" Gene checked his watch. "—*an hour and a half* ago. You left at least three hours before I did. How the *hell* did I beat you to the office?"

The other detective, a member of the Alcohol Enforcement Division, pressed her lips together and made a hasty exit from the room. Gene put his hands on his hips and stared at Jack expectantly. He stood a few inches taller than his partner and, at times like this, felt like a parent scolding a child.

Jack folded his arms across his chest and his left leg over his right. "I made a pit stop. Had to take care of something."

Gene resisted the urge to close the distance between them and wrap his hands around this man's neck. "Listen, I know you've got some weird bad-boy vibe going for you, but—"

"You think I'm a bad boy?" Jack asked, an amused glint in his eyes.

"*But* some of us are trying to work here."

Jack raised his hands in surrender. "Sorry...I thought we were working a case with no evidence, so..."

Gene sagged against the counter next to his partner, their biceps a hair's width apart, making his skin flush with goosebumps. He ran a hand over his face and shifted away from Jack slightly. "You're impossible."

"*Hmm.* And yet you're stuck with me." Jack laughed. "Did you find anything on the grid search?"

"Yes and no. We found an abandoned truck eight miles away. No plates, no prints...and no connection to the case." He let out a groan of frustration. "You're right. We're working a case with no evidence."

Jack patted him on the shoulder, giving it a small squeeze before dropping his hand. "Eh, we'll crack it." With that, his partner walked toward his desk.

Gene watched him go. *Yeah, we'll see.*

*

Leaving Gene sulking in the break area, Jack pulled out his sister's sticky note and dialed Dana's number. It had been a while since he'd talked to them, and against his best wishes, his palms began to sweat in anticipation. *Jeez, what am I, a teenager?*

The phone rang and rang, eventually going to voicemail. *Hey you've reached D.M. Can't come to the phone right now. If this is some fucked up shit, you know who to call. Otherwise, leave a message, and I'll get back to you...BEEP.*

"Uh, hey, Dee, it's Jack Cartwright. Um, give me a call when you have a sec. Maggie said you might be able to help me out with something...uh, yeah. Okay, talk to you later." He winced as he ended the call and relaxed into his chair, rocking a little before pulling himself closer to his desk. It was time to work.

Eventually, Gene rejoined him, and they worked in silence for a while until something needling at Jack couldn't be ignored anymore. He turned to face his partner.

"Hey," Jack said. "What are you thinking? Like, about this case?"

Gene took a deep breath and tilted his head from side to side. "I don't know...it's hard to say."

Jack leaned forward, resting his elbows on his knees. "But what does your gut say?" He paused, giving his partner a scrutinizing once-over. "Animal attack?"

"Honestly?" He looked up at the ceiling as if he couldn't believe he was about to say it. "I don't think so. I've seen animal attacks. I worked as a park ranger a while ago in Bryce and remember finding bodies after they'd been eaten on by wolves and birds, but *this*? This is a new one for me."

Jack hummed an agreement. "You've never had a weird case?"

"Sure, who hasn't? Weirdest body I saw before today was when I first joined the Bureau, and we were called in on this string of murders. There were a couple in Provo and Salt Lake, so, you know, jurisdiction fell to us. And I remember the victim... Her throat had been ripped out, but it was cleaner than an animal attack. And almost *all* the blood had been drained from each person. I was only a rookie, so I didn't work the cases. I mostly handled crowd control and stuff." He closed his eyes. "I'll never forget it though. It was gruesome."

"I think I remember reading about that. It was, what, almost ten years ago?"

"Uh, yeah...good memory."

Jack flashed back to Maggie staking a vampire above him, its eyes going wide, a screech piercing the cool night air. *Gotta be more careful, Jackie*, she'd said to him.

That's what you're here for, he'd said with a smile as she helped him up.

Jack cleared his throat. "Yeah...the killer was never caught, right?"

"Nope. Stopped killing though."

What a coincidence. "So you think a person could do what we saw this morning?"

"I don't want to believe it, but...we don't know enough yet to say anything definitive, so." He regarded him in a manner that said *so what else is there to do*? and turned to his computer.

This wasn't an animal. Jack had been at this long enough to know when it was something else. He was a little impressed Gene had the same intuition, but it wasn't human, whatever killed this person. It was something else entirely.

And for the first time in his life, he had no idea what it could be.

Chapter Three

It took until the next day for the medical examiner to call and tell them he hadn't found much. Jack and Gene were the only ones left in the office, and Gene put the ME on speaker.

"Nothing?" Gene asked. "You can't even tell me who it is that's dead?"

Jack moved over to Gene's desk and sat on the corner.

"If I had identified the person lying on my autopsy table, I would have led with that."

"What about fingerprints?" Jack asked.

"Yeah, can you tell how they were removed?" Gene chimed in.

"Now, that appeared to have been done surgically, not with the skill level of a trained medical officer, but purposefully nonetheless."

This news seemed to excite Gene. He sat up a little straighter and scooted his chair half an inch toward his desk as if moving closer to the phone would get him answers quicker. "So that rules out animal attack, right?"

"Well..." The doctor's tone sounded skeptical. "I can't tell how long ago the procedure occurred. There's enough scarring to indicate that whenever the victim's fingertips were removed, they were alive when it happened. They may have done it themselves for all I know. Maybe they're a criminal." Jack could practically hear the doctor shrug. "That's for you to find out."

Jack could see the frustration growing in Gene, and he stepped in before he could say something to piss this guy off. "Hey, well, thanks. If you could send a copy of the autopsy report over to us, that'd be great. We'll call you if we have any more questions."

"Sure, no problem. Good luck with this one," the doctor said and ended the call.

Gene leaned back and covered his face with his hands. "You've gotta be kidding me," he muttered.

As their computers each *dinged* with an email notification, Gene sat up and opened it. Jack thought about offering some encouraging advice, but truth be told, he didn't have any, so he pressed his lips together and retreated to his desk, eager to read the ME report.

As they'd found at the scene, there was no evidence of animal activity on the body. Now that he thought about it, that, in and of itself, was pretty odd. Gene had said it himself earlier, "bodies that had been eaten on by animals." In the middle of the desert, how likely was it that a body would be found by people before it was found by bobcats or vultures?

Jack pulled out his notebook and scribbled it down, something for him to follow up on later. He flipped through the autopsy photos and then checked the ones taken at the crime scene. Gene had pointed out a patch of dirt to him that morning and said it looked like "signs of a struggle." He found that same patch photographed with an evidence marker next to it. It was still just dirt to Jack, but something struck him about the picture—about *all* the pictures. For all the trauma the body had been put through, there was no blood around it, suggesting it had been moved.

At that realization, Jack spun around and yelled, "The body was *moved*, Gene!"

Gene jumped and turned slowly to face him. "Well—"

Jack was up now, pacing between their desks. *A monster* moved *the body? That never happens. What the hell is going on*?

"The body was moved," he repeated. "There's no way a crime scene with remains this destroyed would have no blood around it. It was moved. They were killed somewhere else."

Gene tried interjecting again, "Yeah, I mean—" but Jack was only half listening.

"What if the—the shredding? I guess that's the best way to phrase it—what if that happened *after* our victim was killed? What if they were killed somewhere else, moved, and *then* the killer did that to them? Blood wouldn't flow the same way if they were alive."

"No, it wouldn't. But I'm trying to tell you, we know—"

Jack's ringtone cut him off. He pulled out his cell and picked up when he saw Maggie's name flashing on his screen. "Hey, why are you—"

"You just *had* to tell me what the body looked like, didn't you? You couldn't let me go live my boring life, could you?"

A wide grin spread across Jack's face. "So you're interested?"

"Yes," she groaned. "Yes, I'm fucking interested. And I spoke with Dana. They tried calling you back, by the way."

Jack checked and saw a missed call from a few hours ago. "Shit, my phone has been on silent."

"Well, turns out they worked a similar case in Kansas City a few years back."

"Wait, seriously? Do they know—"

"Nope. No idea. They worked it for a few weeks. All their leads were dead ends, and they eventually moved on. I reached out to a couple other people, and there was another one in Ohio six years ago."

Jack pressed the phone between his ear and shoulder and swiped his notepad. "What city?"

"Some town about an hour from Toledo called Bryan."

He scribbled it down. "I'll try to get some info on that. So are we doing this? Are you in?"

Maggie was quiet on the other end of the phone, and then, "You know I hate you, right?" She said it without much heat, making him smile. "Ugh. Fine. I'm in. Do you have the autopsy yet?"

"Yes. Do you want me to—"

"Of course, send it to me now. I'll skim through Granddaddy's journal. I think I have Mom's around here somewhere too."

"Oh, I have hers. I can come by in about—" He checked the clock on his computer. "I can probably make it to you by eleven thirty? Is that..." It was pretty late.

"Good. Bring Mom's journal. And send me that autopsy." With that, the line went dead.

Jack stuffed his phone in his pocket. "Sorry, Gene, but I've got to go," he said as he quickly forwarded the autopsy to his sister's secure email account. After it was sent, he pulled his coat from the back of his chair and slipped it on. When he turned to face Gene, he found him with his hands and arms spread in a *what the hell* gesture.

"We were in the middle of a conversation!"

Shit, we were. "Uh, yeah, yeah, sorry. My sister called. Family emergency."

He waited, allowing Gene some time to challenge the excuse, but he didn't, so Jack grabbed his keys and headed for the door. "I'll call you!" he yelled over his shoulder, leaving a dumbfounded Gene staring after him.

Chapter Four

Hunting Journal
October 3

Day 6—new case. The short of it is, a woman was killed in her house. Driver's license says her name is Shelly O'Donnel. Pretty brutal scene, victim had scratch marks all along her arms and legs. At first, it seemed to be a normal murder, but during the autopsy, the ME found a long black nail embedded in one of the wounds on her left arm. He wasn't able to identify it, but I could. Ran a couple of tests (Maggie was always better at this part than me) and found abnormally high levels of sulfur. Thought it might be a Were, maybe a goblin or a ghoul, but since the victim was killed inside her house, it seems unlikely. Not sure what else it could be. I'll figure it out. I always do. I'll have to evade my new partner. He's a little over-eager, always breathing down my neck. Probably have to ditch work to get him off my back, which won't win me any awards, but what the hell, who cares?

Jack wasn't exactly sure how he'd gotten here—or rather, how he'd let his sister drag him into this. He buried his face in the collar of his coat, which was zipped all the way up; he'd never been too fond of the cold. It didn't help they were currently in the middle of the Moab desert at three in the morning.

Maggie shined her flashlight over the brush. "You're right. No blood around here." She refocused the light on the bloodstained patch of earth in front of them. "Just this."

"I know," Jack gritted out.

"Kinda seems like something your tech guys shoulda picked up."

"Maybe they were too distracted by the shredded human body."

She scoffed. "If that's all it takes for them to be bad at their jobs, no wonder murder and rape cases so rarely have helpful forensic evidence in this state—"

"Mags—"

"Or maybe you didn't read the report. Is that it? You never liked reading the forensics reports, even before you became a pig."

Jack pressed his lips together. He, in fact, hadn't finished reading the report, but that didn't mean he wasn't *going* to. Instead of rising to her taunt, he tried to brush it off. "Come on. You were always more into the science stuff than I was. I'm more of a history guy."

Maggie squatted over the area where the body had been found. She pulled a small collection kit from her coat pocket—a simple plastic biohazards bag with a few vials inside. One was a regular, plastic tube that a nurse might use to collect blood. The other two were silver-lined and wooden. She scooped up some of the dirt with one of those before sealing the container in the bag and returning it all to her pocket. Once Maggie finished, she stood and turned off her flashlight.

Jack's eyes adjusted quickly, and the half-full moon high above them provided plenty of light to see their way to the main trail. They walked up a gentle incline leading to a ridge overlooking a deep yet narrow canyon below. At the top, he could see for miles. The light and darkness played off each other, casting shadows here and there, none of them appearing natural due to various rock formations. Jack looked up.

Thousands of stars danced above him. He could barely make out the Big Dipper and Orion. If the moon wasn't so bright, he wasn't sure he'd be able to make them out at all, the constellations swallowed up by the endless cosmos.

Maggie came up beside him and turned her gaze skyward. She took in a small breath at the sight. He smiled.

For a while, they didn't speak. They simply stood on top of the ridge and observed the night.

Maggie broke the silence. "It's so quiet out here—so quiet, it's loud. As if it's just me and my thoughts, and I can't escape them… Wonder if Mom ever saw it that way."

Jack hummed.

Suddenly, Maggie threw her head back and let out a high-pitched scream. It rang into the stillness of the night. A flock of bats screeched and flew out from the rocks before swooping down into the canyon.

"Jesus, Maggie," Jack groaned, rubbing his ears.

She grinned at him. "Sorry. I had to."

Her grin faltered, and her eyes drifted, staring past him into the expanse behind him, and he recognized that expression. It mirrored their mother's when she was young, distant yet focused. Suddenly, it seemed Maggie was somewhere else, in her own head, contemplating everything about the world and their place in it. And in a blink, it was gone.

Jack shifted his weight from foot to foot. "Maybe we should get going."

He turned and started descending the other side of the ridge. Maggie stifled a laugh behind him, but she followed all the same.

As they made it to the bottom, she caught up to him. "I forgot how weird you are about doing all this at night." She giggled as if they were teenagers again.

"*Sue me* for thinking that the pitch-black darkness makes our line of work a bit creepier than it already is."

She laughed as she danced past him. "We, of all people, shouldn't be scared of the dark. We know what's out there. And how to kill it."

By this point, she'd put a decent bit of distance between them, and Jack muttered under his breath, "Clearly, not *everything*."

*

Jack drifted in and out of sleep on the return trip to the Salt Lake suburbs. He expected they'd return to Maggie's house, so he was surprised when they passed the Provo exit and continued north. Half an hour later, Maggie pulled into their mother's driveway. Neither of them said anything as she shifted into park. As Jack stared up at the house, his mouth went dry. It had been a while since he'd been here.

Another car idled in the driveway, and once Maggie cut the engine, the driver turned off theirs and stepped out.

Dana.

They looked good. It'd been about six years since Jack had seen them, but they seemed the same as always—short-cropped black hair, big wire-frame glasses, and a wardrobe out of the forties, suspenders and all. Despite his best efforts, his heart rate ticked up with nerves.

As Jack stepped out of Maggie's car, he offered a smile. "Hey, Dee, long time, no see."

They returned his smile. "Wouldn't have been so long if you weren't a cop."

Maggie cough-laughed behind him.

Jack glanced up at the sky, exasperated already, and continued toward the house. Maggie hurried ahead to unlock the door. As he stepped over the threshold, Jack scanned the room. No one had lived here in over seven years, but Maggie still used it. The sun shone through aged curtains, its rays illuminating the dust hanging in the air. The only areas in the house that appeared well-used were the kitchen and basement. Despite Jack's stomach growling loudly, they bypassed the former and headed straight for the latter.

Maggie led them through the cold and dusty basement to her lab— the one finished room. At the center of the pristine room stood a work-table with a microscope and its own sink. Scientific equipment lined the walls, ranging from the mundane to specialized. One wall held a basic collection of tools such as hammers, wrenches, pliers, and tweezers, while a fumigation hood sat against the opposite wall.

"Damn, Maggie," Dana said, "when'd you build this?"

"A few years ago." In response to Jack's and Dana's surprised faces, she added, "What? I had a few weeks to myself."

Dana chuckled and stepped to the side as Maggie pulled out the tube of dirt collected from the desert. As she prepared a dish to examine the contents under the microscope, Jack joined Dana against the far wall. He hadn't seen them in a while and hoped they could let their differences go. The three of them had been close once, like family; surely, they could move past it.

"Mags said you worked a case like this?"

"Yeah, 'bout four years ago now... Never thought I'd see another one. Otherwise, I don't think I've ever come across this type of thing."

"Me too."

Dana's eyes locked with his. They shared a brief moment of uncertainty before averting their gazes. "I don't have this set up though. I'm sure Maggie'll figure it out."

"Yeah," Jack whispered, focusing on his sister in the middle of the room. He shifted closer to Dana, and their biceps brushed together in a silent gesture of comfort. "I'm sure she will."

Maggie continued to work in the quiet room. As time stretched, Jack and Dana fidgeted in their own ways. Dana wandered around the room, picking up random tools and inspecting them before returning them to their places. Jack scrolled on his phone, trying to ignore the urge to check his work email. Gene wouldn't have emailed him anything new anyway. Jack did feel a little bad about abandoning him at the office yesterday.

Thankfully, it wasn't long before Maggie pulled away from the microscope with a dissatisfied wrinkle between her eyes.

"What?" Jack asked.

"I got nothing. There's nothing abnormal about the blood or the clay." Maggie paused. "I need to see the body."

"I'm sorry?"

"I need to see the body," Maggie repeated.

"I...don't think that's a good idea."

"Why not?"

"I can't invite my sister to the morgue to see a murder victim's body."

"What's the point of you being a cop if you can't help us skip the line?"

Jack heaved a deep breath, ready to argue, but...she was right. This was the whole point of his being a cop. And if he wanted her and every other goddamn person in her network to stop giving him shit about it, he might as well show them how useful he could be. He deflated. "Fine. Fine, I'll make an appointment for us to go see it later today."

"Sounds good!" Her cheery tone was annoying so early in the morning.

He checked his watch. "The office doesn't open for another couple hours, so can we— oh, I don't know—take a nap before doing anything else? Or at least eat something? I'm starving."

Dana laughed. "So grumpy when he's hungry and tired, isn't he?"

Maggie grinned. "He's always been like that."

"Ha. Ha." Jack headed toward the door. "I'm gonna go make pancakes."

Maggie gasped dramatically. "Don't you dare!"

"Gonna have to stop me," he said before mustering up the last bit of energy he had left and dashing up the stairs.

Jack was out of breath as he reached the kitchen, laughing and smiling so wide his cheeks hurt, Maggie not five feet behind him. For the first time in a long while, he felt at home, and Jack couldn't help but let her drag him out of the kitchen and sit him on a bar stool near the doorway.

"*I'll* be making breakfast," she said.

"Don't want a repeat of 2004, do we?" Dana asked, joining them at a normal pace.

Maggie looked pointedly at Jack, and he pursed his lips, offended.

"So, I set *one* cabinet on fire. I can cook *now*. I'm not completely dysfunctional." He paused. "Frankly, I don't think I get enough credit for *containing* the fire."

Dana and Maggie exchanged a sidelong glance before bursting into laughter.

Chapter Five

Case Notes, Case #187.2210.03.FS.6892
October 9

Our victim, Shelly, has a brother, David, who claims he hasn't spoken w/ sister in over a month, but phone records show otherwise. (Why would he lie? Feuding w/ victim over money? Something else?) No evidence yet that D was in area at the time of the murder. Will continue to dig. He doesn't seem the killing type, but in a rage, anyone's capable.*

**Note to self—ask Jack to dig into brother's alibi and whereabouts for time of murder. (If he bothers to show up to work today. Man hasn't been into the office in three days...maybe requesting him for a partner was a mistake.)*

Gene trudged into his house, shrouded in darkness. He'd had a couple of long days back-to-back, and now with the disappointing autopsy report, he expected he was in for more. If he wasn't careful, he'd fall asleep on his feet. And as he shuffled through his home, dragging his feet toward his bed, he thought back to his partner abandoning him in the middle of a conversation. The body was moved? he thought to himself as he kicked off his shoes and shed his clothes.

"Of course it was moved, Jack. And if you had stuck around long enough to hear it, I would have told you it's in the *fucking* forensics report."

He let out an agitated groan and flopped onto his bed face-first, where he promptly fell into a deep sleep.

Hours later, but far too soon, his phone's ringtone made its way into his dream—one where his partner was dedicated and helpful—and jolted him awake. Fumbling for it, he knocked it off his nightstand. He swiped the cell from the floor and flipped it open to answer just in time.

"Bradshaw," he said, one eye open, hair sticking every which way.

"Uncle Gene?"

If the ringtone hadn't fully woken him, the sound of his eldest niece's voice definitely did. Slightly deeper now, its tone more mature, there was no doubt it was her. "Prudence?"

"Yeah, it's me... I, uh, go by Prue now, not that it's important. But, well, it's what I prefer and—"

"Prue." He gently cut in. Seemed she hadn't outgrown that habit. "What's up?"

After a lull, she said, "I, uh, need your help."

Gene sat up a little straighter. "With?"

A commotion sounded in the background of her call. She covered the mouthpiece of the phone and said something on the other end. And then, she was back.

"I can't talk for long. Can you meet me for breakfast? That place on West Temple we used to go to? Around nine?"

He hadn't seen Prue in almost ten years, and apart from a few birthday cards and a handful of phone calls, he hadn't talked to her either. An image of her popped into his mind from the last time. She'd been seven and going through a pigtail phase. It was Easter, and she wore a green dress with white polka dots. Cake smattered over her round cheeks, she ran up to him, giggling and poorly hiding the handful she had for *his* face.

The memory seized him, and he had to swallow before he could speak again. "I'll be there."

"Thanks," she said, sounding relieved, and hung up.

He closed the flip phone and stared at it. Although Prudence was the last person he should be nervous to meet with, the thought of interacting with any of his family made his palms sweat. She'd always been his favorite niece, but that didn't make it easier, dredging up his past.

Doing his best to push his nerves aside, Gene got up and readied himself for the day. When he returned from his shower, he had a text from Jack.

8:32 AM: Not coming into office today. Running down some field leads.

Typical. Gene didn't bother responding. He finished getting dressed and headed out the door by a quarter to nine. Gene lived close enough to the restaurant to walk, and it was such a beautiful morning, he might as well. As he reached Temple Square, he paused at the intersection and stared up at the somewhat palace-like structure of the LDS Church. He tensed. How many times had he come here as a boy with his family? How many times he must have passed it since then. Why did guilt nag him now?

When the light turned, Gene hurried past the imposing institution and continued down the street until he finally reached his destination. About a hundred feet from the entrance, he saw his niece—now seventeen years old—standing outside, waiting for him. Prue wore jeans with a cerulean-blue sweater and her long hair tied in a half-ponytail. She worried her bottom lip between her teeth as her eyes danced from face to face. When they landed on Gene, she visibly relaxed, and a tentative smile spread over her features.

"Hey," he said when he reached her.

She stared at him before crushing him in a tight hug. Shocked, he didn't react right away, but he quickly recovered and wrapped his arms around her. The hug only lasted a second before she eased away and said, "Shall we?" before leading the way into the restaurant.

His curiosity piqued, Gene followed her in.

It wasn't until after they had ordered and were waiting for their food that he finally decided to dive into what had brought him here. "I don't want to sound as if I'm not happy to see you—I am—but..."

"But you want to know what you're doing here," she finished for him.

He tilted his head and lowered his voice. "You didn't commit a crime or something, did you?"

She laughed. "No! Of course not."

He relaxed in his chair. "Then, what is it?"

Her smile slowly faded, and she shifted her gaze to the table between them. "I called you because I know you're the only one who would consider helping me."

Depends on the request. Though, if he was being perfectly honest with himself, he would probably do about anything for her. "What is it?"

She released a heavy breath. "I need help getting something my parents won't pay for."

"Prue, I'm not buying you alcohol if that's what this is—"

"I need birth control," she blurted, flushing a deep shade of red.

Gene's mouth went dry. Right. Right. His seventeen-year-old niece, who was *seven* the last time he saw her, was now old enough to have sex, and apparently, she *wanted* to have sex, and *thank God*, she wanted to have *safe* sex, but good God, was this really a conversation for nine in the morning?

The silence dragged between them, during which time their waiter brought their food. In the awkward quiet, Prue picked up her fork and pushed her potatoes and eggs around on her plate.

Gene took a few sips of coffee—boy, was he tempted to order a Bloody Mary—giving himself time to come up with a response. He cut into his sausage, took a bite, and swallowed.

"Okay," he said. "Listen." He took a breath. "I'm glad you're trying to do this safely, but you *are* still pretty young to...you know. Plus, you're in a bit of a legal gray zone when it comes to consent. You're technically legally able to consent, though if your partner is under eighteen, he technically isn't, so—"

"Uncle Gene?"

"Yes?"

"I don't want to have sex with anyone."

"What?"

Prue's face remained flushed, but she seemed amused. "I'm not dating anyone. You think my mom would let me even if I wanted?"

Thought they'd be practically shoving you toward the altar by now.

"No, I need birth control pills because I..." Somehow, her face burned redder. "I haven't had a period in, like, three months. I'm a virgin, so I don't know what's up, but I know birth control can help me regulate it."

Gene shifted and basically gave up on his food. "Did you tell your doctor?"

Prue bit her lip and shook her head.

He closed his eyes, releasing a breath through his nose. "Honey. I'm glad you reached out to me. I'd be happy to help you with whatever this is, but you should talk to a doctor about this, not your uncle."

"But how do I do that without my parents finding out?"

"You have a legal right to privacy regarding medical matters, even as a minor."

"You know my mom will be with me though. She'll assume—" Prue shifted in her chair and crossed her arms.

"Hey, I know it's hard," he said. "And as much as I disagree with your—*our* family's beliefs, I can't stand behind lying to your parents. Trust goes both ways, Prue. You have to trust them enough not to judge you."

"But they will!"

Gene gave her a level look. "You honestly think your mom never had a late period in her life? She *may* jump to conclusions, but if you tell her what you told me, she'll likely be more concerned than anything else."

Prue remained silent, continually worrying her bottom lip with her teeth.

"And hey, if they do react as badly as you think, you call me, and I'll come give 'em hell. Okay?"

Finally, Prue met his eyes and gave him a small smile. "Okay."

He reached across the table, laughing, and ruffled her hair, making her giggle, groan, and push his hand away.

"Eat up," he said as the mood lightened. "I gotta get to work."

*

By the time Gene made it into the office, he was in a weird mood. The out-of-the blue meeting with his niece dragged some memories to the surface that he'd rather not think about. So, he sat at his desk and threw himself back into the case. One thing he hadn't had a chance to do yesterday was search for similar cases in the national database. He doubted he'd find anything, considering how odd this one was, but it was worth a shot.

To his surprise, he turned up two others, one in Kansas and one in Ohio. The case in Ohio had been determined to be an animal killing, and the Kansas one simply remained "undetermined." Gene found the lead detectives' names and numbers for both cases and scribbled them in his notebook. The Ohio killing was older, so he called them first.

The phone rang for a while before a receptionist answered. "Ohio State Police, how may I help you?"

"This is Detective Gene Bradshaw with the Utah State Bureau of Investigation. Could I speak with Detective Jameson?"

"Would you mind holding please?"

Gene grunted an affirmation. A few minutes passed before the phone started ringing.

"Jameson," a gruff voice answered.

"Hi, Detective, I'm—"

"Yeah, yeah, Carol told me. What can I do you for?"

"You worked a case a few years back—uh, number 2487—and I

was wondering if you could tell me a little more about it. We caught one pretty similar, and I'd appreciate any insight you might offer."

"Let me pull it up." There was a pause, and then, "Oh. That one. Yeah, that was a weird one."

"Yeah?"

"Mm-hmm. The body was completely unidentifiable, never got an ID. And the way it looked—brutal."

Gene grunted an understanding. "You mind if I ask how you were able to definitively rule it an animal killing?"

On the other end, Gene heard the sound of a chair squeaking as if the other detective had reclined in his. "That's probably more a question for the medical examiner. But I mean—there's no way a human did *that*, you know?" There was a pause. "You think yours *wasn't* an animal?"

"We're still trying to figure it out. Our body appears to have been moved, though, which at least suggests some human involvement."

The other detective hummed. "Well, ours definitely had not been moved."

"Would you mind sharing your case file with me? I'd like to explore the similarities some more."

"Sure. My email should be listed with the case on the national database. You send me your badge credentials, and I'll respond with the full case details."

"Sure thing. Thanks for your time."

"Course." And the line went dead.

Gene hung up and immediately sent the detective his credentials. He then dialed the Kansas City detective. This time, the call went directly to him.

"Kansas City PD. This is Detective Barnes. How can I help you?"

Gene ran through his spiel as he had with the Ohio detective and asked about Barnes's cold case.

"Ah. That one," he said, eerily similar in tone to the other detective. "You got one like that?" He sounded skeptical.

"Yep. Caught it early yesterday morning."

"Well, I wish you better luck than I had."

"Thanks. Can I ask why you didn't rule yours an animal killing?"

"There are two answers to that. One is the bureaucratic answer that the specific ME has a policy not to declare a death an animal killing unless he can definitively say what *type* of animal it was—or at least, narrow it down to a few possibilities. Something about him being burned before. I don't know. Anyway, the other answer is— Well, simply put, I didn't feel it. Sounds stupid, but it *felt* wrong to blame an animal. As much as I didn't want to consider that, you know?"

Gene knew the feeling. "Any signs your victim's body was moved, killed somewhere other than where you found it?"

"No. Definitely not. We could barely move it from the crime scene to the ME's office. Find it hard to believe a killer could do it all by themself."

"Well, I appreciate your time, Detective," Gene said, and he struck a similar deal to send his credentials to get access to his case files.

Before hanging up, Barnes said, "If there's anything else I can do, or if you find anything new, please don't hesitate to get in touch."

"Will do. Thanks," Gene said and hung up. He sent his credentials over to him and relaxed in his chair.

He pulled out his cell and typed out a message to Jack, asking him about his "field leads," but he hesitated sending it. After staring at it, he deleted the text and put his phone away. If Jack didn't want to share what he was up to, whatever.

Across from him, Gene noticed Jack had left behind the pocket notebook he used for crime notes. Maybe it could give him some answers. He swiped it and perused the latest entries. The seemingly disordered amalgamation of letters in Jack's neat hand stared up at Gene. Jack had an annoying habit of keeping everything in code. When they'd first started working together, it drove Gene crazy, especially since he was the one who did all their paperwork. Now, after six months of working together, Gene found he hardly noticed the code. But it still drove him up the wall.

Finding nothing new in Jack's notes, Gene switched gears and logged on to the ME's appointment scheduler. After all the talk with the other detectives, he wanted to see the body again and have a face-to-face discussion with the medical examiner. He was surprised to see an appointment already scheduled in the system for later this afternoon. Gene checked his watch—*dammit*, in forty-five minutes.

"Son of a—" He hastily stood, grabbed his jacket, and made his way to the ME's office.

Chapter Six

"We need more brains on this," Maggie said as Jack and Dana helped her put the breakfast dishes away.

"Agreed," Dana said.

Jack hesitated. "I...don't know."

Maggie turned to him. "You were practically begging for my contacts the other day."

"Yeah, but honestly, I only wanted *your* help."

She left the kitchen, only to return moments later with her journal. She flipped open the leather-bound book and set it on the counter. "Okay, so we've got Dana, obviously... What about Kurt?"

"Aww, little Kurt Taupin. Haven't seen him in ages," Dana remarked.

An image of a young twenty-something with sandy blond hair flashed through Jack's mind. Oh.

"You ever meet him?" Maggie asked Jack, oblivious to his discomfort.

"Uh, yeah. I think I worked one case with him a while back, almost fifteen years."

She must have heard the trepidation in his voice because she said, "Oh, well, he'd obviously have to get used to you being a cop, but I think he'd get over it." She thumbed through a few pages. "As much as you *can* get over that."

"Yeah, that's not what I'm worried about, Mags."

"What else would you be—oh." Realization dawned on her face. "Well, I mean, he's...he's okay, right?" She gestured to Dana for confirmation.

"I've never had a problem with him."

"It should be fine," Maggie said. Then, more seriously, "And if it's not, he'll answer to me."

Dana snorted.

While his sister's offer to defend him was touching, Jack didn't want to deal with someone he hadn't been in contact with for so long. And to go fifteen years without talking...well. Jack had changed a lot. Old insecurities flared up, gnawing at him, picking away at him like a scab.

Instead of voicing any of these concerns, he asked, "Who else?"

Maggie scanned the page and glanced up ruefully as if she knew Jack wouldn't agree to what was about to come out of her mouth. "Well, there's always Argus."

"That Scottish bastard's still alive?"

"He's technically Greek."

"I don't care. He has a Scottish accent... He's seriously still alive? The guy's older than Mom."

"Oh, yeah. He's still kickin'."

"Mostly does background work now," Dana added. "Sending people place to place, helping with fake IDs and all that." They paused. "Heard he worked a case a couple years ago though. Took out a whole goblin den by himself."

"Dude's still a badass," Maggie said.

Dana hummed an agreement.

"Ugh, fine. I guess we have no choice, then. I'm not a fan, but—"

"I never understood why you don't like him," Maggie said as she continued down her list.

"Believe me, it's mutual." Jack checked his watch. "Hey, we gotta get going if we want to make it to the morgue today."

Maggie closed her journal and stood. "Okay, let me grab my kit, then we can go." She disappeared into the basement.

Dana came up to Jack and gave his shoulder a light squeeze. "I'm gonna head out, go through some of my old files. See if I can't find anything to get us through this. Y'all keep me in the loop, all right? Was good seeing you."

"Yeah, you too."

Dana paused at the door. "I wouldn't worry about Kurt. He's a good guy."

Jack gave them an appreciative smile. Once they were gone, he slumped against the counter as an odd, irrational sense of foreboding washed over him.

*

The morgue was a little less than half an hour from Sandy, straight up I-15. As the sun rose over the valley, the Wasatch Mountains came into clear, crisp view, their snowcapped peaks glistening in the sunlight. The mountains had always looked funny to Jack. Something about the way the sunlight hit them, they appeared two-dimensional, as if they were made of cardboard. Like part of a movie set that could be toppled and taken away at the drop of a hat. Didn't make them any less beautiful though.

Before long, they pulled into the ME's office parking lot, and standing beside the door was—

"Shit," Jack said.

"What?"

"That's Gene, my partner. By the door." He should have known Gene would see the appointment in the system. Jack pulled into the parking space as far from the door as possible. It didn't seem Gene had spotted his car yet, but it was only a matter of time.

Maggie peered at him, eyes narrowed. "Huh. He's kinda hot."

Jack decidedly ignored that comment. "Okay. You can't go in with me."

"Like hell, I can't. You can't get the samples."

"I can—"

"No, I need to do it, and I need to see the body. Don't worry. I planned for this." Unperturbed, Maggie rummaged in her purse before producing a fake ID badge.

Delilah Owens, Forensics Specialist.

Jack scoffed. "No. No, forget it. He'd never buy it. We're twins!"

"Come on. We look nothing alike. You have a beard!"

Not even close. On instinct, Jack ran his hand along his stubbled jaw. He tilted his head up at the ceiling. *Was this really happening?*

"Gah, I forgot how chickenshit you are about all this stuff. Okay, here's what we're gonna do. Remember how we did it when we were kids, and Mom wouldn't let us go on a hunt?"

"Yeah, but—"

"So you're gonna go over there and talk to your partner, keep him distracted, while *I* sneak in behind you."

"You can't see the body without one of us."

"Easy. Call the ME and let him know I'm legit. Tell him I'm with the forensics unit or whatever. It'll be fine. Trust me."

Jack let out a long breath. "Fine. There's a backdoor by the bathroom. Go out that way."

"Don't worry about me. I got this. Now, go."

"Can't believe I let you talk me into this," he muttered, getting out of the car. As he made his way over to Gene, he called the ME and quickly relayed the information about "Delilah Owens" coming to see the body without him.

Gene paced near the entrance, and when he caught sight of him, Jack tried not to halt his approach. Gene was mad, possibly madder than Jack had ever seen him.

Once he was close enough, Jack offered a laissez-faire smile. "Sorry. I, uh, meant to call you about the appointment. You know how I forget."

"Maybe that's the problem. We've been working together for six months, and I still feel I don't know you at all."

Okay, this was going to be easy. Now that they opened this can of worms, right out the gate, keeping Gene distracted should be a walk in the—

"Six months, man! And not only do I not know you, sometimes I wonder if I can even trust you."

"Wait...you don't—you don't trust me?"

Gene closed his eyes briefly. "I mean, can you blame me? You're not exactly dependable."

"Okay, but come on. It's not like I'm crooked." Jack ran a hand over his face, turned, and took a few steps away from him. *My own partner doesn't trust me*?

"Jack...I think it's a compatibility issue more than anything else."

Jack faced him again. "Trust's a pretty big thing. It's not a compatibility issue if you don't trust me. That's... Hell, I don't know what it is."

Jack caught Gene's gaze, his partner's brown eyes wary and angry and...soft—a softness that was almost always there, but Jack had never noticed before. And now it stood so starkly against the negative emotions darkening Gene's gaze that Jack couldn't help but notice. "Do you truly believe I don't have your back when we're out in the field? That I won't fight for you? Come on, man."

Gene tore his eyes away from Jack's. Jack was surprised he could feel their loss.

"It's complicated," Gene said. "Do I think you'd be there for me in the moment? Sure, but sometimes you're simply *not there*."

Jack nodded and pinched the bridge of his nose. "If that's how you feel, maybe this should be our last case together."

A heavy silence fell between them.

Gene winced. "It's not that simple."

"Why not?"

"No one else...wants to be your partner."

Jack opened and closed his mouth a number of times, the words sticking in his throat.

Gene continued. "You have a reputation around the office of being a bad cop..."

"Well, why do *you* work with me, then?" Jack retorted, and when Gene's expression turned sheepish, "You feel sorry for me?"

"No...well, that's part of it, but—no one wants to work with me either."

While Jack took the dig at his reputation as more of a compliment than an insult, the implication that no one wanted to work with him—including his current partner—hit him somewhere else. He deflated, glaring down at his shoes, and kicked the ground. He let out a cynical laugh. "I'm such an idiot to think I could do this," he said more to himself than Gene. "To think I could *fit in* here...god dammit."

"Hey—" Gene sighed. "Hey, you're smart. I know you're a good detective, okay? I wouldn't have agreed to be your partner if I didn't think that. You're observant and pretty damn good at considering all the facts before drawing a conclusion."

He paused. "But being partners? That means sharing information and thoughts and ideas. And it means telling me about the, quote, unquote, 'field leads' you're running down, instead of saying you're not showing up for work because of some vague reason that may or may not be true. If you could do that just 70 percent of the time, I think we'll be okay."

Jack regarded Gene, his partner's eyes softer now, still wary, but not as angry, and Jack could tell he was being earnest. Offering an olive branch. So, he extended a hand and said, "Deal."

The corner of Gene's lips quirked up, and he shook Jack's hand. "Deal."

For half a heartbeat, their hands lingered, clasped between them.

Then, Gene gave Jack a pat on the shoulder and headed for the entrance to the morgue. "Come on. Let's go inside."

Gene disappeared before Jack could think to stop him. And then he remembered Maggie.

"Oh, shit," he said and scrambled after his partner.

Chapter Seven

Case Notes, Case #187.2210.03.FS.6892
October 12

*Asked Shelly's brother, David, to come in again. I was able to confirm his alibi, so he is definitely not our guy. Asked him why he lied about not talking to his sister for a month when his phone records indicate otherwise. He claimed he misunderstood the original question and meant he hadn't seen her in that long. Still a little suspicious, but I don't think he killed her. Exploring other leads—David says his sister broke it off with a boyfriend a couple months ago, a Jason Miller. Digging deeper into her finances and personal life.**

**Delegate social media scraping to Jack*

***Side note—may need to talk to Captain Smith about reassignment for Det. Cartwright. He was MIA for last two days. Tried calling him last night and got nothing. He did show up* *today but is not very collaborative. Keep track of behavioral issues in case of the need for IA involvement.*

"Detective Bradshaw?" Dr. Jackson greeted him, his voice a tad higher than usual.

"You seem surprised to see me," Gene said.

The doctor's eyes moved past him to his partner behind him, and he seemed more confused. "Well, I am," he said. "*He* called not ten minutes ago to tell me you weren't coming but rather a member of your forensics team."

Gene turned to his partner and put his hands on his hips. He leveled him with a look that said, *something you wanna tell me?*

Jack turned a bit sheepish. "I was going to tell you. But you practically ran in here..."

"Jack. Who did you authorize to examine the body?"

"Delilah Owens."

"Right. And who is that?"

"She's a new member of the forensics team."

Gene narrowed his eyes. "So if she was going to see the body and not you, what are you doing here?"

Jack stood there with his mouth open for a good few seconds, but he didn't say anything. Gene waited.

Finally, Jack said, "Because...we were going to get lunch...together afterward."

Gene faced the ME again. He gestured toward the back. "Well, as long as we're here."

"Oh, sure." Dr. Jackson turned and led them to the area of the morgue where the bodies were kept. "Ms. Owens came in only five minutes ago. I'm sure you'll be able to—" He stopped as they entered the exam room—no sign of life. "Huh...that was quick... I didn't see her leave."

"That's Delilah," Jack muttered as he moved past Gene and circled the body.

Gene eyed his partner before focusing on their victim.

What remained of the body lay across two autopsy tables. Gene had to give the medical examiner some credit—the body seemed almost identical to how it had been situated at the crime scene. The only difference was the hands; they lay on a separate table, mostly intact save for the fingertips.

"Still no luck on ID?" Gene asked, focusing on the hands.

"No."

Gene circled the body, searching for anything he might have missed the other day. He bent close to the body and caught a whiff of an odd scent—odd not because it was sour or putrid, but because it was *nice*. Out of place. He wrinkled his nose, frowning as he straightened up, then beckoned Jack and the doctor over.

"Do either of you smell that?"

Jack came closer and stopped opposite him. He shared a questioning glance with the doctor before he tilted forward and sniffed. And then he shot up with a confused expression on his face.

His eyes locked with Gene's. "Lavender?"

"That's what I smell too. I thought I smelled it at the crime scene, but I wasn't sure. Could it be a perfume or something?"

"Eh. Unlikely," Dr. Jackson chimed in. "With the amount of decay and trauma the body has gone through, I'd be surprised if we could still smell it...though, I suppose it's not impossible."

Gene gave Jack an exasperated look. This guy had a tendency to say something that added nothing to the conversation. The ghost of a smile played on Jack's lips, and he moved the conversation along before Gene could call the doctor out on it.

"Did you do a tox screen?" he asked. "There wasn't mention of anything in the report you sent over last night."

"That's because I hadn't gotten them yet. The results came through this morning. All normal."

Gene wanted to turn the table over and scream in frustration. *Dammit.* No ID, no cause of death, nothing. He heaved a long breath. "We should get going." He thanked the doctor and started heading out, assuming Jack would follow.

When they got outside, Jack paused. "Well, I was going to—"

"Run down field leads?" Gene interrupted. "Was that actually what you were doing earlier today?"

"As I was saying before I was so rudely interrupted—" Jack continued. "I'm meeting that forensics lady for lunch, so…"

Gene ran his gaze over his partner's face. He seemed nervous, his brow dotted with sweat, his skin a bit flushed, his eyes darting about, not resting on anything for long. "Is it a date or something?"

"What? Oh, God, no, definitely, *definitely* not a date. Why would—why would you think that?"

"You seem nervous."

"I'm not nervous…" He released a breath. "It's not a date."

Gene gave him a disbelieving look, though, truth be told, relief flowed through him. He wasn't an idiot; he knew what the feeling in the pit of his stomach was, but he wasn't ready to dig into that. Not when it was his work partner that was causing it.

So he teased him instead. "Whatever you say. I'll be at the office. You know, doing my job. I'll call you if I figure anything out."

With that, he headed for his car. As he made it to the driver's side door, Jack called after him in a muted voice so quiet Gene almost missed it.

"Not if I call you first."

Gene smiled and strapped himself in. He paused and watched Jack make his way to his own car, that same feeling gnawing at him. Lightly slapping himself on the cheek, he said, "God, get a grip, Bradshaw," before shifting into drive and heading back to the office.

When he got there, one of the uniformed officers from the grid search was waiting to greet him. They'd identified the truck's owner.

"Only, he's been dead for five years," the officer said.

Gene accepted the file from the rookie. "Good work. I'll look into it."

When he returned to his desk, he pulled up the DMV database. Sure enough, the owner, Victor Thompson, had died five years ago at the age of seventy-six. With no next of kin, his truck should have gone to an estate sale. Digging a little deeper, Gene found that Thompson was declared legally blind when he was sixty-three, making it unlikely the guy had been driving five years ago.

Gene reached for his office phone but hesitation crept into him. His talk with Jack had felt...good, as if they'd turned over a leaf, but he still wondered how much he could rely on his partner. *Gotta give him the chance, I guess.*

The phone rang a few times before Jack answered, "Cartwright."

It sounded like he was driving. "Are you on the road?"

"Uh, yeah. I just wrapped lunch. What's up?"

"We got a hit off the truck. Found a partial VIN. It belonged to Victor Thompson, who's been dead for five years."

"Did you check—"

"Insurance? Yeah, and DMV records. But there was nothing."

"Probably sold under the table for cash."

Gene smiled. For a second there, it was as if they were reading each other's thoughts. "That's what I'm thinking. Can you come to the office? I know you said something about checking field leads, but I could use some help running stuff on this Thompson guy."

It was quiet for a second too long, and Gene had an odd flare of anxiety that Jack would say no.

"Yeah, of course. Uh, I'll probably be another hour or so? I have to drop Delilah off."

Gene tried to brush off the way his heartbeat kicked up a notch. *Coworker,* he told himself. "Yeah, yeah, no problem. Tell her I said hi." He winced at his attempt at teasing and, sparing both of them the need to say anything else, hung up.

Gene rubbed his eyes and refocused. He combed through the truck's records, going back ten years. As he'd found with his first read through, there wasn't much of note—no parking tickets, no traffic violations of any kind. It seemed to be a dead end. He clicked over to the forensics report and opened the pictures of the crime scene. He'd studied them so much over the past couple of days he practically had them memorized. Scrolling through them, he didn't see anything near the body that would have given it a scent. He ran his fingers through his hair and pulled at the ends. It was getting long, the curly bits by his ears becoming more unruly by the day.

"Fucking lavender," he muttered to himself as he sat up straighter.

He unlocked the top drawer of the filing cabinet next to his desk and pulled it open. He debated with himself before taking out the file hanging at the front of the pack. Setting it in front of him, Gene chewed his bottom lip. He shouldn't open this up again, but dammit, it was the one case he couldn't put behind him.

The folder flipped open easily as it always did, and he paged through the documents until he found the pictures.

Animals, killed like sacrifices. Sprigs of flowery herbs scattered around them and placed delicately on their bodies.

He didn't truly think there was a connection, but the thought lingered like the scent of lavender on the wind. So, until Jack showed up, he'd let himself get sucked into this old mystery.

Who knows? Maybe I'll finally have a breakthrough.

*

A week later, they still had nothing.

Jack shuffled around Maggie's lab, and he halted, hands on his hips. "What do you mean *inconclusive*?"

Maggie switched slides under her microscope without looking his way. "I mean inconclusive. Do you need me to pull out a dictionary?"

"What did you run?"

"The basic tests! The only abnormal thing was that the victim's blood lead levels were high, but that could be from anything. Likely from a bullet."

"Well, couldn't that be something?"

"Eh... It could be from an old injury. And I think it's safe to say they weren't shot to death."

"Do you have anything we can use to narrow down what this is?" he pleaded.

Maggie finally focused on him. "This is why we need more brains on this one, Jack. You, me, and Dana can't handle this on our own."

Jack groaned.

"I know you're worried about Kurt, and I know you don't get along with Argus, but we *need* them."

"Fine. Set up the meeting."

"I already did. It's in three days. I'll send you the calendar invite."

Jack's phone rang—Gene. He checked his watch; it was barely past eleven.

"Bradshaw," he greeted with an edge of teasing in his voice. "Thought you'd be in bed by now."

"Usually, I would be," Gene remarked with little of his usual humor. "Another body turned up."

Chapter Eight

Jack stared up at the star-studded sky and wished he wasn't at a crime scene. The techs' bright floodlights polluted the darkness, and despite the fact that he was a good two hundred feet away from the body, they were still overpowering. This time of night—or rather, morning—was the best time to stargaze, and he could barely see them.

"So," Gene said, stepping up beside him, "you planning to come look at the body sometime soon, or do you study stars now?"

Jack's focus didn't stray. "I'm not studying the stars. I'm looking at the planets." He pointed. "Jupiter and Saturn."

After a long pause, Jack shifted his gaze to his partner. "Oh, come on, Gene. Give it a try. Look up. What do you see?"

Gene glanced up, made a small *hmm*, then returned his deeply un-amused attention to Jack. "A bunch of stars, lightyears away. Breathtaking. Now, would you please come over and do your job?"

"Fine."

Jack followed Gene to the taped-off area up the hill. The scene wasn't all that dissimilar to where they had found the other body. As with the other, the remains, horrendously shredded and torn up, had been found in the middle of the Moab desert, miles off the beaten path. They appeared fairly fresh, with little decay. Unlike last time, though, only the ankles and feet remained intact. The hands were nowhere to be seen.

Jack squatted next to the body and took a deep inhale. "Lavender again."

"Yeah, I smelled it too. Also, no signs of a struggle. No blood around the body, same as before. The scene is almost identical, save for the location."

Jack stood and circled the body. "No animal activity?"

"Not as far as we can tell."

Odd. Jack halted, his eyes catching something. "Hey, look at this." He beckoned to Gene and pointed at the ground. "Those are probably coyote or fox tracks, right?"

"Presumably."

"Okay. And they seem fresh too. Wind speeds were reported up to sixty miles an hour the past couple days, so they would have blown away. But look." Jack pointed again. "They walk up toward the body, stop, then turn and descend the hill." He checked the other side of the body. "No tracks over here... Why didn't it stop? Why didn't it feed on the body?"

Gene stayed quiet while Jack worked through what it could mean.

Finally, Jack muttered, "Something's repelling them."

"That doesn't make any sense."

"Yeah, maybe," Jack said, lost in thought. He shrugged. "Just a hunch."

Gene continued scribbling in his notebook, then put it in his breast pocket. "Well, I think we're done here."

"Oh, yeah?" Jack asked, surprised.

"It's too dark to do a grid search right now. The forensics guys are handling everything, so, yeah, our job is done for now."

Jack tried to hide how excited that made him. As he and Gene made their way to the car, he checked his watch, and his excitement grew.

"Perfect," he said. "If we leave now, we'll make it to Salt Lake by seven-thirty, eight o'clock. You know what that means? Pancakes! On me." He reconsidered. "Well, wait—we'll split it. I got ahead of myself there. But still. Pancakes!"

Gene paused, making Jack turn toward him.

"What?"

"We're not going back to the city tonight."

"You said we were done—"

"I know, but they're taking the body to the regional hospital before transporting it up to Salt Lake tomorrow. We have to stay so we can sign all the paperwork."

"Dammit," Jack groaned. "Why can't anything ever be easy?"

Gene hummed in agreement as another thought dawned on Jack.

"Wait. Where the hell are we supposed to find a room? It's the middle of the night."

Gene smirked and patted his shoulder as he passed. "Don't worry. There's a place up the road."

"Bet they don't have pancakes," Jack muttered grumpily as he turned and followed his partner to the car.

*

The motel was dingy, but it would do. *And* it was the only one close by that didn't have an illuminated "NO" on their vacancy sign. Jack's main concern was a place to sleep...and pancakes. Damn, now that he couldn't have them, he couldn't stop thinking about them. But it was pretty clear that wasn't going to happen, at least, not until they were in Salt Lake again.

A bell above the door chimed when they entered, but there was no one behind the counter. They waited for someone to come greet them. When no one did, Gene rang the counter bell, its metallic tone much louder than Jack expected in the silent room.

Sounds of shuffling came from the back office, and a middle-aged woman emerged. "Oh, hello. How can I help you two gentlemen?"

"Do you happen to take late check-ins? We need a place to stay the night."

"Well, sure. Let me see what we have available…" She checked her computer. "You're in luck. We have one room left."

"Great." Gene gave Jack a satisfied look that seemed to say, *See? Told you we'd find a room.*

Jack had the feeling Gene would be gloating about this for a while.

"I need a credit card and form of ID, please." As she began to put their information in, she asked, "Would you like a cot for the room?"

"A cot?"

"Yes, well, there's only one bed. Pardon the assumption, but you two probably don't want to share."

Gene's eyes darted to Jack's and held for a beat too long, a low-simmering heat flaring between them. Jack blinked, and Gene's gaze was gone. Frowning, he wondered if he'd imagined it.

Gene cleared his throat and faced the employee. "Yes, a cot would be great. Thank you."

As she finished getting them set up, she gave them directions to their room and told them about the complimentary breakfast in the morning. "Nothing too special, coffee and pastries."

After he got their keys, Jack turned to leave, but Gene hung back to ask about a convenience store. The lady kindly gave him directions to a 24/7 shop up the road. With that, they thanked her and made their way outside.

Jack veered toward the stairs, and Gene offered to run up to the shop and pick up some necessities while Jack settled in. Jack was happy with that plan since it gave him time to call Maggie.

Without further ado, they went their separate ways, and Jack trudged up to their room. The small room held one lone double bed, tucked into an alcove to the right of the door, taking up most of the space with the wall AC unit taking up the rest. A narrow path led from the door to the bathroom, and a small chest of drawers sat along one wall. Jack wondered where they would squeeze the cot in as he took a seat on the bed and called Maggie.

She answered on the third ring. "Well?"

"It's another one," he confirmed.

"Damn."

Jack yawned. "I know… They're not transporting the body to the state morgue until tomorrow, so I won't be back in Salt Lake till then."

"You mean later today?"

"I haven't slept yet. Tomorrow."

Maggie chuckled. "Can you get the samples I need? Or does Delilah need to make another visit?"

"I could have handled it last time, but *someone* didn't trust me. I can do it. Text me exactly what you need, and I'll do my best."

"Will do… How'd the body look?"

An image flashed through Jack's mind—ground flesh, the same color as the red clay beneath it. "Worse than the other one."

He could practically hear his sister's wince when she said, "How could it get worse?"

The quiet enveloped them as they each stewed in the disturbing reality they lived in.

Then, Maggie changed the subject. "Dana heard from Kurt today. He's definitely coming to the meeting. Do you want to get here early so that you can meet him before everyone else shows up?"

"You think I should?"

"I figured it might be more…comfortable for you to meet him that way. But if that's not how you want to play it, that's fine."

"I'll think about it."

"Okay." She yawned. "I'm going to bed. Bring me those samples when you get back."

"Goodnight," he said and hung up.

Yawning himself, Jack went to take a shower in the tiny bathroom. He stripped as the water heated and caught a glimpse of himself in the mirror, making him pause. He looked tired, but that was to be expected, considering it was 4:00 a.m. The bags under his eyes were practically permanent at this point in his life. What made him pause was the sight of his barely-stubbled jaw. He wished he could grow more than his current smattering of peach fuzz, but he was incapable of it, and it frustrated him beyond belief. For the entirety of his adult life, Jack had struggled to grow a beard. Now, as he approached his midthirties, it made him feel like a kid. What thirty-five-year-old man couldn't grow a beard? As he allowed himself to wallow in his insecurities for the first time in years, he absentmindedly ran his fingers along twin scars on his chest.

It wasn't until the mirror began to fog that he shook himself out of it and stepped into the hot spray of the shower.

*

Gene could barely keep his eyes open as he picked out some deodorant for him and Jack. The store also had plain socks and T-shirts, so he picked up a couple packs of those too. By the time he'd returned to the motel, all he wanted was to plop face-first onto the mattress and pass out. But Gene couldn't seem to get his limbs to move, so he sat in the blissful quiet until he started to doze off. He managed to jolt himself out of it. Blinking a few times to clear his blurry vision, he grabbed his purchases and went up.

Jack was pulling on a T-shirt when he walked in. To Gene's amusement, his face flushed pink. His hair was wet from a shower, and his shirt clung to his lean, wiry frame.

Gene averted his gaze, setting the bag on the bed. "Didn't know what scent you liked, so I picked up two that I liked, and you can choose whichever you want. They also had socks and T-shirts. Figured we could use some fresh clothes for the morning."

"Thanks."

"Right. Well. I'm beat." As if to emphasize his point, a yawn interrupted him. "So I'm going to bed."

They had brought the cot to the room while he was out, and he wasn't sure he could squeeze past it to get to the bathroom anyway.

"I can take the cot if you want," Jack offered.

"Sounds good with me." Gene didn't need to be told twice. He took his jacket off and had started on his button-down when he paused. "Uh...you don't care if I sleep in my boxers, do you?"

"Nope...that's fine."

Right. Okay. Gene turned away from his partner and finished getting undressed as quickly as possible. The silence stretched until he heard Jack climb into the squeaky cot behind him, the sound making him relax a bit. Gene didn't know why this was so weird. They were two dudes sharing a hotel room. It didn't have to be weird.

He mentally groaned.

Finally, *finally*, he climbed into bed. Gene didn't care that it was a lumpy old mattress or that the room smelled vaguely of mildew and bleach. As soon as he was situated, his eyes drooped. *Just* as he was about to fall asleep, Jack broke the silence.

"Gene? Can I ask you a question?"

"If it's a quick one," he said with his eyes closed.

"When did you know you wanted to be a cop?"

Couldn't have waited till morning, huh?

"Kind of always did. My dad was a cop, dad's dad was a cop. Always thought I'd be one too." He shifted in the bed. "Not much of a story." Curiosity scratched at his mind before getting the best of him. It was odd they'd never talked about this before. "What about you?"

"I never wanted to be a cop," Jack said.

"But...you are a cop."

"I became one out of necessity."

"Necessity?"

"Yeah, you know, stability, monthly paycheck, health insurance."

"You could have done anything to get that."

"I know. I only wanted...well, I wanted something where I could do some good."

"Yeah, but there are other things you could have done for that too," Gene said.

"Now you're starting to sound like my sister."

"She not happy you're a cop?"

Jack laughed. "Oh, definitely not. She's about as anticop as you can get, which... Can't say I disagree, but I don't know. I guess I want to try to fix the system from within, whereas she thinks the only way to fix the system is to blow it up."

Maybe that's why he's a "bad" cop...

It was quiet for a little while, then, "Was your family proud when you became a cop?"

Gene huffed a laugh. "Not exactly." He flashed back to the graduation ceremony and his father's stern handshake afterward. Had that been pride?

"But you come from a cop family," Jack said.

"That doesn't mean I come from a functional one. My dad was happy I became a cop—I think. But he wasn't necessarily happy with what I chose to *do* as one."

Jack hummed contemplatively.

Silence dragged on, and Gene began to nod off when Jack broke it yet again.

"Can I ask your advice on something?"

Gene resisted the urge to groan in frustration. "Man, I'm so tired. Can it possibly wait until morning?"

"Right. Sorry."

Another long pause.

Gene couldn't quite say how, but he knew Jack's eyes were wide open, his mind racing with whatever it was he wanted to talk about. Gene said, "Fine. What is it?"

"So my sister and I haven't talked much in the last six years, but we recently made up, sort of, and we're doing good, but... She wants me to get together with a couple of her friends. I can't stand one of them, but the other one is nice, I guess. I met him when I was, like, nineteen? I've changed a lot since then, and I'm worried."

"I'm sure it'll be fine. You don't strike me as someone who has trouble getting along with people."

"Really? Because it took us over six months to talk about why we became cops. And the other week, you told me how no one likes me in the precinct."

"I didn't say no one *liked* you. I said no one wanted to work with you. There's a difference. If you're worried he won't like you because you're a cop—"

"It's not that. Well, it's not *only* that."

When he didn't elaborate, Gene asked, "Then, what is it? We all change, Jack. It's not—"

"I'm trans."

Gene's words died in his throat. In the silence, Jack started to ramble.

"The last time he saw me, I hadn't come out yet, and I— Look, I'm finally at a point where I don't care. I'm perfectly comfortable with myself, but I also don't have to meet people who knew me pretransition very often."

Gene was still recovering from his shock, so his brain was slow to respond.

"I just don't want him to think any differently of me," Jack said quietly.

"Is your sister...supportive?" Gene asked hesitantly, thinking he knew the answer.

"Oh, yeah, a hundred percent."

Not the answer he was expecting, considering the six-year distance. "Do you think she'd ask you to meet someone she thought would be unsupportive?"

"Well, no, but—"

"Then, I think you have nothing to worry about, Jack. Trust your sister's got your back."

Jack fell quiet. "You're right. I'm working myself up for no reason. Thank you."

"Of course," Gene said sincerely. "And Jack?"

"Yeah?"

"If you say one more word, I'll smother you with a pillow. Now, go to sleep."

Jack laughed. "Aye, aye, Captain."

Gene threw a pillow at him, which only made him laugh harder. Eventually, it faded, and Gene fell asleep with a pleased smile on his face.

Chapter Nine

FORTY MILES NORTH OF MOAB, UTAH

Sunlight streamed in through windows high-up on the walls in the vast hall, touching tall ceilings and casting shadows in the open spaces among the pews. If not for the musty smell, one might even call the place clean. It felt odd returning here after years of being away. Knowing all that I knew now.

I came to a stop in front of the altar along a side wall. A portrait of one of the Founders adorned the wall above it. I didn't know his name. On the altar itself sat a silver bowl of holy water. A placard next to it read, *Cleanse yourself. This is a place for all to heal.*

I looked down at my bloodstained hands. After a slight hesitation, I dipped them in the sacred water—and turned it red. Once they were clean, I wiped my hands with one of the towels laid out next to the bowl. Returning my gaze to the Founder, I noticed another placard placed next to his portrait. *Pray for your forgiveness, for we all lack Salvation.*

For the first time since I was a child, sitting in this very room in one of these very pews, I put my hands together and closed my eyes. I wasn't entirely sure to whom I was praying, but the time passed, and I made the usual. One for forgiveness, one for strength, and one for guidance.

"You should not be here," a cold voice interrupted me.

I opened my eyes, unclasped my hands, and moved them behind my back. Without facing her, I said, "Oh? I thought this was a 'place for all to heal.'"

She didn't rise to my taunt. Instead, she asked, "Why are you here?"

"Felt like a chat."

I turned and revealed my face to her, and her open surprise thrilled me. In a flash, she stood inches from me and took hold of my chin in a painful grip. She moved my head from side to side, tilted it up toward the light, inspecting every inch of my face with intense scrutiny.

"Impeccable," she muttered, releasing me. "You have not aged a day since I last saw you... Pray, you have not aged at *all*."

I smirked, stepping away from her. "Must be my new skin-care routine."

As I started to take a turn about the room, pretending to take note of the various decorations and elements, she continued.

"Those bodies they found... That was you, wasn't it?"

I paused before the confessional booths and opened a door to peer inside the empty space. "So what if it was?"

"You didn't even try to hide the bodies!"

I let the door to the confessional slam as I faced her again. "Please. I dumped them in the middle of the desert, *and* I shredded them. Did you see that? How much more hidden can you get?" I resumed circling the room as she began lecturing me.

"You cannot be so cavalier about such things. We are a Collective. I don't know how many times I must tell you that. Your actions affect *all* of us. If the hunters caught wind—"

"The hunters don't know about us. And if they did, they wouldn't know what to do with us." I picked up a candlestick and inspected the design before setting it back down. "They don't know who we are, what we are. They don't know how to kill us. Besides, I disguised my kills. They won't know what to make of it."

"I wouldn't be so sure. Their archives span centuries."

"Well, the last two I met were absolutely clueless. And quite easy to kill." I finally circled around to where I'd started and stopped before the altar.

"You *killed*—" She paused to fully understand me. "They were hunters. You're killing hunters?"

My silence spoke for itself.

"You *foolish* child!"

I gritted my teeth at her tone but held my tongue.

"If you're killing hunters," she continued, "it's only a matter of time before they're onto you. And then they'll be onto all of us. You have endangered us all. And for what? Your actions are irredeemably selfish. You will lead them straight to us. They'll kill us all."

"Oh, no. I won't let that happen."

She scoffed. "You've sentenced us all to death, and yet you treat us with sarcasm! Why am I not surprised? You have never had the best interests of the Collective in your heart."

"Hmm, for once, you're right."

"I won't let you get away with it. Not this time. I'll alert the elders, and you will be— *ahhhhhhh*!"

Her scream perforated the still air of the room, echoing off the high ceilings. It was beautiful in its agony.

"Not so fast," I said as I turned to face her yet again. Her eyes were wide with confusion and fear.

"Impossible," she spat through the pain.

"No," I told her, doing my best to emulate her condescending tone. "Just very, *very* old magic that you and all the other *elders* are too chickenshit to use."

"*Forbidden* magic," she corrected.

"A perfect lie you crafted for us."

"You cannot—" She stopped as another agonized scream ripped out of her.

I *tsk*ed. "I wouldn't struggle against those bindings if I were you."

Her breathing became labored as her pain undoubtedly worsened. "You cannot...you can't do this."

"Oh, but I can."

She screamed as I tightened my hold on her being.

"You see, I tried doing it the way you taught me. I went after the young, the ones *you* said would be the most nourishing. I didn't toy with them, didn't *play with my food*. In other words, I only consumed the power you *let* me consume."

"If you consume too much," she gasped through heavy breaths, "there will not be enough—"

"Another beautiful lie." I cinched my hold a little more. She whimpered. "But I've learned the truth. And, well, as you can see, I've learned some new tricks."

"You haven't learned the truth. You're lying to yourself now."

"One of the hunters I killed was in his fifties," I continued, ignoring her. "And he was...*delectable*."

I stepped up to her, frozen in place, bound to my will. I lifted her chin and inspected her face as she had mine earlier. Her eyes held so much within them, so much light, so much energy.

"Now, tell me," I said. "In all your time, how many years have *you* consumed? Hundreds? Thousands?" I dropped her chin and closed the distance between us even more. "Imagine...what I'd gain from killing you."

She was trembling now, and still, she tried to plead her case. "You cannot kill us. As one, we persevere; alone, we perish."

"Hmm." I contemplated what she'd said. "Such a shame your last words are a lie."

Chapter Ten

Hunting Journal
October 16

Caught a break last night—an old journal of Mom's mentioned a similar case. People killed in their homes, scratch marks all up and down the body, black nails embedded in the wounds. She and Granddaddy narrowed it to a type of water spirit similar to a Kelpie, usually found in Scotland and Ireland. According to her, the bodies had remnants of salt water on them, which seems odd since there was no such evidence on our victim. I'll need to go back to the morgue and take another look at the body to confirm this is the same creature, but it's a solid lead.

Gene seems annoyed with me, but as long as he's chasing his tail and distracted by the victim's brother and her ex, I think we'll be good. He seems like a good detective, but he doesn't know what I know. Which is probably good, all things considered.

Jack woke in the morning feeling sore the way one only feels after sleeping on a rollaway cot. He stretched his limbs in opposite directions, an embarrassingly high-pitched squeak escaping his lips as he did so. Despite the uncomfortable bed and the few hours he was able to sleep, he felt well-rested. He lay there for a few minutes, his eyes drifting closed every now and then—floating in peaceful limbo between waking and sleeping—before memories of the previous night flooded his mind. A wave of mortification washed over him, effective as a bucket of cold water, and woke him fully.

He pushed himself up onto his elbows and peeked over the edge of the bed. It was empty. Gene had gotten up already.

Jack collapsed onto the cot. Coming out to Gene hadn't been in his plans, full stop, and it certainly hadn't been in his plans to do it in a random hotel room in the middle of the Utah desert. After his talk with Maggie, and with the hunter meeting coming up, he was more anxious than usual. He'd been amped up and talkative last night and remembered Gene was less than pleased he'd kept him up chatting. But he still indulged him. Jack wondered why.

Then, an image of Gene's molten gaze flashed through his mind, the way his eyes had lingered on Jack's half-dressed frame the night before, and warmth spread through him.

The door opened suddenly, and a bright stream of sunlight hit him square in the eyes. He winced.

"Morning, sunshine," Gene greeted him as the door swung closed behind him. He tossed a brown bag to Jack, but his reactions weren't quite up to speed yet, so it hit him beneath the sternum. Jack grunted softly at the impact, not that it hurt—simply unexpected. "Got you a muffin."

Jack sat up and opened the bag. A blueberry muffin sat inside. "Thanks," he said and dug into it.

"Coffee's in the car. We should probably get going."

Right. Not needing to be told twice, Jack scrambled out of bed. He pulled on his discarded slacks as he stood. He sniffed his button-down from yesterday—*not too bad*—and put it on. As Jack buttoned up his shirt, he let his attention drift over to his partner, who stood by the door reading over the case file quietly. Gene seemed determinedly focused on the papers in front of him, and Jack's stomach sank. See, *this* was what he didn't want to happen.

He finished getting dressed, slipped his phone into his pocket, grabbed the muffin, and headed for the door.

"Let's go," he said, pulling it open and leaving the room without another glance at his partner.

A moment later, Gene followed.

The ride to the county morgue—which was in the basement of Moab Regional Hospital—was quiet. Once Jack finished off his muffin, he sat and watched the desert pass by. Miles and miles of open space, not a human to be seen. Every ten miles or so, there'd be a gas station on the side of the road, but those were the only signs of civilization on their journey to Moab proper.

As they pulled into the hospital parking lot, Jack couldn't take it anymore. Gene parked and cut the engine.

"Hey, before we go in..." Jack started.

Gene looked at him expectantly.

"About last night." Jack couldn't quite bring himself to meet his partner's eyes. "I'd appreciate it if you don't...if you—"

Gene held up a hand. "No worries. It's your business."

Jack caught Gene's gaze. "And you don't mind?"

"Well, I'd be lying if I said it didn't take me by surprise, and I'm sorry if that sent the wrong message, but to be fair, it *was* four in the morning." Gene laughed. "Honestly, though, it doesn't change how I feel about you at all."

Jack released a breath of relief and quirked a smile. "So you're saying you still barely tolerate me?"

Gene chuckled, his soft brown eyes radiating a sense of safety. "Exactly. Now, come on. Let's go sign this paperwork and get back to Salt Lake."

*

*F*inally, Gene pulled into his parking space at the office around four in the afternoon. Jack slept in the seat next to him, but his eyes flickered open as Gene put the car in park, and it rocked in place. He'd slept most of the drive. Gene had thought about waking him a couple of times and asking him to take over, but he didn't. It wasn't only because Jack had looked so damn peaceful that Gene couldn't bear to wake him, Gene had also heard him last night, tossing and turning. He knew Jack hadn't slept much—granted, he hadn't either, but he was more awake than his partner.

But now, it was time to sleep, he thought as a yawn ripped through him.

"God, I'm about to pass out," Gene said, rubbing his eyes.

Jack sat up and stretched as best he could within the confines of the passenger seat. "You could have woken me. I wouldn't have minded."

"Nah. It's all right. I enjoy driving."

Jack gave him a small smile, a hand on the door handle. "Well. I'll leave you to it, then. See you tomorrow."

"See you," he said through another yawn.

Jack waved as he got out of the car and went to his own a few spaces down.

Gene watched him and then downed the last of his coffee. The dregs of an hours-old brew tasted like tar, cold and bitter, and he couldn't help a cough and a *yech*. The taste alone gave him enough of a boost to drive home.

It only took him fifteen minutes, but Gene couldn't tell you how he got from point A to point B, so tired he'd zoned out completely, and drove home on autopilot. *I should not be driving.* He stepped down from his company-issued SUV and staggered up the front steps. He didn't make it to his bed, collapsing right then and there on the living room couch.

When Gene woke sometime later, he didn't know why. There was a crick in his neck and his left arm was asleep, but they weren't bad enough to have woken him. He shifted off his arm and closed his eyes. Sleep, he thought.

Five loud raps on his door jolted him awake, and he sprang up like a weed. *"Shit!"*

He released a deep breath when he realized it was only someone at the door. Gene swung his legs over the side of the couch and caught his breath before answering it. When he pulled the door open, he immediately regretted it. It was times like these that he wished his front door had windows beside it or at least a peephole.

His sister, Mallory, brushed past him without invitation.

"I'm sorry, did I say you could come in?" he asked.

She turned to him, arms crossed, face angry. Gene closed the door, trudged into the living room, and collapsed into the couch cushions, hopeful they might swallow him whole. Mallory followed him into the room but remained standing. She looked much as she did ten years ago, save for some extra wrinkles around her eyes and mouth. She wore a pair of brown slacks and a plain, pale blue T-shirt, a gray zip-up sweater over it.

"Want to take a seat?"

"When, exactly, did you speak with Prudence?"

"Last week."

"And you didn't think to tell me? To ask me if it was okay to, to—"

"To what, Mal?" Gene sat up and rested his elbows on his knees. "She's my niece. She called me and said she needed help. So I helped… I'm sorry, but did I tell her to *lie* to you? Did I tell her to hide this from you—as she *has* been doing for the past three months? No! I seem to remember telling her to talk to you!" He let out a small laugh. "She's so scared of you that she didn't bother trying to—"

"You don't know anything about our family!" Mallory screamed. "You haven't been a part of it for *ten* years, Eugene. You don't get to waltz back in and pretend nothing's happened."

Gene pushed himself off the couch. "You and your husband are raising your kids how Mom and Dad raised us. What is it that I don't know, Mal? Huh?"

"You don't know *us!*"

The exclamation hung in the air, the weight of it palpable. They stared each other down for a few heartbeats before Mallory averted her eyes to the floor. She paced a few steps backward before returning her focus to Gene.

"Despite what you think of us, Prudence is *my* daughter, and I will raise her the way I see fit."

"She's practically an adult, Mallory. You can't control every little thing she does."

"It's not about control," she said exasperatedly. "You don't know anything about raising a child. It's not about control; it's about protection."

Gene considered his next words carefully before he said them in a gentle but firm tone. "If it's about protection, why won't you give her what she needs to protect herself?"

"It's not that simple."

Gene released a cynical laugh. "Of course it's not. Nothing ever is." He turned away from her. "There's clearly something wrong, and she needs medicine to treat it." He spun to face her again. "But you won't to take her to see a doctor because you're afraid they'll give her birth control pills, which is condemned by the Church. You're so worried about what other people will think—"

"That's not it! It's not how it used to be. It's not as...condemned as it once was. But it's seen as something that should be decided between husband and wife. It's not for me to interfere with—"

"With your daughter's health? Jesus, Mallory! Do you hear yourself? Prue needs this. She *needs* it. If you don't help her, I will."

Mallory clenched her jaw. "I'm taking her to the doctor tomorrow."

"You are?"

"Yes." She kept her eyes trained on the floor. "I'm here because..." She took a seat on the sofa chair next to the couch. "Joseph works for the Church; our insurance doesn't cover..."

Understanding dawned on him as he sat on the couch again, and he bristled with annoyance. "So you came here to yell at me, argue with me about the *morality* of birth control, and then...ask me to help pay for

Prue's medication?"

"Well?"

"She's not on my plan. My insurance won't cover it either. And if it's money you need..." He huffed. "Mallory. You said it yourself. It's been ten years, and this is how you want to rekindle our relationship?"

"Frankly, I don't want to rekindle it at all."

"Doing a great job of asking for my help."

"Please," she said, looking at him in earnest now.

He wanted to say no. He almost did. But then he thought of Prue. Not the seven-year-old girl he knew a decade ago, but the seventeen-year-old he'd met last week. Prue's eyes had sought his imploringly, the same way they always had. He could see himself in her—the desperate need to get out, hoping something would open for her, to give her a push.

He inhaled deeply and held the breath deep in his throat before exhaling in a rush. "Fine."

Mallory nodded, and when the tense silence stretched, she stood. "Thank you." She headed for the door.

In the fifteen seconds it took for her to make it there, in the five it took for her to open it and leave, Gene thought about stopping her. About asking her to stay to catch up, to see how she was doing, how everyone was doing. But that wasn't why she came here. And quite honestly, he didn't want to entertain her blind selfishness.

Somehow more tired than before, he returned to his bedroom. Sunlight streamed in, and he pulled the curtains closed before sinking into the soft sheets and falling asleep.

Chapter Eleven

Jack stared up at his sister's house. It sat in an idyllic neighborhood, every other house identical to one another, Utah mountains off in the distance behind them. He wondered how Maggie had ended up here. It was nice, no doubt, but it wasn't her, no matter how much she claimed it to be. He wondered where she hid her machetes.

He clocked Dana's car in the driveway; they'd likely already been here for hours. Even before all this, Dana'd been close with Maggie. And Jack. They'd all been close, once upon a time. Dana had stopped talking to him when he'd decided to join the force. Maggie hung on, tried to make it work for a year or two, but she, too, eventually gave up and cut him off. They'd talked here and there over the years—what to do with Mom, mostly—but Maggie had largely been silent.

And now...well, now, it felt as if everything was almost back to normal. Jack worried though. When this case was said and done, would they all return to being strangers? Maggie to her cookie-cutter life, and Dana to their wild one?

Jack didn't know. But as long as they had this case, they'd be together.

His phone buzzed with a text message from Gene.

ME's taking his sweet time with this report. Gonna go apply the pressure. Want to come?

Jack smiled despite himself. He didn't fully understand the beef his partner had with the medical examiner, but he found it endearing, truth be told. A movement in his peripheral vision made him look up—Maggie waved him in. He typed out a quick response.

Can't. Taking care of some personal business this morning. Be in after lunch.

With that, he cut his engine and went inside to join Maggie and Dana.

"Been sitting out there long?" Maggie asked by way of greeting. Her dog came wandering around the corner and, at the sight of Jack, picked up her pace, her tail wagging.

Jack gave the dog a few scratches behind the ear as he said, "Had to answer a few texts."

She closed the door behind him.

He looked around. "Is your husband *ever* home?"

"Yes...he travels a lot for work."

Jack gazed at her, knowing it would say more than any words could. She waved a dismissive hand and led him to the living room, where Dana sat on the couch, leaning forward, elbows resting on their knees. Old tattered journals lay spread out on the coffee table before them.

"Hey," they said with a smile, turning to Jack.

He gestured to the table. "Yours?"

"Some. Most of these are yours and Maggie's. Kurt's bringing his."

Jack took a seat on the floor and pulled a random journal toward him, this one, his mother's from before he was born. It had to be at least forty years old. Her writing was almost indecipherable, not because the script was untidy—quite the contrary—but because she used a code. Luckily for Jack, he could read it. His mom had taught it to him when he was a kid, and since he'd become a cop, he'd started keeping his own journals in code too.

"Not much in that one," Maggie said as she moved past him to sit on the couch.

"I didn't know you could read Mom's journals."

"I can read 'em well enough."

He hummed and started reading. An hour or so later, he closed the book and put it on the table with a sigh. He swiped another, one of Granddaddy's. Unlike Jack's mom, his grandfather didn't use a code, but he might as well have—his handwriting was horrible. Jack passed it to Maggie, whose script was as atrocious, and picked up another one of Mom's. They continued this way for a few hours. Finally, around noon, a knock sounded at the door.

Dana closed the journal they'd been reading—one of their dad's—stood, and headed for the door. "That'll be Kurt."

Jack scrambled to his feet and positioned himself so that he wasn't immediately visible to their new guest. He waited through sounds of the door opening, loud, happy greetings, and footsteps drawing closer. Maggie smiled and stood, and there Kurt was.

The first thing Jack noticed about him was that he looked like a verifiable hunter in his dark brown cargo pants, a camouflage jacket, and a bright orange hat, which sat backward on his head. And what had Dana called him? *Little Kurt Taupin.* Right. He *was* little. Granted, Maggie was taller than the average woman, and Dana stood at almost six-foot-two, but still. Kurt couldn't be taller than five-foot-three, with a lithe, slender frame. He had sandy-blond hair and a bit of scruff along his jaw. It had been about fifteen years since Jack had last seen him, but he didn't seem that different, to be honest. Maybe some crow's feet around his eyes, but that was it.

"Maggie Cartwright," he screeched, his Southern accent breaking his voice. "C'mere, it's been too long!" He opened his arms and, despite his shorter stature, managed to barrel her in a hug.

They pulled away from each other with smiles on their faces and exchanged some small talk. Eventually, Maggie's eyes drifted over to Jack.

"Oh, Kurt, this is my twin brother, Jack."

Jack sent her a grateful look for sneaking the word "twin" in there, and he hoped Kurt would put the rest together himself.

Kurt faced him with a smile, though confusion shone in his eyes. "I thought you had a sist—" Kurt cut himself off as realization dawned on his face.

Jack watched him puzzle it out. He'd always hated this part, sitting in this silent limbo, waiting for someone to decide what to do with him. What should they say? *How* should they say it? What people chose to say after learning about his identity was always telling of how their brain worked and how truly accepting they were. His sister, for example, hadn't blinked an eye and teasingly told him, "Always wanted a brother." His mother hadn't said anything, just cupped his cheeks and smiled.

And now, he awaited Kurt's response to meeting someone with whom he'd already been acquainted but had never technically met.

After an instant of shock passed, Kurt extended a hand. "I'm Kurt. Nice to meet you, Jack."

Relief flooded through him. He released a small breath and shook Kurt's hand.

"So," Kurt said, "what do we got?"

And with that, they brought Kurt up to speed on the case and their progress thus far—or lack thereof. Kurt blended well into their little group. He was of the same age and similar to Dana and Jack in that hunting in his family went back generations. Jack hadn't crossed paths with him much because Kurt's family mostly stayed in the Southeast, covering the cases that popped up there. While Jack and Maggie had traveled the country and the world with their mother and grandfather, their "home base" had always been Utah. Dana's too. As Kurt talked and told various stories, Jack had to admit he was impressed. The guy knew his stuff. He was happy to have him on the team.

"Y'all sure it's not a Were of some kind?" Kurt asked sometime later.

"Definitely not," Maggie said. "There's no pattern to the kills."

"Well, if the bodies are being moved as you say, maybe they're being killed on the lunar cycle, and we don't know it."

"They're fresh kills," Jack said. "Plus, do you know of anything that would bother to *move* the body of their kills? A Were certainly wouldn't care."

Kurt weighed that. "True."

"Then there's the lavender."

"*Hmm*. It's a pickle, ain't it?"

With an amused smile on their face, Dana said, "Which is why we called your dumbass to help."

He grinned at them. "Alrighty, then. I got some of my journals in the truck. Gimme a hand?"

Once the two of them had gone, Maggie said, "See? No big deal."

Jack hummed in agreement. "I'm only glad Argus isn't here yet."

Maggie snorted. "He'll be here soon."

Jack mentally groaned.

"What's your partner think you're doing right now?"

"Told him I had some personal stuff to take care of, but I don't know. He probably thinks I'm ditching work. Apparently, I have a reputation around the office that I'm a bad cop."

That made Maggie laugh. "Good for you."

Yeah, good for me, Jack thought as Dana and Kurt returned, each with armfuls of journals. Trailing behind them, looking old as shit, was none other than Argus Vasil himself.

Upon spotting Jack, Argus smiled. "Ah, Detective Cartwright. It's been a while."

Argus definitely looked like he'd seen some shit, with skin like aged leather, wrinkled and discolored in some places but, on the whole, fitting for his face. Unlike many men his age, he still had most of his hair, though its once bright red hue was now white as a freshly cleaned bone. His faded eyes had only a few specs of green pigmentation standing out against the gray. Dressed in a plaid three-piece suit, he stood stooped lower than the last time Jack had seen him, with a small hunch at the top of his back. He walked with a mahogany cane, the handle intricately carved into a lion. His stature, his small limp, his frail body, none of it made him appear any less deadly. The man simply had a murderous air about him.

When Jack didn't acknowledge his greeting, his smile widened, and his eyes slithered over to Maggie.

"Magdalena," Argus said affectionately, arms outstretched. "Why, I thought you had left the business."

Maggie shook her head at his use of her full name and gave him a brief hug. "I did. Jack pulled me back in."

"Did he?" He faced Jack again, seemingly pleased by that.

"We going to work, or what?" Jack asked as he gestured to the journals.

"Straight to business, I see," Argus mused. He took a seat on the couch across from where Jack sat on the floor.

Everyone else took a seat around the coffee table and started catching Argus up. Jack had been through it all so many times at this point that he zoned out, his mind wandering elsewhere. He was on edge, unable to sit still. He kept bouncing his leg and fidgeting with his hands. It didn't help that he could feel Argus casting amused glances his way, fully aware his presence was making Jack uneasy. Argus had been akin to a parent to Maggie and him. But sometimes, no matter what, parents and kids didn't get along.

Jack tuned in again when they began spitballing ideas.

"What about a changeling?" Jack asked.

The rest of them chorused their universal dissent.

"Seriously," Jack said.

"I can guarantee you," Argus said, "they are a myth."

"I know we don't have any record of them, but that doesn't mean they don't exist. This *thing* isn't anything we've ever come up against. We have got to start thinking outside the box."

Argus gave him a level look. "Changelings do not exist because for them to exist, faeries would have to exist, and for fae to exist, you must be ready to believe in a realm parallel to ours in which they live. Now, are you willing to believe in such a thing?"

Jack scowled at him.

"Exactly." Argus settled further into the cushions. "No, this is not the work of faeries.”

"Okay, well, what about a hybrid of some kind. We know it's not a Were, but what if there are hybrids we don't know about?"

"And what exactly would you have in mind?" Argus said.

"Maybe a dhampir."

Argus laughed. "I do believe you've been reading too much fiction." His eyes gleamed with amusement. "Dhampirs do not exist. Vampires are nearly extinct, as you know, and they certainly cannot breed with humans. This isn't some ridiculous romance novel."

Jack bit his tongue to keep from remarking further. Then he said, "Well, what about you? Got any bright ideas, old man?"

Argus gave him a smile. "Perhaps," he said cryptically.

Jack huffed and focused on Maggie. He refused to rise to Argus's taunt. "Come on. Don't you think we should start entertaining ideas outside of what we normally think?"

"Of course... But I think we should start with things we *know* exist and work from there."

Jack released a frustrated groan and pushed himself off the floor. "It's pointless. Completely pointless. We know—we *know* it's not anything we've faced before. Or anything Mom's faced, or Grandaddy, or you." He pointed to Argus. "We know in our guts this is something new. But none of you are willing to use your goddamn heads." He checked his watch. "So be it. I have to get to work anyway."

With that, he fled the house. God, he hadn't lasted twenty minutes with Argus. He didn't know why he let him get under his skin, but he did. He always did. He threw himself into his car and drove away before anyone could stop him.

He needed not to be there anymore.

*

Gene returned from the coroner's office with an autopsy report. The ME hadn't been all that pleased at his lack of patience, but Gene couldn't care less. The report, though—while he was happy to have it—didn't reveal much. A lot like the other one. The ME had a specialist coming in to examine the X-rays in hopes they could get something from the bones, but Gene knew a cold case when he caught one. Not to say he wouldn't try, but…he wasn't holding his breath.

He'd made it to his desk and draped his coat over the top of his chair when the captain called to him and beckoned him into his office.

"Yes, sir?" Gene said as he entered and shut the door behind him.

Captain Smith, a portly man, stood behind his desk with his hands on his hips. "Where's your partner?"

"He's taking care of some personal business. He said he'd be in after lunch."

"So let me get this straight," Smith said. "You're in the middle of two cases with no leads, and you're giving your detectives personal time?"

"Sir—"

"You're a sergeant, are you not?"

Gene sealed his lips and nodded.

"Right. You're the leader of this team, and as a leader, I expect you to *lead*." Smith's voice left no room for argument.

"Yes, sir."

"Now, you better get your house in order, you hear?"

"Yes, sir."

"And you tell Cartwright if he wants to keep his job, he better show up to work on time, especially on briefing days."

Oh, shit. Gene had completely forgotten.

"Now, get." The captain shooed him out, and Gene left without another word.

He went to his desk and collected his files before heading to the briefing room. Detectives from the other divisions were already there, sitting around and making genial conversation. Gene took a seat by himself near the front.

"Hey, Bradshaw, how's it feel going two months without closing a case?" asked Gomez, a detective on another Major Crimes team.

Gene didn't let himself rise to the taunt. Gomez's partner strolled in and stopped by Gene's table.

"Where's your partner?" Daniels asked. "Leaving you high and dry already?"

Gene met the other sergeant's challenging stare head-on. "Running down field leads, actually."

Daniels gave a short laugh. "Right. I'm sure he's being super helpful...especially considering you're working a case with, what, zero evidence?"

Gene offered a small smile. "More than you might think."

"That's interesting. Because as I remember it, we can't even officially declare it a crime. You sure it wasn't an animal attack? Why waste the resources?"

Gene didn't have the time to explain to him why it was important to run down every possible lead before drawing a conclusion. Didn't have time to explain why they, as law enforcement officers, should care about the victims they investigate—whether their deaths were accidental or not. Instead, he was saved by the bell as the captain walked in and called the meeting to order. Daniels smirked, gave him a wink, and continued to his seat next to his partner.

"I want round-table updates from all of you, but before we get into it, here's Lieutenant Michaels with the AET."

The lieutenant stepped up to the podium as one of her detectives passed out files to everyone. Gene flipped through it as she talked.

"Thank you, Captain. Alcohol Enforcement's been working a TRACE investigation, delving into a couple of recent alcohol-related fatalities on I-15." She clicked a remote, and an image of a car wreck flashed up on the screen beside her. "We've been able to track it all to the same bar near the U."

Worry flared up and chewed at Gene.

"Seems simple, right?" The lieutenant chuckled. "If only. Turns out this bar's been buying apple vodka from an LLC called The Brewing Company. Well, surprise, surprise, it's a shell. I mean, *The Brewing Company?* Come on, fellas, that doesn't come close to sounding legit. Anyway, my detectives have tracked the company to a couple a guys in Sandy. And before we bring them in, we want to be sure we got them dead to rights. Their moonshine's killed two people and injured six others. So. The AET's set up a stakeout for tonight and tomorrow."

Understanding dawned on Gene.

"And since we're a little short-staffed, we need each of you to offer two detectives to take a shift."

Gene raised his hand, directing his comment to Captain Smith. "All due respect, sir, but my team's got two active murders on our desks too—"

"I'm not asking," Smith said. "Besides, you got something new on those murders? Huh?"

Gene's silence spoke for itself, and whispers rippled throughout the room. He ignored them.

"Didn't think so. No. Tonight, you can work this stakeout."

Gene seethed but didn't say anything else. The rest of the meeting passed in a blur, and an hour later, he left the room in a gloomy mood.

Nothing screamed, "I have confidence in you," like assigning you and your partner to a completely random other case. He took a seat at his desk and tried to push his anger aside. Déjà vu rolled through him, and he opened the top drawer in his filing cabinet. His old case, the one he obsessed over, rested atop neatly kept hanging folders. He stared at it and grew cold thinking about it. Clenching his jaw, he slammed the drawer shut.

With Jack still MIA, Gene headed down to the gun range. He needed to blow off some steam.

Chapter Twelve

Case Notes, Case #187.2210.03.FS.6892
October 17

[DO NOT INCLUDE WITH COURT-REQUIRED NOTES]

I think I'm about ready to wring Det. Cartwright's neck. He is currently off running around God knows where supposedly chasing down leads from our victim's recent credit card purchases, but I don't believe him. So far, he's had nothing to show for any of these so-called leads, and I'm sick of it. I'm his superior officer, for crying out loud! The least he could do is respond to a direct order.

"Thought I'd find you down here."

Gene had just taken his earmuffs off and jumped at the sound of his partner's voice coming out of nowhere. "Jesus. Way to scare a guy." He pressed the button to pull his target paper toward him.

"Good shooting," Jack said, stepping closer.

Gene could feel his breath on his neck, and he tried to ignore the goosebumps that arose from the sensation. Jack's voice carried a slight hint of surprise and, if Gene wasn't mistaken, approval.

Gene shifted as he deconstructed his gun and placed it in the return tray. "Thanks."

He dropped off all his gear at the check-out desk, Jack following quietly behind him. As they made their way up to the bullpen, Jack spoke up.

"So what's this stakeout I hear we're going on?"

"A dumb TRACE investigation Alcohol Enforcement needs more hands on."

Jack groaned behind him. "Those investigations are so...ridiculous."

When they reached the top of the stairs, Gene turned to him and walked backward a few paces. "Hey, that's the job." He faced forward again and led the way to their desks.

Gene rifled through the papers on his desk before finding the file he'd gotten during the briefing. He handed it over to Jack. "Apparently, there are a couple of guys in Sandy who are making illegal moonshine and selling it to bars and clubs under a fake business. It's a registered LLC, but it doesn't have any of the proper liquor licenses or anything."

"And we hope to get what from the stakeout exactly?"

"Intel, I guess."

Jack released a long breath as he took a seat at his desk. "What a *great* use of our time."

My thoughts exactly.

*

Jack parked across the still, dark street, three houses down from the house in question. A large tree with overhanging branches helped conceal their plain black sedan. It also helped that, of the three lamp posts on the street, they parked closest to the one that flickered, weakly casting light along the sidewalks.

He cut the engine and relaxed in his seat. "And now we wait."

Gene hummed.

The silence between them stretched. Jack reached for the binoculars. The house was dark, too, not much activity; in fact, he'd wager they weren't home.

Bzz-bzz. Gene pulled out his phone. He flipped it open and typed out a quick text before shoving it in his pocket. A second later, it buzzed with another text. Gene's texting went on for a few minutes before curiosity got the best of Jack.

"Still amazes me you can text with one of those," he said.

"This thing cost a *tenth* of what yours did, and it won't shatter if I happen to drop it."

Jack laughed, setting the binoculars on the dash. "I'm sorry; how old are you again?"

Gene shoved him playfully. "Shut up," he muttered as another text came through. He groaned this time, and his brows drew closer together. He stared at the message and then closed his phone without responding.

"Clingy girlfriend?"

"Definitely not... It's my sister Mallory."

Jack wracked his brain for what his partner had told him about his family. "Your sister... Wait, the one you don't talk to?"

"I don't talk to any of my family," he said. "But, yes. She's been texting me about my niece... I got roped into helping her pay for a medical treatment for her, and—" He rubbed his eyes. "It turned into more of a pain than I was expecting. And *now*, she wants me to go to Prue's birthday party, and I—I love my niece, I do, but I'm not sure I want to see everyone else. Besides, I'm sure Prue doesn't want her uncle crashing her eighteenth birthday party and making it all about his drama."

Jack wasn't sure what to say to that.

He was relieved when Gene tapped his bicep, nodding toward the house.

"We got movement."

And for a little while, that was all they did: their jobs. They tracked comings and goings from the house, noted license plates of cars that drove by, took pictures of the suspects. For the most part, they did it in silence, only speaking when needed. After about an hour, it went quiet again, and they relaxed in their seats.

"It's not a good sign, is it?" Jack asked.

"What?"

"Getting reassigned to another case. We've got nothing on our murders, and by the looks of it, we're not going to have anything new anytime soon. They're going to take the case from us."

Gene was quiet for a while. "I don't know." He paused. "As gruesome as it is, as long as bodies keep turning up, they can't declare them cold cases."

"They could rule them animal deaths."

Gene tilted his head side to side. "I suppose, but I don't think they will." He leaned his head against the head rest and stared up at the roof of the car. "What bothers me..."

Jack prompted when he didn't continue, "What?"

"What bothers me is I've had a case like this before. Obviously, not literally, with the murders and the way the victims were killed, but...it was similar."

"How so?"

"Well—" Gene frowned as if trying to decide how to tell the story. "I told you, right, that no one wants to work with me?"

Jack had been curious about this ever since that talk. "Yeah, which makes no sense to me, by the way. Me, I get. I know I'm not the easiest person to work with, but you? You're a straitlaced, by-the-books kinda guy."

"Yeah, well, when I graduated from the academy, I went straight to the State Bureau of Investigation which, while not unheard of, is not usual. Most of the time, people work local police, sheriff's offices, get some experience in the field, and *then* apply to the SBI. Now, a lot of people liked to say it was my name, you know my family, that got me this job. And truth be told, I'm not sure if it was my name or if it was me. I mean, I worked as a park ranger for a few years before I went to the police academy, so I did have some law enforcement experience, different as it was... The short of it is, a lot of people didn't like me for that reason—dumb nepotism shit. They felt I hadn't earned it or whatever."

He paused and took a heavy breath before continuing. "And around the same time, I...started questioning my faith and growing apart from my family. I started— There was a lot going on.

"Then I got assigned this case. Nothing seemed that big, to be honest, only some suspicious farm animal deaths that needed to be investigated. I was working with this guy from animal control, and all I was supposed to do was investigate the farms' finances. Unlike the case we're working now, there were a good number of leads and avenues to go down, and pretty much all of them led to the Church. The Mormon Church. And as you can imagine, here in shiny, bright Utah, that was pretty big."

"You don't say," Jack muttered.

"You know how in movies and TV shows, they show those cops that go against the grain, the ones who aren't afraid to investigate the politicians or the rich people or whatever, how they always say 'yeah, that's a good cop'? It's always seen as something that should be done."

That's because it should, Jack thought.

"Well, in real life, if you're one of those cops, you don't always end up on the right side of things. Or, at least, in other cops' eyes, you don't." Gene gazed out the window. "So, I pushed. I investigated. I poked my nose where people didn't want me poking it. And I took one step too far, and the case was taken away from me. It was put on a shelf and not much later called a cold case. It was never fully finished or solved. I still dig into it from time to time, but a lot of the leads are dead, a lot of the evidence gone."

"Doesn't seem right."

"It's not," Gene said. "I know it sounds completely unrelated, but when we had this briefing today, and they told us about this dumb, fucking TRACE investigation, I went to my desk, and...I swear it was like I was there eight years ago when all that happened. It was as if it was that day again, and I got the feeling they were going to take it away from us.

This case. Because that's what happened last time. But. This case is different. It's murder—murders, plural. And, again, as ugly as it is, I think as long as we have bodies, we'll keep the case."

Jack let the dark thought hang between them for a while. He had so many questions and comments running through his mind that it wasn't a matter of not knowing *what* to say, but rather which to say first—if at all. Eventually, he settled on attempting to lighten the mood.

"Hmm, I can see the headline now—*Homicide Detective Roots for the Killer in Order To Keep His Job*," he said in his best news-anchor voice.

Gene laughed at the dark joke. "Ah, God, we're going to hell, aren't we?"

Jack smirked. "I definitely am. I don't know about you."

Gene looked over at him, a relaxed smile on his face. "If you go, I go. Besides, if you're there, I'm not sure I'd call it Hell."

Something twinged in Jack's chest, and he held Gene's warm gaze for the length of a breath before he cleared his throat and averted his eyes.

Jack refocused on the house. "Seems pretty quiet now."

Gene shifted beside him. "Yeah."

"If you, uh, want to get some shut-eye, I can take first watch."

"Yeah, that'd...that'd be great." Gene reclined his chair a little farther, crossed his arms, and closed his eyes.

Jack let his attention linger on him before he shifted back to the house, but his mind remained elsewhere.

*

Come midnight, Gene was snoring, and Jack was getting bored. Right as he was about to wake Gene and have him take over, the streetlamp in front of the suspects' house blew out. Bright sparks drifted to the ground. Jack went still. Seconds later, the flickering light went dark too. That left one streetlamp at the end of the lane. Farther back, where they were parked, the street was cast into darkness. The wind picked up and began to whistle as an eeriness washed over him. Jack glanced at his partner—still sleeping—and climbed out of the car.

He closed the door as quietly as possible. Gene didn't stir. He turned to face the street. This time of night was usually quiet, but an odd quality hung in the stillness of the air. It didn't feel real, almost as though all the noise around him was suppressed; trees thrashed in the wind, but he couldn't hear them. It was as though the sounds hit a wall before reaching his ears—as if he were wearing earmuffs. Jack pulled his silver knife from his ankle holster and ventured into the shade.

His eyes had grown accustomed to the dark, and he was able to make out details. Down the street, on the dark end, another car sat parked along the side of the road, but it had been there before they arrived. Toward the working light, the street was empty. As he surveyed the area, he began cautiously making his way over to the first light that had blown, so he couldn't be spotted. The black windows of the suspects' house didn't tell if they were asleep or not.

Jack stepped over a crack in the sidewalk, and sound crashed into him so suddenly, he was hit with an instant headache.

"Fuck," he whispered, putting a hand to his forehead. Now, he heard an owl hoot down the street, the wind whistling, his own breathing. Curious, he stepped back over the crack, expecting his hearing to go again, but nothing happened. *Interesting.* He continued to the lamp post. As he reached it, a blur in his peripheral vision caught his attention, and he spun toward it.

Nothing.

He stared into the black space between the houses, willing himself to make out something, anything, but he didn't. Cursing under his breath, Jack walked into the yard. He was nearly at the fence when a low sound hissed behind him. He took a deep breath and turned around slowly.

Jack expected a multitude of dark creatures of the night—a werewolf, a goblin, some kind of spirit or ghost. Alas, it was a deer that returned his stare with big, black eyes. She emitted another warning sound when suddenly, a fawn jumped out from behind him and ran to her. They turned and trotted across the street and into the woods behind the neighbor's house.

Jack released a pent-up breath. His shoulders lost their tension, and he lowered his knife. Had it been all in his head? No, the sound thing was real…right?

When he returned to the car, Jack paused to scan the area and found no signs of anything hinky going on.

The streetlights flickered on again as he climbed into the driver's seat. As though nothing had happened.

Chapter Thirteen

A couple weeks went by, and Gene grew more worried every day that his dark words wouldn't hold up. *As long as there are bodies, they won't take it away.* And yet, it had grown quiet. For two weeks, nothing happened. Their absent leads dried up, and the case truly began to feel cold. And then, after a two-week drought, a body turned up.

Cameras flashed, reporters screamed questions—city police, rookie cops held them off behind wooden barricades. Gene stared up at the Temple, its towers looming over him, casting him in shadow. He took a deep breath and approached the crime scene.

This one was different. The body was fully intact, for one, but that didn't make it any less gruesome. In fact, it might have been worse.

Her mouth hung open in a silent scream, eyes wide open, clouded, and dry. Her pale gray, leathery skin clung to her bones so tightly it was as if someone had sucked all the blood and flesh from beneath. Like a vacuum seal.

"Can we get a sheet here?" Gene yelled, transfixed on the soulless eyes staring up at him.

A moment later, a sheet fell over her face.

"I'm gonna need a minute," he muttered when Jack stepped up next to him. Gene turned away from the body and sought refuge behind one of the ambulances. His breath came rapidly, his knees felt weak, and his heart thudded. He leaned against the side of the ambulance, trying to quell the rising need to puke.

He'd been a cop for close to ten years, and he'd never had a crime scene get to him this way. But this one was... It hit too close to home. A body displayed for all to see on the steps of the holiest institution in the state, a place he used to come with his family, a place that was sacred—or used to be. Now, what was it to him? A tie to his past. It was like a different life—hell, it had been. And he wished he could do away with it completely, wished he could forget the guilt, the distinct otherness he felt while sitting in the pews among his peers. Even before he understood why, Gene knew he didn't belong there, that he was different. And he wondered if he'd ever be able to shake the feeling, or if he was stuck with it forever.

Bit by bit, his breath slowed, and he shook himself out of it—or at least, managed to push his troubled emotions aside—and returned to the scene. He found Jack squatted close to the body, roaming over it as a curious animal might.

"Anything?" Gene asked.

Jack shot up, a gleam in his eyes. "Smell her."

Gene didn't hesitate to lean close and take a sniff of the body. The action felt inappropriate, but then the feeling fled. His gaze locked with Jack's. "Lavender."

He straightened up, his mind reeling. The MO was different, but... this couldn't be a coincidence, could it? This body must be connected to the ones they'd found in the desert.

Before he could say anything, two other detectives from Major Crimes strolled up.

Daniels said, "Bradshaw, Cartwright, what are you doing here? Is your case so cold you jump at any opportunity to leave the office?"

Gomez smirked. "Sorry, but this one's ours. Captain's orders."

Jack seemed ready to push back, but Gene held up a hand.

"No, you're right. We were simply curious." He jerked his head to the side, gesturing for Jack to follow. "Come on, Jack." Thankfully, his partner followed quietly. Until they were out of earshot, at least.

Jack grabbed his arm, the touch nearly searing Gene's skin, despite the layers of his coat, and forced him to turn around. "What was that? This is *our* case."

"No," Gene said, "it's theirs."

The statement seemed to enrage his partner. "You smelled it! This has to be connected to the others, and you know it!"

Gene gritted his teeth before he rattled off the company line. "It doesn't matter. What matters are our orders. Which are to stand down and let the others handle it. So that's what we're going to do."

"God. Do you hear yourself, Gene?" Jack wasn't yelling, but his tone had the same effect. "Come on, man. You got to trust me on this."

Butterflies fluttered in his stomach as he met Jack's eyes. For once, it was Jack standing over him, his smaller frame somehow imposing as he stood higher up on the hill. Where had the issue of trust come up? This hadn't been a matter of trust; it had been a matter of protocol and logic. But now? Now, it was all about trust. Oddly, Jack's insistence to do so almost made Gene do the opposite. *What isn't he telling me*?

Keeping his doubts at bay, Gene said, "This isn't about trust. It's about protocol. The captain wants them on the case, not us. And that's...that's final."

With that, Gene turned and retreated to his car. This time, Jack let him.

*

Jack paced in front of Maggie in her home office. "This is insane! We have a *normal* body for once, and it's given to someone else. Just when we might be able to get some answers, we're pushed aside. And Gene fucking let it happen!" He threw his hands up. "Unbelievable."

"Well, that's what you get for—"

"For being a cop. Yeah, yeah, I know." He stopped before her, his hands on his hips. "But I..."

"What?"

"I'm sick of lying to him. It's been better these past few weeks, but I can still tell there's something there. That he doesn't fully trust me."

She gave him a sympathetic grimace. "That's the life."

"What if...what if I told him?"

"No. No, you don't know how he'll react. You want to lose your job? I know I give you shit about it, but you at least seem to enjoy it."

"You're assuming he'll react badly."

"And *you're* assuming he'll accept it, no questions asked. Telling people never goes well."

"I get that, but..." Jack plopped down on the couch opposite her desk chair. "I can't lie to him anymore."

He felt Maggie's inquiring stare but kept his trained on the floor as he toyed with a loose thread on one of the cushions. He couldn't shake the distrust he'd seen in Gene's eyes, which was bad enough. He didn't need Maggie piling on.

She leaned forward, resting her elbows on her knees. "You remember what Mom told us when we were little? About Dad?"

They hardly ever talked about their father, let alone called him "Dad." Jack gestured for her to go on.

"When Mom told him, he threatened to have her committed, to take us away from her. All because he'd rather live in denial than accept the truth. If it hadn't been for Granddaddy, who knows what would have happened?"

"I told you I remembered. What's your point?"

"My point is that people who didn't grow up in this life don't take the truth very well." She paused. "My husband still doesn't know. And I don't plan on telling him."

"Yeah, and how's that working out for you? You think he has no suspicions that you're hiding something from him? Doesn't it get to you, lying to him every day?"

Maggie's jaw pulsed. "Never said it was easy. But that's the job. It's what we signed up for, and you know it."

Jack knew she was right, but he couldn't help the feeling that he could trust Gene implicitly, the one that twisted every time he lied to him. An opposing feeling plagued him, though, one that urged him to protect Gene, to keep him out of it. Some part of Jack wanted to keep him ignorant to reality as long as he could because maybe then, he'd be safe from it. But Jack knew that wouldn't protect him. Only the truth would.

He took a deep breath. "I still want to tell him."

"If you trust him, and you want to do this, I can't stop you. But be prepared for the high possibility that he won't react well."

"Message received."

Maggie swiveled toward her computer. The screen showed a spinning wheel, and a progress bar inched ever so slowly along the bottom.

"So, uh, what exactly are you doing?" Jack asked.

"I'm running the DNA from the two desert victims through the hunter database. Thought it was worth a shot."

"And you think it'll find someone who's not in the police database?"

"First of all," she said, "this database is international. Secondly, we scrub DNA and fingerprint records for any hunter who might have one. Helps us stay out of trouble if we ever get caught on anything shady."

"Well, that's new."

Maggie chuckled. "It was in beta around the time you joined the force."

"Still. It's pretty impressive—"

A loud *ping* from Maggie's computer cut him off.

"Holy shit," she muttered. "It worked."

Jack stood and peered over her shoulder as she clicked the blinking *99% MATCH* button on the screen. Two DMV-style photos popped up, both men, both in their late forties, early fifties. One appeared Hispanic, the other white.

"Pablo Ferrara and Michael Taupin."

"Wait, Taupin as in Kurt Taupin?" Jack asked.

"It's a big hunting family, no telling if they're closely related..."

Jack's world tilted. This didn't feel real. They had IDs. Real, honest-to-God victims that they could investigate.

"They're both hunters," Maggie said. "That can't be a coincidence."

"One, maybe. But two? Definitely not."

"I have to call Dana."

Right. Now, how in the hell was he supposed to keep *this* from Gene?

As if on cue, his phone rang, and his partner's name flashed across the screen.

Man, he has bad timing. "This is Cartwright."

"You have to help me." Gene's voice lacked his usual confidence, wavered, seemed almost panicky.

Jack was already in motion. He grabbed his keys and slipped on his shoes, all thoughts of the case gone from his mind.

"Please," Gene said, "I need your help."

"Where are you?"

Chapter Fourteen

Hunting Journal
October 22

Another body discovered in a house near Wendover (on the Utah side), not 3 miles from our other victim. Same MO. This time, there was definitely evidence of salt water—victim was practically drowned in it. ME says the cause of death is the same too: asphyxiation and blood loss. I've been digging more into Kelpies and other water spirits. They're usually found in bodies of water; it seems odd that they're coming so far onto land to do their killing. Luckily, Mom's journal says you kill them how you would any Were—silver bullet to the heart and decapitation. But you have to find them in their shifted form, and apparently, they tend to spend their days like that, as opposed to nights. So, I'll be ditching work tomorrow so that I can do some hunting around the Salt Lake. (Sorry, Gene.)

Jack screeched to a halt on the quiet suburban street, his blue lights flashing. As he stepped out of the car, he spotted Gene. Searching for any sign of danger, Jack spread his arms wide when he didn't find one.

"Why'd you call me here?" he asked.

Gene approached him, his hands stuffed in his front pockets, looking sheepish—*young*. He glanced over Jack's shoulder at his police lights and shook his head, muttering something under his breath. "I'm sorry... I, uh, I shouldn't have called you." He started to backtrack. Jack caught up to him and grabbed his arm, forcing him to face him as he had at the crime scene earlier.

"What's going on? I thought you needed backup."

"I *do* need backup...just not the kind you're thinking of."

Jack raised an eyebrow.

Gene didn't say anything. Instead, he passed Jack on the way to the car. He opened the driver's side door and switched off the police lights. Jack eyed him as he then closed the door, rounded the vehicle, and opened the passenger-side to dig through the glove compartment. He then stuffed something in his pocket. Eventually, Gene reemerged and leaned against the car, an airplane bottle of whiskey in his hand. He opened it and downed it. He capped the empty bottle and shoved it into his jacket pocket.

Now, Jack was even more confused than before. He cautiously approached his partner, stopping a few feet from him.

Gene exhaled a sharp breath. "This is my parents' house."

Oh.

"I'm here for my niece's birthday, and—" He laughed derisively. "I don't know what I was thinking, why I thought it'd be a good idea to come, but..." He stared blankly in front of him.

"So, you need a buffer?" Jack asked.

Gene closed his eyes and nodded. "I need a way out—an excuse to leave when I'm ready. I've been here half an hour, and I already want to shoot something."

Jack almost found Gene's hotheadedness funny, but he could tell by the rigidity in his shoulders and the shakiness in his voice that he wasn't being hyperbolic.

"Plus, you have booze," Gene said, pulling another bottle of whiskey from his jacket pocket.

This time, Jack did laugh. "Hey, save some for me. If I'm going in there with you, I ain't going in sober."

Gene tossed him the bottle after taking a sip. "See, that was my first mistake."

Jack was antsy to return to Maggie and the others, the new information weighing heavily, but he couldn't help it. He couldn't say no to Gene. As they started heading into the house, he said, "I'll text Maggie to call me in an hour to give us an out."

"Maggie?" Gene asked.

"Yeah, my sister."

"Right," Gene mumbled.

Heat crept up the back of Jack's neck, but before he could say anything more, they stepped into the bustling frenzy of a teen girl's birthday party.

*

Gene wasn't entirely sure what he was doing, or more specifically, why he had called Jack. After their tiff this afternoon, he wasn't sure Jack would come, and yet here he was. In some part of his brain, Gene knew why he'd reached out to him, but he still wasn't ready to admit any of it to himself.

His mother was the first to spot them when they entered. A short woman with graying hair and wrinkled skin, she wore her typical Nance Bradshaw outfit: a conservative, quarter-sleeve, blue dress that fell a few inches below the knee, paired with two-inch black heels and a simple silver necklace.

"Eugene," she said once she reached them, and he heard Jack stifle a laugh. "There you are. I thought you had slipped away without saying goodbye."

Her words and tone were polite enough, but Gene understood the implied "and how rude that would have been." He guessed she probably expected such behavior from him, and though the ruse he and Jack had concocted wouldn't necessarily disprove her expectations, it still made Gene happy to know he wouldn't fill them to the letter.

Her eyes moved to Jack, and she offered him a tight smile. "Who's your *friend*?"

"This is my partner, Jack." Gene had planned to offer some explanation as to why his partner was at his niece's birthday party, but he drew a blank.

Thankfully, Jack stepped in with, "Sorry for crashing the party. I caught a lead on one of our cases and tracked Gene down. Thought it'd be the polite thing to at least say hello." He offered a kind, genuine smile and held out his hand to shake, and if Gene hadn't known it was all a lie, he would have believed him no questions asked.

His mother certainly seemed to. "Ah, you're a cop. Yes, well, I understand the business... You can call me Nance. It's nice to meet you, Jack." She clasped her hands together. "You're welcome to stay, of course," she said, slipping into good-host mode. "We have punch over there, cake, sandwiches. Help yourself."

She gave them another smile before leaving them be. Gene exhaled a long breath once she was gone. Jack gave his shoulder a small squeeze as he made his way to the refreshment table. "You think anyone's spiked it yet?"

Gene caught up with him, and Jack fixed them both a glass. "Don't even think about it," Gene said, seeing the mischievous glint in his partner's eyes.

"I would never." His voice dripped with fake innocence. "We'll just have to sneak off somewhere to spike our own."

"Yeah," Gene muttered, glancing around the room filled with family he hadn't seen in years. Most of them were avoiding him, some threw him indecipherable glances here and there as if deciding what to do or say. And then there was Prue, the only reason he was here. She stood amongst a group of friends, all of them gathered around a phone screen and laughing at a video, and he suddenly missed that little girl with pigtails and cake on her face. He'd missed the other eras of her life—when had she stopped liking pigtails? When did she start going by Prue? He wished he had seen it all, been there through it.

"Hey, come on, let me introduce you to the birthday girl," he whispered to Jack and led him through the crowd.

He paused a few paces away from her friends and caught Prue's attention. She excused herself and came over, her eyes alight.

"Hey, Uncle Gene, I thought you'd escaped."

"Nope, still here. I, uh, want you to meet someone. This is my partner, Jack."

Jack gave her a smile, repeating the same lie he'd told Gene's mother. Although, as Prue looked between them, her eyes glinted with a sense of understanding, and Gene knew she didn't buy the lie the same way his mother had.

"Rumor has it you got into BYU?" Jack asked.

Gene turned to him, surprised. *How did he know that*?

Prue tucked a stray lock of hair behind her ear. "Yeah, yeah, I found out the other day."

"It's a good school," Jack said encouragingly.

"It is." She lowered her voice. "Only, I'm not sure I want to go there. I heard from UC Boulder, and I got in there, too, but...well, I doubt my parents want me going out of state. They'd rather I take a year or two off anyway. Do a mission, but...well."

"My sister went to Boulder. For undergrad anyway. She went to Boston for everything else."

"Everything else?" Gene echoed. He couldn't help but butt in as curiosity got the better of him.

"Yeah, she got her other degrees there."

"And how many others does she have?"

Jack closed one eye and made a thinking face. "I think two? No, wait, three. She never completely finished her MD, only the didactic portion."

Gene blinked, absorbing the information. And then he put together the Boston reference. "Your sister went to Harvard Medical School?"

"Only for a couple years."

"Why didn't she finish?" Prue asked.

"Oh, for various reasons. She went to college when she was fifteen, and nearly ten years went by before she realized she'd rather get hands-on experience. And then, we had to take care of some family things here in Utah. That's all to say my sister could get away at *fifteen*, so nothing's impossible."

Prue seemed doubtful. "Yeah, but were your parents overprotective?"

Jack choked on his drink. Once he'd gotten ahold of himself, he said, "Definitely not. Quite the opposite, but my mom hardly wanted her daughter to move across the country. She definitely put up a fight in her own way."

"Besides, you won't know until you talk about it with them," Gene added with a pointed look.

Prue sighed. "I know."

One of her friends tapped her on the shoulder, wanting to show her something on their phone.

Gene took that as a sign they should let her get back to celebrating. "Go on, have fun," he said, allowing her to easily end the conversation. She smiled and rejoined her friends a little ways away.

Jack gave him a small smile. "Good kid."

Pride swelled within Gene. "She is."

"Ah, Eugene."

Gene stiffened at his father's voice. He'd managed to avoid him thus far. He took a deep breath before turning to face him.

"We weren't sure you would show," his father continued.

Unlike his mother, his dad was unable to hide his contempt for his son.

Yet, similarly to his mother, he echoed the same question, "Who is your *friend*?"

Before Gene could say anything, Jack stepped beside him and placed a hand on his nape, almost putting his arm around his shoulder. "I'm Jack. His partner."

This time, he didn't explain further, simply letting the statement linger in the air between them.

Gene's father's lips drew into a tight line. "Right," he said, reaching out to shake Jack's outstretched hand. "Hope you enjoy the party. Excuse me."

And he was gone.

Gene stared after him as he made his way to the refreshments, greeting other guests with charming smiles and genial hugs and handshakes. The weight of Jack's hand on his neck had made everything else in the room fade to the background. Its sudden absence snapped him out of it.

"Bathroom?" Jack was saying.

Gene turned to him, Jack's green eyes closer than he expected. He simply stared at him before swallowing and averting his gaze. "Uh, yeah, I'll show you upstairs."

He led Jack to his childhood bedroom, which had a Jack-and-Jill bathroom between it and his sister's old room. He took a seat on the edge of the bed while Jack used the facilities. After a couple of minutes, he returned, and Gene watched as his eyes swept around the room.

Jack cast him a playful smile. "This was your room, wasn't it?"

"How'd you know?"

"It's got Gene written all over it," he said fondly. "They've changed it some, though, yeah?"

"Pretty much everything, honestly."

"Not these paintings, though." Jack stepped closer to one of the landscapes.

"That one's my favorite."

"Hmm."

"And I'm pretty sure the books are all mine, still. Don't know why I left them here." He gestured to the short bookshelf below the painting.

Jack squatted before it as he muttered, "And what was teenage Gene reading?" He scanned the bookshelf, then swiped a book off the middle one. "Vonnegut?" His voice held a hint of surprise. He'd picked out Gene's well-read copy of *Slaughterhouse Five* and now flipped through the pages, pausing every now and again to read his scribbled notes in the margins.

"Don't sound so surprised," Gene teased. "That happens to be one of my favorite books."

Jack hummed as he finished perusing the book before replacing it on the shelf. He strolled around the room and paused at all the parts of it that were Gene's, taking note of each little knickknack. It amazed Gene how he ignored every piece of decor that was placed there by his parents but caught everything that was his.

Once he'd finished, Jack turned to him. "Should we head back?"

Gene wasn't ready to return to the party, so he pulled the last little whiskey bottle from his jacket pocket. "Figured we could have another drink first."

Jack gave him a wicked smile and joined him on the bed. He sat close, his leg a hair's breadth from Gene's, and held out his hand. Gene cracked the lid, took a sip, and passed the whiskey to Jack.

They sat in silence for a while, sharing the bottle. Gene tried to ignore how close they were, how his palms had grown sweaty, how he could still somehow feel Jack's hand on his neck, though it hadn't been there for some time now. He resisted the urge to shift away from Jack—as well as the urge to shift closer to him.

Eventually, Jack broke the silence, "Can I ask you a question?"

Gene had a sneaking suspicion of what it was.

"Why are you still a cop?"

"What?"

"You said you became one because your dad was a cop, and I got the impression you did it to get his approval, right? To make them proud. And yet...they're clearly not swelling with pride for you." He paused. "Probably in more ways than one," he added hesitantly.

A knot formed in Gene's throat.

"I'm not sure why you're *still* a cop," Jack continued. "You told me there were other things I could have done to help people or to do some good in the world. Well, so can you." He shifted beside him, his leg now pressing up against Gene's, solid and warm. "I'm just not sure I get it."

Gene swallowed the lump in his throat enough to say, "I think you do get it. You basically hit the nail on the head. I mean, somewhere deep down, it's all for their approval, you know?" He paused. "Besides, I'm pretty good at it. Might as well be some good cops out there."

"Maggie would say there are no good cops."

Gene almost laughed. "Ah, maybe she's right. I'm not exactly a cop for the *right* reasons, am I? Just after Daddy's approval. And you're in it for the paycheck, right? Maybe she's right."

Jack didn't say anything to that, only took a sip of the whiskey. His arm came to rest against Gene's, and warmth spread out from the contact. Gene looked down at where their arms touched before his gaze danced up to Jack's profile—his strong jawline, a hint of stubble, the beginnings of crow's feet around his green eyes.

As if sensing Gene's stare, Jack turned his head and met Gene's gaze, and for a brief instant, the world came to a grinding halt. Sitting this close together, Gene could smell the spicy deodorant he wore, a light sheen of sweat mixed in. Could see the small flecks of brown in Jack's otherwise grassy irises. Felt small puffs of his breath on his cheeks. Every one of Gene's senses zeroed in on Jack, and for a breath, nothing else mattered.

Gene tore his eyes away, then stood. "Maybe we should, uh, head back."

Jack's eyes narrowed, but he nodded. They both headed downstairs, Gene vaguely aware of Jack following after a bit of distance was put between them.

As they returned to the fray, Gene wandered over to the refreshments table to get some punch. He wished he had another whiskey to calm his nerves, but at this point, it was probably a good thing he didn't. He turned to face the room and noticed Jack speaking with his dad in the opposite corner. His father said something that made Jack's back straighten, and his partner stepped closer, imposing on his father's personal space, and made a retort. Then, Jack turned on his heel and strode straight to Gene, a satisfied smirk on his face.

"What'd he want?" Gene asked, briefly locking eyes with his dad across the room.

Jack perused the table, picked up a couple of cookies and shoved one in his mouth. "Nothing," he said around the food, an action far too gross to be endearing.

Gene decided not to press it; he probably didn't want to know.

Jack's phone rang. "Ah, our escape plan," he whispered as he answered. He made his voice loud enough to carry to those standing nearby without being too disruptive. To Gene, it was obviously a fake one-sided conversation, but as with earlier, he was struck with how well Jack lied. And again, if Gene hadn't been in on the ruse, he'd have bought it as the truth.

Jack turned to him after he hung up. "We caught a homicide downtown. Got to go." Again, he spoke loudly enough for others to hear.

Gene played along. "Well, duty calls. Let me say bye to Prue."

Jack trailed behind him as he found Prue among the same gaggle of friends as before.

"Sorry, we have to go so soon," he said as they pulled apart from their hug.

She waved a hand. "I understand. Thanks for coming!"

Gene was hit with a small pang of guilt for lying to her, but he needed to get out of there. The last thing he wanted to do was ruin her birthday with a blowout fight, which became more and more inevitable the longer he stayed. With a final wave to his niece, he and Jack fled the party.

Outside in the quiet of the night, the cold struck him, and Gene slowed as they reached Jack's car. "Thanks," he said.

Jack gave him a smile. "What're partners for?"

Gene chuckled. "Yeah, I think it's fair to say you went above and beyond the job description tonight."

"Eh. It wasn't that bad."

Gene kicked at the ground awkwardly. "Well...see you tomorrow, I guess." He turned toward his car down the street.

"Hey, Gene?"

He paused and looked back. Jack hadn't moved from under the

streetlight, and the soft amber glow made his eyes appear darker than usual.

"We never got those pancakes. You know, the other week?"

"No, we didn't."

Jack walked a few paces closer to him. "Want to get breakfast tomorrow? I think…I think we need to talk about some things."

Gene was briefly at a loss for words.

"And you may not like what I have to say," Jack continued, "but I think you should at least hear me out."

"Yeah…you're probably right. The diner down the road from the office. Say, eight o'clock?"

"I'll see you then."

Gene watched him return to his car, fire it up, and drive away. He was left standing on the quiet suburban street, the light from the lamps catching his breath. As he trekked back to his car, a small smile crept across his face, and giddiness radiated through him.

*

Maggie called as Jack merged onto the interstate.

"Hey, we got a hit on that truck you found near where Taupin's body was dumped."

"He was the first victim?" he asked.

"Yeah. Turns out Victor Thompson was an alias of his, so we ran some of his others, and he had a cabin up in Little Cottonwood. You're pretty close, can you go check it out?"

"Uh, I mean, I *can*, but wouldn't it make sense to go during the day?"

Maggie laughed. "You really are scared of the dark, aren't you?"

"No, but if we want to do a search, it'd be nice to have, you know, *light*."

"Come on, Jack. You're less than half an hour from it."

He signaled and took the exit for Little Cottonwood Canyon. "Fine. Send me the address."

"If it's *that* shady, we'll head that way. Don't go in without backup unless you're sure." Her teasing tone was gone, replaced with concern.

"Of course," he said before hanging up.

She was right. It only took him twenty minutes to reach the cabin, which was a generous word for it. The house wasn't much of a house anymore. It seemed part of it had been burned out, and parts of the roof had caved in. As he sat staring up at the building, he felt the need to document it, so he pulled his journal from the glovebox and scribbled a few brief notes about the cabin, the lead, and his plans to divulge the truth to Gene tomorrow. Once finished, he tossed it on the passenger seat and stepped out of the vehicle.

He shivered as the cool stillness of the air surrounded him. He wasn't lying when he said he wasn't scared of the dark. He *wasn't*. But that didn't mean he was comfortable in it either. After a brief hesitation, he dialed his sister.

"This place is creepy," he said when she answered.

"Do you think you should wait for us?"

The property was remote, but...well, it gave off an eerie vibe. It didn't necessarily mean anything hinky was going on. He pulled his knife from its holster, clicked on his flashlight, and slipped a Bluetooth earbud in his ear. "I think it's okay, but stay on the line with me."

"Seriously, if it's that bad—"

"Shh, I need to listen. If you want to start heading this way, go for it, but I don't want to wait an hour for you to get here."

With that, Maggie stopped talking. He heard her breathing on the other end, but it was comforting. He took a deep breath and stepped into the cabin.

The house was gutted. All that remained were structural supports. In some ways, it seemed more like a barn. There were no interior walls, no floors, nothing. He swept his flashlight around the space and spotted a wooden chair in the middle. As he crept closer, he noticed a dark, dark spot in front of it. He squatted next to it and gathered the stained dirt on his fingertips. He sniffed them. *Blood.*

He stood and surveyed the scene. A large pool of blood had been absorbed into the dirt in front of the chair, enough that the person it belonged to couldn't be alive.

"Hey, Mags?"

"Yeah?"

"Looks like someone was killed here..." He turned away from the chair, and his flashlight caught something else in the dirt. "...or maybe not." He tracked bloody footprints from the chair to the corner of the room. "Okay, there's a table here with an assortment of weapons. Silver knives, stakes, you name it."

Curious, he circled back to the chair. Scratches ran along the legs, as if chains, or something akin to chains, had rubbed against them, scuffed them.

An image, an idea started forming right as all the noises around him stopped. Maggie's voice was muted as if she was speaking through a thick wall of glass.

Suddenly, something struck him on the head, and he fell to the floor, his knife slipping from his fingers.

He was faintly aware of Maggie screaming his name but only barely. Her voice was the last thing he heard before his attacker delivered a final blow, and he blacked out.

Chapter Fifteen

"Jack! Jack!" Maggie pulled the phone from her ear to check whether the call had dropped. It hadn't. "Jack!" A muffled noise sounded, and then the line went dead.

Dana's face was unreadable as they gathered keys, put on shoes, and holstered weapons. "Come on. Let's go."

Maggie shoved the phone in her pocket and followed Dana out to their car. The drive up to Little Cottonwood was quiet and tense. Dana drove well above the speed limit, swerving in and out of traffic, skilled and controlled, yet still earning a few honks from disgruntled drivers. An hour later, they screeched to a halt in front of the cabin. The sight of Jack's SUV only made Maggie's already uneasy nerves worse. She and Dana exchanged a worried glance before exiting the vehicle and making their way into the house.

Dana brandished a hunting crossbow fitted with silver-tipped arrows and a flashlight on the sight. Maggie wore a standard headlamp and carried a light metal baseball bat, posed at the ready, along with numerous concealed throwing knives. As they approached the door, Dana held up a fist, then silently indicated for Maggie to go right while they went left upon entering. Maggie nodded.

Dana pushed the door open, and they both entered swiftly, Dana first with Maggie close behind. There didn't appear to be any immediate danger, and as Maggie strode farther into the right side of the house, she found few potential hiding places.

"Jack?" she whispered into the space.

There was no reply.

Finishing their sweep of the left side, Dana joined her. "Doesn't appear to be anyone here."

Maggie caught sight of the chair Jack had mentioned on their call. As she approached, she noticed fresh drag marks along the dirt.

"Dana, look," she said, pointing at the ground.

Dana followed the drag marks with their flashlight until they stopped cold a few paces from where they stood. Dana swung the crossbow toward the chair, the light catching a reflection of something along the ceiling. "What's that?"

Maggie walked over to it. Jack's phone. The screen was cracked, and when she picked it up, it wouldn't turn on. Reality came crashing into her. The nerves that had gripped her since they left her house finally released their hold, but the feeling was soon replaced with a different one. A vast emptiness spreading throughout her body.

*

Gene woke up an hour and a half before his alarm. After an hour of tossing and turning, he finally decided to get up. It wouldn't take him long to get showered and dressed, but it didn't matter. So what if he was early for breakfast with Jack?

At least, he would have been early if he hadn't changed his shirt three times. If he hadn't brushed his teeth for an extra minute on account of zoning out halfway through, thinking about what Jack wanted to talk to him about. And now, he wasted time staring at himself in the mirror, trying to tame his unruly black hair. Still damp from the shower, its drier ends curled up in all the wrong ways, Gene knew that once it was completely dry, it wouldn't be a good hair day.

He mentally gave himself a slap on the cheek. *Enough.* He turned from the mirror and headed out to meet Jack.

Gene made it to the diner a couple minutes after eight, and when he didn't see Jack at any of the tables, he snagged a booth for them in the far corner of the room. A waitress stopped by to ask if he wanted some coffee, and he ordered two. As she left him, he pulled out his phone and sent a quick text to Jack. *In a booth at the back, near the jukebox.* He set the phone on the table and waited.

And waited and waited and waited. Jack's coffee grew cold, and Gene eventually ordered a breakfast sandwich to go when the waitress asked for the fifth time if he was ready.

The icing on the cake was when he walked into the office—thirty minutes late, by the way—and found his partner's desk empty. Gritting his teeth, Gene pulled his phone out and called Jack.

It went straight to voicemail.

"If you want to stand me up, fine. The least you could do is show up to work." He slammed his phone shut.

He was so fired up that the sounds of the station were all drowned out. He had so many questions he couldn't sort through them all. Gene didn't know where to begin. Clenching and unclenching his fists, he stood in the middle of the bullpen between his and Jack's desks, boring holes into his partner's blank computer screen.

As his anger waned, the sounds of the office returned to him. He was about to take a seat at his desk when he heard his name from down the hall, so he veered toward the voices.

"Please, I need to speak with Detective Bradshaw. It's important—"

The cop working the front desk cut the woman off, trying to calm her down. "Ma'am, I need to see—"

"Ugh! I'm his *sister*. Please. Please, I need to talk to him!"

Gene walked over, and rounding the corner, he saw a tall, muscular woman in the lobby area, yelling at the desk attendant. Her frizzy hair spiraled and fell to her shoulders. When she caught sight of Gene, her eyes widened, and her pleas became more demanding.

"It's all right, Officer," Gene said. "I'll see her."

The woman brushed past the officer and gripped Gene's forearm as soon as she was close enough.

"You have to help me," the woman said desperately.

"Please let go of my arm."

She dropped it and huffed. "Please. He's missing."

Gene started leading her to his desk, but she grabbed his arm again to stop him. "Hey, lady," he said, "please stop grabbing me."

"Would you listen to me for two seconds?"

Gene turned to her and was about to send her back out to the waiting area when he was struck by her eyes. Pale green, round, small crow's feet around the corners—identical to Jack's. He swept his eyes over the rest of her face, noticing similar features, *shared* features with Jack—a long, narrow nose, a square jaw, thin lips. "Maggie?" he asked disbelievingly.

Her shoulders relaxed. "Jack's missing."

"What?"

"He's missing," she repeated.

"No, I saw him last night... It's not exactly unlike him not to show up to work on time or altogether."

She pulled a phone out of her pocket and handed it over to Gene. It was Jack's, cracked and broken. "I found that where he was taken."

"I'm sorry, *taken*?"

Maggie cast her eyes around them as if checking if others could listen in on their conversation. She stepped closer to him. "I was on the phone with him when it happened."

"When?"

Maggie checked her watch. "About ten hours ago."

"*Ten* hours? Why didn't you call 911?" Gene's mind reeled, his anger forgotten.

"I came here, didn't I?"

Gene took a deep breath to calm his nerves. Something inside him burned to go searching for Jack, procedure be damned. But the cop part of his brain kicked in as it always did in a time of crisis. Procedure was there for a reason.

"Come on. I'll take you to Missing Persons," he said, stretching his arm toward the bullpen.

"No."

"No?"

"I don't want them involved."

"You do realize you came to the police, right? If you don't want our help, why bother coming?"

"I don't want the police's help. I want *yours*."

"Maggie—"

She held up a hand. "I know how it sounds, but…look. Do you trust my brother?"

It was too early for this. He thought of last night and the ease with which Jack lied. How naturally the tall tales had fallen from his lips. Then, yesterday morning at the Temple when Jack had brought up this issue of trust out of nowhere. Gene thought of the stakeout when he'd woken up to find Jack's seat empty and him standing outside the vehicle staring up at the streetlights. Despite it all, despite an instinct telling him Jack had something else hidden beneath the surface, he found himself answering, "Yes."

"Then trust me. Please. Come with me, and I'll explain everything. But we can't do it here."

Gene hesitated for half a second before nodding. "Okay. Let's go."

*

He followed Maggie to an older house in Sandy, its windows dark. No one appeared to be inside, but a green pickup truck idled in the driveway. The driver cut the engine, and two people stepped out as Maggie climbed out of her car, the first, a short guy with sandy-blond hair, and the other person, taller with short-cropped black hair and big wire-frame glasses. As Gene pulled to a stop in front of the house, he could clearly see the worry etched on their faces.

He wasted no time unbuckling and going to meet them. As he drew nearer, he noticed them arguing with Maggie in hushed tones, which cut off as soon as he was within earshot.

"Gene, this is Dana." She gestured to the person wearing glasses. "A friend of mine and Jack's. And this is Kurt."

"They know anything about Jack's disappearance?" he asked, unsure why the two were there.

"No, but they're here to help. Come on, follow me." She turned on her heel and headed into the house.

Kurt and Dana watched him as he passed them and followed her. He grew more confused by the minute.

The house didn't seem lived in, with cobwebs in the corners and dust covering almost every surface, which immediately made Gene's throat scratchy. As they walked farther in, and as Maggie turned on more lights, Gene noticed a few well-used and clean spaces.

"This your house?" he asked.

"Technically, it is, I guess."

"Technically?"

Maggie paused before a closed door and turned to him. Her eyes swept the area in a manner eerily similar to Jack. "It's my mom's house. Jack and I grew up here."

"She doesn't still live here, does she?"

Her eyes saddened. "No."

With that, she went into the room before them.

Gene barely held in a gasp as he took it in. A library, it had shelves reaching to the ceiling, going up two or three stories. He couldn't help but get sucked into it and approached the shelves to inspect the ones at eye level. Leather-bound books lined them, some that looked centuries old, some newer. Most didn't have lettering on the spine, and the ones that did were too faded to read. His finger twitched as he fought the urge to pluck one from its shelf. This wasn't why he was here. He was here for Jack.

"Why did you bring me here?" he asked, turning to Maggie, who stood in the middle of the room.

She gestured to a leather sofa along the right wall. "Sit."

He would have preferred to stand, but her tone left no room for argument. Once seated, she handed him a book.

"These are journals, most of which have been written by my family, going back generations."

The room took on a whole new meaning. Gene examined the book in his hands. Now that she'd said it, it did seem more like a journal.

"That's one of mine. I filled it years ago."

"What does this have to do with your brother?"

She ignored the question. "Jack said you worked a string of murders when you first joined the force. Men and women, their throats slashed, blood drained. He said they were never solved."

"And?"

"Open to page fifty-seven. Read the date and the entry." When he made no effort to follow her directions, she said, "Trust me."

Gene turned to the page in question. Maggie's handwriting was absolutely horrible. If not for his own being equally bad, he didn't think he'd be able to read it. Though initially difficult, he got the hang of it quick enough.

June 12, 2013— Hunting with Jack today. Been home for three months and already wish I was back in Boston...been missing the normal life lately. Haven't had the spine to tell Jack yet. But maybe after this one, I'll finally call it quits. We'll see.

String of bodies keeps coming. New one found right outside of Salt Lake today. Girl was only nineteen. Blood drained, just like the rest of them. Pretty sure we know what we're up against. Now, we gotta go out and kill it.

The thing jumped us when we went to where they found the body. Luckily, it was only one of them. Knocked Jack to the ground but didn't see me. Able to stab it through the heart before it got him.

My first vampire kill. Always thought it'd be harder. :)

Gene closed the book with a snap and pushed himself to his feet. "What the hell is this?"

"The truth," Maggie said.

"No. This is ridiculous."

"The murders stopped, didn't they? Ever wonder why? It's because we caught it. We took care of it."

"What, you're telling me you seriously believe a *vampire* killed those people?" He couldn't muster the energy to laugh. This had to be some sort of sick joke.

"This is what we do," Maggie said. "We track, research, and kill monsters. Things that aren't human."

Gene turned away from her. *What the hell am I doing here?* "Your brother is missing. I don't have time for this bullshit."

"Come on, Gene, you've been a cop for, what, close to ten years? You have to feel it in your gut by now. The thing that killed those people in Moab, the body on the steps at the Temple? You've got to know, deep down, the killer isn't human."

"I've been a cop long enough to know the real monsters *are* human." He headed for the door. "I don't have time for this. If your brother is missing, someone should start looking for him."

Maggie called after him as he wrenched the library door open, "You should know. You leave now, you'll be proving me right. Jack trusted you. He had faith in you. And you're letting him down."

Gritting his teeth, Gene stormed out of the house.

Chapter Sixteen

Jack blinked his eyes open. He lay face down on a hard surface, his arms pinioned behind him, his wrists pressed together at the base of his spine. He tried pulling them apart to push himself up and immediately seized in pain. Electric, it shot out from his wrists into the rest of his body. After an indeterminable amount of time, the pain subsided, and he instead rolled onto his back and rocked himself up into a sitting position.

He was in a small, dark room similar to a jail cell, with concrete walls and floors and no exit in sight. He scooted toward the wall closest to him and leaned against it, his breath coming raggedly.

Jack tried pulling his wrists apart again, and this time, he fell to his side as a silent scream ripped from his throat. The pain seemed to last longer this time, but as before, it eventually subsided, and he was left panting, gasping for breath.

"I wouldn't do that if I were you," a metallic voice rang out in the cell. Jack tried to sit up again but settled for rolling halfway onto his back when it proved to be too troublesome.

He scanned the room but didn't see anyone else with him. He did, however, notice a speaker tucked away in the far-right corner.

"The more you struggle, the more it will hurt," the voice continued.

Jack was in too much pain from his last attempt to even consider moving his hands. He didn't need to be told twice, but still, his body seized up tight as a charged pulse moved from the tips of his toes to the top of his head and back again. His spine arched, his heels dug into the cold, grimy floor, and when the blinding pain receded, he tasted the signature coppery taste of blood in his mouth. It slowly dripped from his lips onto the floor.

He fought to keep his eyes open, but it was a futile effort.

As he blacked out again, his captor spoke once more.

"Rest up, detective. You're going to need it."

*

When Jack woke next, his hands were in front of him. He slowly sat up, careful not to move his wrists apart. He pulled his knees to his chest, resting against the cool wall behind him, and examined his wrists. Nothing bound them, yet...it *felt* like they were, and Jack knew if he tried to pull them apart, it'd hurt.

At least with them in front of him now, he could use his hands, even if only a little. His body ached from earlier, but he forced himself to stand anyway. He needed to figure out how big the room was—and if there was any way out. He found the closest corner and started from there. Measuring out in footsteps, he estimated the room to be about eight by nine feet. He had no way of guessing how high the ceiling was. As he counted, he pressed his hands along the wall, feeling for any cracks or openings. There were none.

He slumped against one wall and slid to the floor. *Idiot. I'm an idiot for going in alone.*

Jack wondered if anyone was looking for him. They were bound to be, right? Maggie had been on the phone with him when he'd been knocked out. She would surely enlist Dana and Kurt's help to find him. That only left...

Gene. He winced, imagining him sitting at the diner, waiting for

Jack to show up, growing more and more annoyed as the time passed and he didn't show. He pictured him walking into the office, seeing his empty desk and undoubtedly thinking *nothing's changed.*

How am I going to come back from this? If I survive, that is.

He peered around the damp, dark cell. *If I survive.*

Chapter Seventeen

Case Notes, Case #187.2210.03.FS.6892
October 24

Medical examiner called this morning with an interesting finding. Our second victim, Laura, was drenched in salt water, yet no water was found in her lungs, and when he ran chemical tests on it, he found the water had high levels of sulfur in it. He says it's somewhat normal for sulfate to be present but not pure sulfur, especially since it's not soluble in water. So, I researched what sulfur is used for—largely in production of paper and insecticides, which doesn't narrow much. Maybe our killer worked with these chemicals?

Subordinate behavioral note: Second day in a row that Det. Cartwright has failed to report for duty. Continue to monitor before reporting to IA.

It wasn't until Gene had returned to the station that he realized he still had Maggie's journal. He didn't know what to think of it. He paused at Jack's empty desk, and a heaviness settled in him. *He had faith in you.* Maggie's words echoed in his mind as Gene walked over and started rifling through Jack's notes and files. He searched thoroughly but didn't find the notebook Jack always wrote his crime notes in.

Gene didn't know what to think. Part of him wondered if this was all an elaborate prank. If he stopped to think rationally for half a second, he would know Jack would never do that. But what Maggie had told him was too incomprehensible, too impossible, to be true. And that left him paralyzed, unsure what to think, what to do.

He plopped down at his desk. There was one thing he knew for certain: Jack was missing. And to think, he'd been angry when he hadn't shown up this morning. Gene felt so stupid now. The least he could do was try to retrace his steps after he left the party last night.

He dialed the technical department. "This is Sergeant Bradshaw in Major Crimes. I need the last known location on Detective Jack Cartwright's cell phone and vehicle."

The tech said it would take some time, but he'd check now and promised to return Gene's call once the information was in.

Gene picked up Maggie's journal, opened it to the same page as before, then turned back a few to read previous entries.

May 27, 2013— Third body in two weeks. Things are not looking good. Victim only had half a liter of blood left in her body. Puncture wounds on the neck are evenly spaced (measuring roughly 35.6 mm apart), almost how teeth would be. We're thinking vampire, but they're rarer nowadays, so could be a Were of some kind. It's the amount of blood loss, though, that screams vampire. Calling in Argus for advice. Times like these make me miss Grandaddy. And Mom...though she's still here, but it's different, I guess. She's not all there.

Anyway, Jack was able to track down an old journal from the 1500s, and we read some...

Gene stopped reading. He didn't have the file in front of him, but he quickly pulled up the autopsy report from all those years ago…and there it was. Wounds, 35.56 millimeters apart. *How the hell did she know how far apart they were?* He continued reading, and she was right about the blood loss too. None of this had been released to the press. How did Maggie know?

His head was about to explode. This was impossible. Just because she knew about the blood and the wounds didn't mean there were vampires in the world. But the murders—they *had* stopped. And he had to admit, some part of him was relieved. Some part of him screamed that she was telling the truth. As insane as it was.

If this was all true and Jack had been taken by a monster, how the hell were they supposed to go up against that? How were they—

His office phone rang, cutting off his anxious thoughts. It was the tech department.

"Bradshaw," he answered.

"Sir, the last known location of the cell and the vehicle are the same. An address up in Little Cottonwood—1289 Elk Haven Lane."

"You're sure?"

"Yes, sir."

He hung up and immediately started digging through his file drawer. He pulled out the cold case file he knew too well and flipped to the last page, though he knew that address by heart. Gene had to be sure. *Coincidence. It's a coincidence.*

"No such thing," he muttered to himself.

He closed the file as a plan formulated, then jumped into action. He went to the captain first.

"Have a second, sir?" Gene asked as he knocked on his office door.

Captain Smith waved him in with a grunt.

"I have reason to believe Detective Cartwright is missing."

The captain's eyebrows shot into his hairline. "Missing, huh? The boy's almost always late to work. You sure he's not AWOL?"

"I saw him last night. He was checking out some field leads, but he hasn't gotten back to me, and I can't reach him. It's not like him."

Smith considered this, then stood and put his hands on the desk. "It's a bit flimsy, but if we do have an officer missing, I'm not taking any chances." He ran his finger down the current shift list. "I'll get Gomez and Daniels on it."

"Sir, I can—"

"You got enough on your plate. Besides, he's your partner. You're too close to it."

"Sir, the case from yesterday. The body at Temple Square?"

The captain grunted as if to say *what about it?*

"I believe it's connected to the other two—"

"No. That one stays off your desk till we have conclusive evidence it's related."

"But—"

"That's final. Now, get."

Gene steeled himself and left Smith's office. Returning to his desk, he stacked the cold case file on top of his newer ones, grabbed Maggie's journal, and headed out of the office. It was time to get some answers.

*

Told you it wouldn't go well," Dana said when Maggie joined them in the living room.

"Yeah, well, it's what Jack wanted...and he was our only hope of figuring out Jack's code."

"Aw, come on, it can't be that bad," Kurt said, an edge of optimism in his voice.

Dana gave him a teasing smile. "Oh, *bless your heart.*"

Maggie tossed Jack's journal to an offended Kurt. "Have at it, genius."

Kurt opened the book and turned a couple of pages. He then closed it and set it on the table. "Yeah, okay, I see your point."

"Even I can't read it," Maggie said. If anyone should have known how to read his code, it should have been her. Jack hadn't used a code the last time they hunted together, and though she could spot the similarity to their mother's, she couldn't seem to figure it out. She wrung her hands and paced in front of her friends.

Then, the door to the garage opened, and Argus came in. As the closest thing she had to a parent right now, he radiated comfort.

"How can I help?" he asked calmly.

"I want you all to keep going through the journals to try to narrow down what this thing is. If we figure that out, maybe we'll find Jack faster. I'm going to…I'm going to try to find him. Somehow…"

Sympathy welled in Dana's and Kurt's expressions, and they immediately jumped into it, pulling out journals and discussing theories between themselves. Argus, however, pulled her aside, lines of worry etched onto his face.

"Perhaps I could assist you," he offered.

"No. You have the most experience of all of us. You're better suited to research."

He reached out and placed a gentle hand on her elbow. "Are you sure you're all right, dearie?"

"I'll be fine. Once we find him."

Argus grimaced, but he didn't say anything else. Instead, he joined the others and began pouring over his own journals.

Maggie retreated to the study. There, she allowed herself to lose it. She sank to the floor behind the door and pulled her knees to her chest as panic welled within her. *He has to be alive, he has to be alive, he has to be alive…*

It became a mantra for her as she rocked gently. She would know. She would know if he was dead. Wouldn't she? She would.

Mom would, but I'm not her.

Her hands shaking, Maggie pulled out her phone and opened her contacts list. She hovered her thumb over the first person in her favorites before pressing the call button.

"Hey," Elliot answered.

Immediately, her pulsing heartbeat slowed. Simply hearing her husband's voice was enough. "Hey," she said.

"What's up? You okay?"

"No."

"Just need me to talk?"

She hummed an affirmative.

"Okay. Well, you know my coworker—Lee? He talked to me for an *hour* about types of coffee creamer the other day. It about drove me insane, and then..."

His voice became background noise. She sat and listened to him talk about his annoying coworkers and whatever else came to his mind, and slowly but surely, calm seeped into her. She laughed at the end of a story about one of his coworkers embarrassing himself.

"Feeling better?" Elliot asked.

"I think so."

After a pause, he said, "You know you can trust me, right? That you can tell me anything."

A sad smile touched Maggie's lips. "I know."

Elliot sighed on the other end. "Well, listen, I should probably go. It's, uh, it's pretty late here—or rather, early."

Maggie winced. "I woke you, didn't I? I'm sorry. I forgot about the time difference."

"Yeah, well...it's fine."

Something in his voice gave him away, made guilt spring up. She tried to wrack her brain for information on his work trip... Where was he again? When was he coming home? She couldn't remember any of it, though she knew he'd told her. And the longer she stayed quiet, trying to remember, the more awkward the silence between them became.

"You should, uh, probably let me go. I gotta get at least a couple more hours of sleep."

"Yeah. Yeah, I'll, uh, call you later."

"I'll be home soon," he said as if realizing she needed to hear it.

"'Course you will."

It was quiet, and then— "I got to go. Love you."

"Love you too."

And then he was gone. She sat on the floor for a minute longer before standing up, steeling herself. It was time to work.

Chapter Eighteen

Hunting Journal
October 25

No joy at the Salt Lake, and I kept wondering: why does this water spirit kill so far inland and so far from the actual water? You'd think if it was living in the Salt Lake, it would kill closer to home, like Layton or North Salt Lake, not nearly all the way to Nevada. And it's that brilliant thinking that led me to the Bonneville Salt Flats, the last remnants of a dried-up ancient lake. Located barely outside of Wendover, I might add. Decided to check it out yesterday. I got there in the early morning, and luckily, no one else was around. I drove to the far end of the flats, almost to the base of the mountain on the west side, where I found a large pool of water. Ran a quick chemical test on it and discovered high levels of sulfur present.

I planned to lie in wait for the Kelpie, but the damned thing got the jump on me. It knocked me back, and I fell hard to the salty ground about twenty feet away. I got to my feet as quick as I could and made a mad dash for my car. The thing had the visage of a horse, but its hooves had sharp nails protruding from them, and it was gaining on me fast. I threw open my trunk and grabbed for the first gun I could find. I fired and missed my first shot, but I managed to hit on the second. It let out a loud screech, its gallop interrupted as its legs buckled. When it didn't move, I grabbed my machete and took its head. It oozed black blood that ran toward the pool of water, and its body slowly disintegrated until there was nothing left but a large black stain on the otherwise stark-white ground.

What the hell am I going to tell Gene?

Sunlight kissed Jack's bare skin, stirring him awake. He pushed himself up onto his elbows and looked around his bedroom. As his senses awakened, the smell of fresh coffee and sizzling bacon wafted in through the open door. He smiled, got up, and trudged out to the kitchen. The short walk took longer than it should have, the hallway seemingly stretching on forever, getting longer and longer the farther he went. He picked up his pace, running, until suddenly, he was there. In a blink of the eye. He checked down the hallway, and it appeared normal again.

The kitchen was empty. The coffee pot overflowed with coffee, the fry pan sat abandoned on the stove, the bacon turning black and sending smoke into the air. It rose high above him, filled the space, and set off the fire alarm. He rushed over and moved the pan off the burner, then reached over the sink to open the window above it.

A loud clatter behind him made him spin around. Gene stood there motionless, eyes wide, body frozen in time. A woman, wrapped in light, appeared behind him. She lifted a hand and clenched her fist.

Gene seized. He remained standing as he convulsed, like a puppet forced to dance. It lasted for less than ten seconds, and then he collapsed to the floor, dead. The woman's cruel laugh rang out through the apartment as Jack rushed to him.

"Gene!"

Jack sprang up to a sitting position, breathing heavily. His heart pounded from the nightmare, but there was no relief in waking up. He let his head fall into his bound hands as he reclined against the wall of the dark cell.

"It was only a dream," he told himself. Gene wasn't here. He was safe.

And yet, no matter what he told himself, Jack couldn't shake the image of Gene lying dead. *He's okay, he's okay, he's okay,* he repeated to himself, hoping saying it enough would make it true.

*

Gene had been sitting in front of Maggie's mom's house for a long time, debating with himself. If he went in, there was no going back. He wasn't sure he could trust Maggie, let alone her two companions. Was he willing to risk this case—and the one he'd kept to himself for so long—on the insane idea that some otherworldly creature was responsible for these crimes? He took a deep breath and got out of the car.

When Maggie opened the door, she seemed surprised.

Gene brushed past her and said, "We need to talk."

He walked into the living room and stopped. Dana and Kurt were on the couch, but a newcomer sat with them, an old man dressed in a tailored three-piece suit. His hair, though gray, was thick and well-kept, and he had a scar that ran across his left eyebrow, down the side of his face, and disappeared under the collar of his shirt.

Noticing him, the man smiled at Gene and said in a thick Scottish accent, "Ah, detective. How nice of you to join us."

As Maggie came to a stop beside him, Gene asked, "Who's he?"

"Forgive me." The man stood and crossed the room easily for his age. "Argus Vasil. Pleasure to meet you, Mr. Bradshaw." He held out a hand to shake.

Gene ignored his hand and focused on Maggie. "We need to talk. Alone." In response, Argus released an amused *hmm* and returned to the others.

"Whatever you have to say, you can say in front of them." Maggie gestured to the three people on the couch.

Gene scrutinized them, lingering the longest on Argus before refocusing on Maggie. "No. Alone."

Maggie led the way to the study where they had been earlier. Once she closed the door, she said, "Well, that was quick. Thought it'd take you longer to come around."

"Too many coincidences," he said.

Maggie tilted her chin toward him. "What's in the folders?"

He set one of the files on the table in the center of the room. "These are the case files for the two murders in Moab." He held up the other file. "This is a cold case from when I first made detective. Okay, what I'm about to share with you, stays with you, got it? I trust Jack, and Jack trusts you. It's the only reason I can fathom sharing this with you. Those people out there? I don't know them; I don't trust them. Understood?"

Maggie seemed unconvinced but nodded.

He released a breath and handed the file to her. "The short of it is that I was assigned this case when I made detective, and it was taken away from me right when I started getting somewhere."

"Why were you taken off the case?" Maggie asked as she started flipping through the file.

"Stuck my nose where the Church didn't want it."

Maggie lifted her gaze to his. "And where exactly did you stick your nose?"

"I was supposed to investigate some cattle mutilations. It was a joint investigation with state animal control, and I was supposed to dig into the farms' financials. You know, see if there was anything fraudulent going on. It was *supposed* to be simple." He put his hands on the table and leaned toward her. "Except three of the five farms turned out to be owned by shell corporations, and they seemed to be fronts of some kind. So I keep digging, and I find Sally Pearson. A fake identity, but one used to buy a cabin at 1289 Elk Haven Lane."

"And where exactly does the LDS Church come into play?"

"Well, when I couldn't find anything on this Pearson person, I started investigating the cattle mutilations. The guy from animal control was doing fuck-all. Anyway, take a look at the scenes and tell me what you see."

Maggie skipped to the last section with the pictures and read through the open folder with a skeptical expression. Then, her lips parted, and she examined the pictures more closely.

"Holy shit," she breathed. "Is that…lavender?" She peered up at Gene, wonder in her eyes.

"Lavender was left next to the bodies, almost like a ritual. If you check closely, you can see there are traces of it in the wounds. And on top of that, there was no evidence of insect activity on the bodies. Similar to our human victims." He straightened up. "It took me too long to make the connection. The bodies we found in the desert, the one at the Temple, smelled of lavender, but there wasn't any left nearby. Still, I should have seen it." He ran his hands through his hair, frustrated with himself.

"You still haven't made the connection to LDS."

Gene turned the file toward him and thumbed to an earlier section before showing it to Maggie. "I did a search for ritualistic animal killing. A lot of the stuff I found didn't fit what we had, but there was one thing that did. In the early history of LDS, a sect emerged and branched off— they practiced animal sacrifice—"

"No way," Maggie said.

"It was very short-lived, and the Church has done pretty much everything in its power to make sure this part of their history stays hidden, but it happened. And around the time these animal killings started, there were rumors this sect had reemerged."

Maggie blinked. "Okay. So you're telling me a crazed sect of the LDS Church is responsible for all this?"

"Well, that's the thing. I don't think it has anything to do with the Mormon faith. If you read my notes, there are reports of sects emerging and disappearing within other religions throughout history. The Mormon sect just happens to be the most recent."

"I'm…I don't know if I'm following where you're going with all this."

Gene paused to collect his thoughts. He'd been holding all of this so close to his chest for so long that telling someone about it for the first time made it all come out in a confusing mess.

"Okay," he said finally. "This sect moves through various religions throughout history. They kill animals—sometimes humans—in ways that seem impossible. Isn't it possible this sect is a group of some kind of monsters?"

"I don't know... If they've been around that long, we would have heard about them. We'd have records of them, and we don't."

"Come on," Gene insisted. "Didn't you say you're running out of ideas? That you're stumped on what this could be? Besides, you've got to have, like, *hundreds* of years' worth of journals here!" He gestured to the study around them. "You're telling me you've been through all of them?"

Maggie shifted her feet.

"Maybe *this*—" He shook the case file for effect. "—is the key. And maybe if we can figure out what this thing is, it'll lead us to Jack."

That seemed to do it. Maggie took a deep breath. "Okay. What do you need me to do?"

"I need you to go through your records for reports that match the ones in that case file."

"I can do that...but I'll need help. As you said, there are hundreds of years' worth of journals in here. I can't do it by myself."

"One person can help you. *One.*"

"Good. Argus can help—"

"No."

His interruption seemed to catch her by surprise, and to be fair, if pressed, Gene wasn't sure he'd be able to give a concrete answer as to why he didn't want that man near the case he held so dear. Something about the old man rubbed him the wrong way, and he couldn't put his finger on it.

"He has the most experience, and he's the oldest in our group," Maggie said, then chuckled at his stubborn face. "Damn, you and Jack certainly are alike, you know that?"

He raised an eyebrow at that.

"Fine. Who would you choose, then?"

Gene thought about it. "Dana."

"Okay, Dana it is. Now, here's what I need from you."

"Anything."

Maggie smirked, and a bad feeling settled in Gene. "Oh, you should *not* have said that."

Chapter Nineteen

As Gene took a seat at his desk, he thought about Maggie's request to see the most recent body. He still couldn't believe *she* was "Delilah Owens." He'd been mortified to learn that fact, particularly since he'd thought she and Jack were going on a date. He cringed thinking about it.

Pushing it out of his mind, he logged on to the computer to see if an autopsy had been filed. It hadn't. He was about to check for other details on the new case when he was interrupted.

"So, Bradshaw—"

Gene swiveled his chair around as Detective Gomez strolled up to his desk.

"Did you know your partner changed his name when he was nineteen?" Gomez leaned his hips against the desk behind Gene's, an inquiring gleam in his eyes, but his fake interest was obvious.

Gene shrugged. "So? Perfectly legal."

Detective Daniels spoke up from behind Gomez. "I wonder what it was before. Bet it was something lame. Like Otis."

"Or Eugene," Gomez supplied with a glint in his eyes.

"What's it matter what his name *used* to be?"

"Oh, I don't know," Daniels said, "but it's almost as if he didn't exist before that."

"Makes you wonder, doesn't it? How well you know your partner." Gomez leaned into Gene's space.

Gene met his gaze levelly. "Thought you were supposed to find him, not dig up his past."

Gomez narrowed his eyes and smiled before standing up straight. "Touché, Bradshaw. Touché."

He jerked his head toward the door, and Daniels put on his coat. Before they left, Gomez asked, "Hey, you don't happen to know his sister, do you?"

Gene feigned ignorance. "He has a sister?"

Gomez eyed him before huffing out a small laugh. "Come on, Daniels. Let's go pay her a visit, shall we?"

Gene watched them walk out of view, then shot a quick text to Maggie.

G: 2 detectives on their way to see you.

Her response was instantaneous.

M: I'm omw to my house now.

G: Remember how I told you not to piss them off?

M: Yes. >:(

Gene glanced toward the door where Gomez and Daniels had left.

G: Give em hell.

*

Three hours later, everyone had cleared out of the office, leaving Gene alone. He stood and walked over to Gomez's computer. He waved the mouse, and unsurprisingly, Gomez had left it unlocked. Gene took a seat at the other detective's desk. *Would it bother anyone to follow policy?*

Yet, right now, he was more than happy Gomez hadn't.

Gene quickly pulled up the blueprints to the Salt Lake County Morgue, along with the security plans. The longer he reviewed them, the more it seemed his plan would work. Which unsettled him. Was he really about to do this?

He pushed his doubts aside and grabbed a few tools before he was out the door.

When Gene got to the morgue, the building was dark and the parking lot empty and quiet. He parked in the back, where the security cameras wouldn't see him. Surveying the area, he headed to the seldom-used entrance in the back; nothing seemed out of place. He slid on a pair of gloves before picking the door lock, then let himself into the building. He used his pocket flashlight to illuminate the space, and a few paces down the hall, found the fuse box. Gene cracked it open, exposing the fuse for the cameras. He took a deep breath and switched it off. Carefully, he pulled the switch to the middle so that it appeared it had been tripped, rather than tampered with.

Wasting no time, he entered the morgue.

It was easy enough to find the file for the woman discovered at Temple Square. Her name was Harriet Sparrow, age fifty-four, but beyond that, they hadn't done anything to her. Why, Gene had no idea. She was in chamber thirty-two.

He chewed his lip, pacing in front of the entrance to the examination room, thinking through the next step in his plan. *Now or never, Bradshaw.* He pulled out his cell and dialed Maggie's number.

"You're up late," she said, answering on the second ring.

"Do you have—" He scanned the exam room. "Do you have the facilities to do an autopsy?"

Silence on the other end. Then, "I...might."

"Do you, or don't you?"

"Not *exactly*, but more or less, yes." She paused and then, "Wait, why?"

"I think I have a way for you to examine the body."

"Okay," Maggie said, drawing out the word.

"Why bother trying to get you in here to see the body when we could bring it to you?"

Another long pause, followed by laughter. "You can't be serious. What happened to the by-the-book cop I met this morning?"

"Maybe I'm not as by-the-book as you thought."

She laughed again. "Apparently."

"I'll need help transporting it."

"Kurt has a truck."

He thought about it for a second. "Does it have a cover?"

"Yep."

"Okay, then you and Kurt come meet me at the morgue. Park in the back next to my car and enter through the rear door."

"Jesus, you move fast. We'll be there in twenty."

Gene hung up and leaned against the front desk. He still couldn't believe he was doing this. Letting an unauthorized civilian perform an autopsy on the body of a murder victim... What the hell was he thinking? This plan had been so impulsive; he hadn't thought it through completely. He didn't bother about what would happen tomorrow when the morgue attendant found a body missing. Part of him worried he'd lose his job over this—or worse—but the rest of him didn't care.

It was hard to believe everything that had happened today had only happened today. His whole world had been turned on its head, and now he was throwing all caution to the wind. He hoped it was worth it.

Jack's green, green eyes flashed through his mind like a thunderbolt. Like a curse.

*

Nearly twenty minutes on the dot, Gene heard a car pull up, and then, footsteps sounded in the hallway from the rear entrance. Maggie appeared with Kurt in tow.

"Man, I never been in a morgue at night before...and I don't think I care to do it again," Kurt said as a greeting.

"She's in stall thirty-two," Gene said and led them into the examination room. He stopped by a storage closet on one wall and took out a body bag. "We'll need one of these."

"Well, this ought to be fun," Maggie said under her breath.

"Come on, Mags, lighten up," Kurt teased.

Gene laid the body bag out on the exam table and unzipped it while Maggie found stall thirty-two.

"Harriet Sparrow, that her?" she asked.

"Yep. Let's do this."

As he watched Maggie open the chamber, he noticed both she and Kurt were wearing gloves. *Smart.* He'd forgotten to warn Maggie to bring some, but of course, they'd thought of it. *They're professionals, after all.* God, what had he gotten himself into?

After pulling the body out and examining it, Maggie said, "It's our lucky day. Seems they didn't freeze the body, so we should be able to do the autopsy tonight." She stepped back. "I'm not moving her though."

"You're willing to cut her open, but you don't want to touch her?" Kurt asked, disgust plain on his face.

"I don't want to *move* her."

Kurt turned to Gene expectantly, his eyes narrowed.

Gene nodded and moved the exam table next to the tray. "Okay, so you grab that side, I'll grab this side, and we slide her onto the body bag." He was unsure if the instructions were for Kurt or himself.

"Carefully," Maggie added. "Do it *carefully*. Please."

Gene locked eyes with Kurt as they moved her. The body, though stiff from rigor mortis, felt soft at the same time. Almost *squishy*. This was probably the grossest thing Gene had ever done. But in a matter of seconds, it was over. The body was on the bag, ready to be zipped up and wheeled out to the truck.

"This is the grossest thing I ever done." Kurt echoed Gene's thoughts as he zipped up the bag.

Gene grunted his agreement.

After they loaded the body into the truck, they did their best to make the morgue appear as untouched as possible.

"I'll follow you back," Gene said.

"Okay," Maggie said. "Want me to text you the address in case we get separated?"

"We won't."

She turned and climbed into the passenger seat of the truck.

Gene got into his own car and breathed. *In and out. In and out.* There was no going back now.

Jack would never let him live this down. The thought made his throat tight. It'd been about twenty-four hours since he'd seen him. Gene didn't know how he'd feel if it went another twenty-four.

On that note, he pulled out of his space and followed Kurt's truck to Maggie's mom's house.

*

When they returned to the house in Sandy, Gene helped Kurt carry the body bag inside, following Maggie to a room in the basement.

At the sight of it, Kurt said, "Damn, Mags!" Once they'd set the body down on an exam table, Kurt scanned the space with his hands on his hips, nodding appreciatively. "This here's impressive."

Gene took in the surroundings. It seemed like something out of a TV show—a sterile lab, fitted with all the basic equipment such as beakers and Bunsen burners. She also had an assortment of more advanced tools, many of which he didn't know the name of. Among the tools he recognized were ones that would be useful during an autopsy, and he wondered if they'd ever been used before. As he turned about the room, he caught Maggie observing him.

"You're not going to cite me for not having a permit for this, are you?" she asked.

"Not today. But only because I'd have to explain why I'm here." Gene focused on the body. "We doing this?"

Kurt raised his hands and backed away. "All right. This is where I leave y'all. Holler if you need me." And with that, he made a hasty exit upstairs.

"Everyone's usually pretty squeamish about this stuff," Maggie said. "Not me." She pulled on a blue disposable medical gown before tossing an identical one to Gene. "If you're staying for this part, put that on. I'll get us some masks and gloves."

He did as he was told while she disappeared into a closet in the corner of the room. She quickly returned and passed him the equipment. When they were all suited up, standing on either side of the exam table, Maggie pulled out a voice recorder.

Gene observed as Maggie unzipped the bag and carefully removed it from around the body. First, she took pictures from head to toe and closeups of external wounds, bruises, marks, and anything else of note. As she continued, lifting arms and legs to better examine them, she dictated notes and observations to the recorder, much like a legitimate coroner, and Gene wondered what her specialty would have been had she finished medical school.

Once finished, Maggie retrieved a scalpel and a ribcage spreader. "Okay," she said, "I may need some help with this next part."

Gene pushed any squeamishness aside and nodded.

Maggie took a deep breath and started cutting. Gene had observed autopsies before, but this was different—cruder—the cuts a bit crooked and haphazard. As Maggie peeled the victim's skin and flesh away to reveal her ribcage, bile welled in Gene's throat. He swallowed it.

Maggie reached for the ribcage spreader, then paused, her brows furrowed.

When she didn't move, Gene said, "Um, Maggie?"

She focused on him. "How old did you say she was?"

"Uh, I don't think I did. Let me see…" He skimmed the file on the victim. "Here it is. Harriet Sparrow, fifty-four—"

Maggie abruptly turned away from him and started searching for something in the lab. Eventually, she pulled a couple different pairs of pliers from the wall. When she returned, she asked, "Did they do X-rays on her already?"

Gene hastily paged through the folder. "Um…yes. They did, uh—" He noted the pliers in her hands. "Why do you ask?"

She gave him a look as if not wanting to spell it out.

He hoped this wasn't going where he thought. "You're not going to...to pull out a bone with a pair of pliers, are you?"

"It's not ideal, but I don't have a bone saw."

"What about that?" he asked, gesturing to the ribcage spreader.

"That only moves the ribs out of the way so that we can access the organs, but I need to remove the sternum and get it under a microscope." Gene's face must have conveyed how unsure he felt because she added, as if it would placate him, "I probably won't need to use them. Might be able to do it with my hands."

He released a weighted breath. "Fine."

Maggie set the tools on the counter and did as she said she would—tried to pull the sternum out with her hands. A few tense seconds passed before an ominous *crack* resounded through the room, sending chills up Gene's spine. Maggie, her face shrouded in concentration and without veering from her work, reached for one of the pairs of pliers. Gene turned away and didn't face Maggie again until he heard a soft, relieved exhale from her.

"Got it," she said, holding up the bone proudly. She carried it to a table in the corner and began examining it up close.

Gene followed her. "What're you looking for?"

She didn't respond right away, busy cleaning the bone. After a few minutes, she had it under the microscope, and Gene lost hope of her saying anything until she was done.

"This doesn't make any sense," she murmured before returning to the body and extracting a rib. She cleaned the rib and swapped it for the sternum. A minute or two later, she pulled away from the microscope and slumped in her chair. Then, her eyes darted to Gene and some of the fog lifted. "What'd you say?"

"Not important. What did you find?"

"Well...how much do you know about the human body?"

"Enough."

"Okay. The short of it is the bones don't match up with her age. For someone in their midfifties...her bones should have some wear and tear on them, you know? There should be evidence of fifty-four years' worth of growth and change and—" She cut herself off before trying again. "As we grow, our bones change. They fuse together and become stronger. Then as we begin to age, bones become more brittle, and in some cases, they start to deteriorate. Someone in their fifties should have strong, healthy bones with lots of evidence of remodeling and growth."

"And she doesn't?"

Maggie tilted her head from side to side. "She does, but…"

"But what?"

"Her sternum looks like that of a hundred-year-old. And her rib—" She grabbed it and showed it to him. "This should be from a young adult, someone in their late teens or early twenties."

"Couldn't she have had a graft or something?"

"Possibly, but there's no evidence of one."

"So, what are you saying, then?"

Maggie's eyes drifted to a spot behind him. "I can't say anything definitively, but…something is off about her."

Gene peered over at the remains lying open on the table, then at Maggie. "Let's finish the exam. Maybe it'll give us some answers."

The rest of the autopsy went by routinely, almost exactly as if in an actual morgue, though by the end of it, they had more questions than answers.

"I don't understand," Maggie said, ripping her gloves off and throwing them in the trash. She had reassembled the body, and it now lay on the table under a sheet.

Gene shed his protective gear slowly, thinking everything over. "Me either. I thought this was supposed to be the easy one. We still don't have cause of death."

Maggie groaned in frustration. "I don't do well with not knowing things."

Gene snorted. "'Course you don't."

She rested her hips against the counter, and Gene mirrored the pose beside her. "It's almost like… No, it's impossible."

"What?"

"It's almost as if she's not human."

"Okay, I'm still new to this, but how is that impossible? Don't some of them look human?"

"Some do, but not once you open them up."

Gene shivered.

Maggie tilted her head to the side in thought. "I suppose she *was* different...but not how you'd expect."

She went quiet and then jolted forward. "Oh my God." She tore off her gown, threw it in the trash, and ran out of the room.

Gene followed after her, confused. He found her upstairs, rifling through a leather journal, flipping pages rapidly, her eyes alight in excitement. Maggie paused on a page, her lips moving as she read silently over the words.

"Oh my God," she said again. And then she was rushing back downstairs, clutching the journal. Gene chased after her, and this time, Kurt followed close behind as well.

When they made it to the lab, Maggie had pulled the sheet down, exposing the victim's face. She pried open her right eyelid and studied it before returning to the journal. Her eyes darted between the two a few times until finally, she looked up at Gene.

"She's immortal."

"I'm sorry, what?"

"This victim. She's immortal. That's why the bones don't match her age, why her organs are in various stages of life. I bet if you run a deep enough background check on her, you'll find her identity's fake. She's immortal, not human."

Kurt stepped closer and studied the body. Gene was stuck to his spot on the floor, unable to process it all.

Kurt lifted her upper lip over her teeth. "No fangs. Rules out vamps and Weres. *Hmm.* It's a pickle."

"It also rules out a slew of monsters that *aren't* immortal!" Maggie said. "Don't you see how much easier this makes our job?"

"Well, regardless of whether this victim's immortal, it doesn't mean the thing doing the killing is."

Maggie deflated a bit and cast her desperate gaze toward Gene.

"What do you think?"

He swallowed, forced his feet to move him closer to the table. "I think...I think I'm in way over my head."

All of a sudden, it hit him like a cement truck. Monsters, immortal beings, secret societies of monster hunters, all of it. And he crumbled under the weight of it all. He couldn't weigh in on this because he knew *jack shit* about it. Sure, he could help analyze physical evidence, run background checks; he could be a cop. But he couldn't check a body for fangs—he didn't know *how* to do that. He couldn't be a hunter. He didn't belong here with these people. Why had Maggie asked him for his help? He couldn't help.

"I'm sorry." Gene made for a hasty exit, saying, "I can't help you with this...I don't know what I was thinking."

Maggie stopped him as he reached the door. "Wait!" She came up behind him. "I know this is all new to you. I get it. But I need your help with something else. Please."

He slowly faced her.

She held out a black moleskin journal he recognized instantly. "I can't read Jack's code, and I don't know how to decipher it."

"And you think I do?"

"Do you?" she asked, handing him the journal.

Gene opened it to the latest entry. He recognized the haphazard arrangement of letters, seemingly gibberish to an untrained eye, and read the first few lines easily. He closed it. "What should I be looking for?"

"You can read it? He taught it to you?"

"It's the same code he writes his crime notes in, and who do you think puts together the evidence packages for prosecutors?" Absentmindedly, he rubbed his thumb over the smooth leather cover. "Let's just say, I picked it up pretty quick."

"Well, then, can you skim through it and see if there's anything there we don't know, something he didn't share with us?"

Gene turned toward the door. "I'll let you know what I find," he said and left the room. He made it to his car and sagged against the seat. "What the hell am I doing?"

Tossing Jack's journal onto the passenger seat, he started up the car. Maybe if he got some sleep, he'd wake up and find this was all some weird dream. Maybe he'd go to work tomorrow and find Jack sitting at his desk, smiling up at him and teasing him about how he'd gotten there earlier than him. Maybe it was all a dream.

Man, did he hope this was all a dream.

Chapter Twenty

Jack wasn't sure how long it had been. How long he'd been stuck in the darkness in this damp, cold cell. Could have been days, weeks, maybe even a month, though he didn't think it had been that long. Fuck, he hoped it hadn't been that long.

His captor hadn't made an appearance. Apart from that first night, they hadn't spoken to him at all. He started to wonder if this was it. If their plan was to let him sit and rot in this dark, lonely cell.

He shifted against the wall and winced. His muscles ached. His hands were still "bound" together at the wrists, limiting his ability to move his arms and shoulders. He wouldn't normally think it'd be that bad, but after a while, his shoulders grew tight, his neck sore from slouching. He needed a good long stretch. Jack could picture it now—spreading his arms wide, reaching out as far as he could until a satisfied *squeak* escaped his lips, rolling his shoulders in circles, arching and twisting his torso until his spine cracked. God, he never thought he'd miss something as simple as stretching.

And, oh, was he *bored*. He'd kill for any form of entertainment. A fly flitting around the room, a ball to toss against the wall, a pen to click.

He'd even take a box set of *Keeping Up with the Kardashians* when he'd previously gone on the record saying he'd rather stick needles in his eyes. But right now, he'd take *anything* to take his mind off the monotony of his new life. The sad thing was that he knew if he had something to entertain him, the excitement would eventually fade, and he'd be right back where he was now.

No, what he craved was interaction. Someone to talk to, or at least to hear someone else's breathing, something to know he wasn't alone.

He missed Maggie, missed her annoying teasing. Right now, he'd gladly listen to one of her lectures about how he shouldn't have become a cop, or how he shouldn't be afraid of the dark, or how he should listen to her more because she was the "older" sibling. While those lectures might have previously made him groan in frustration, now, they only made him smile wistfully.

It was different than how he missed Gene—someone he hadn't expected to miss, at least not like *this*. With little else to do, Jack's thoughts drifted to his partner constantly, and when he wasn't thinking about Gene, he was dreaming about him. From nightmares to soppy, domestic fantasies. Jack increasingly jolted awake with such *yearning*, his chest hurt. And when he tried to return to those more pleasant dreams that felt so real, his mind betrayed him and sent him elsewhere. If he was going to die in this cell, couldn't he at least escape to his dreams when his reality was so bleak? But no matter how much he willed himself to dream happy dreams, Jack could never force them.

It was during one of them that he was plucked from the darkness, his cell inundated with light. He closed his eyes, unable to tolerate so much of it after being without for so long. He heard the sound of footsteps and smelled the faint scent of lavender. Jack forced his eyes open to the silhouette of a woman standing before him. It took a while for his vision to fully adjust, but once it did, he was struck by her beauty.

She had an ethereal quality about her, her skin flawless, her body strong and healthy. Her *eyes*, deep, deep navy, almost black, were inhuman, yet alluring.

It was quiet for a heartbeat, and then she said, "Your darkness has been purged. Welcome back to the light." She offered her hand.

As his gaze remained transfixed on hers, her eyes flashed a bright purple, and her hold on him released. She stretched her hand out to him. After a brief hesitation, he took it and let her lead him out of the cell.

The woman took Jack to a larger, brighter room. This one, though minimally furnished, had high wall-to-wall windows, too high to see out of, but the light shining in cast long shadows across the floor. The room wasn't much larger than the cell, but it had a twin cot and a cushioned chair. It was cleaner and smelled that way too.

"Sit." The woman pointed to the chair.

Jack's eyes were still quite sensitive to the light, and he felt pretty gross after being in that cell for who knew how long. He didn't want to stink up the chair. He glanced at the woman and then the chair. For the first time, he wondered if he should try to escape while he had the chance.

As if reading his mind, she said, "I could always make you."

He took a seat. "How long was I in there?"

"A few days."

He studied her. Her frame was slender, yet she radiated power and strength. Her skin, though pale, too pale for a human, didn't make her appear emaciated. Not a vampire, then. Likely not a Were, either. *Wouldn't be that skinny.* If he didn't know better, he'd say she was— No, she was a monster. Monsters didn't look like humans. They *didn't*.

"What are you?" he asked.

She smiled, her eyes playful. "What do you think I am?"

"You're not human."

She feigned offense. "Ouch. Don't I look human?"

He shook his head.

She laughed. "So, what am I, then?"

"You're not a werewolf or a Were of any kind, for that matter. Not a ghost or—"

"Wow, process of elimination, huh? There isn't a quicker way to do this? Come on. Get creative. Take a guess."

He thought of the first meeting with the other hunters and went with his best guess. "A changeling."

That got him a full-bellied, joyous laugh. She threw her head back and everything. Well, she *had* said to get creative.

When she finally stopped laughing, she said, "A faerie? What gave me away? Was it my wings?"

Jack scoffed.

"You got creative with that one, didn't you? I suppose that's on me, but come on. Do you truly believe there's a world parallel to ours where *faeries* exist?" She laughed again. "They're a myth. I guarantee you."

Her words struck a chord, reminding him of Argus's reaction to the same suggestion.

She approached him. "That all you got, hunter?"

He met her dark glare head-on. "You could always put me out of my misery and tell me."

She smiled again, but this time, her eyes turned purple as a familiar sensation overtook him, moving from the tips of his toes upward. It was as though a string wound its way through him, wrapping itself around every vein, every bone, until it was everywhere. And then, it *tightened*. He screamed.

"But that'd ruin all the fun."

When the pain stopped, Jack couldn't move anything but his neck.

"You hunters are so afraid of us you don't even know it. We've been around for centuries, and yet none of you know about us. Why?" She raised her arms up in a questioning gesture. "Could it be that by acknowledging our existence, you would then have to consider there are others like us?"

"Others like you?"

"Like my kind. The first thing out of your mouth was a list of creatures I am *not*. And when pressed for another answer, you turned to fiction. Tell me. What do I look like?" When he didn't immediately answer, she pressed him further. "You listed everything I don't look like. So, what does that leave, oh brilliant detective?"

He swallowed, not wanting to admit it. "Human."

"Exactly. If you acknowledge our existence and that we've managed to evade your notice for centuries, you'd have to confront the possibility that there are others. Other *things* that blend in. That don't fit into your cookie-cutter idea of an inhuman creature. And that terrifies you."

"You seem human enough, but there's still something off about you. Not that dissimilar to other humanoid monsters."

"Right out the gate with the *M* word. Wow. What makes you think I'm a monster?"

"You kill innocent people."

"Innocent people? Do you know what the first hunter I killed did to me?" She appeared to get choked up, and Jack wasn't sure if it was an act or not. "He *hurt* me. I had to protect myself. And the other one was after me too. It's not my fault they didn't know how to defend themselves."

"And what about the victim at the Temple?"

She exhaled roughly through her nose, and anger flashed through her eyes. "Victim. Victim? Honey, I guarantee you, of all of the people I've killed, she deserved it the most."

"So what about me? Why take me? Why not kill me as you did with the rest of them?"

"Isn't it obvious? I need you alive."

Before he could ask why, her hold squeezed him again, and a dull pain threaded through him. Not enough to make him yell out, not enough to make him wince, only enough to make him sweat. And for her to assert her power.

"What am I? What do I want?" she asked. "The answer may disappoint you." She turned about the room. "I'm just a naive disciple. Of a religion that's used me, abused me, lied to me my whole life. One that I will stop at nothing to see destroyed. I suppose you can say I'm lapsed."

Stepping closer, her eyes flashing purple, the hold on him tightened little by little. "And as for you... Well, Detective, I'm afraid you're the key to it all. You're the one who's going to bring us all together."

"What the hell is that supposed to mean?"

She smiled cruelly. "Don't worry. You'll find out soon enough."

As quickly as her hold had tightened, it disappeared, and as she retreated toward a door on the far side of the room, his muscles were no longer stiff and sore. In fact, he felt physically better than he had in months.

"Remember," she said, opening the door a crack, "I brought you out of the darkness; I can throw you back in. Don't give me a reason."

With that, she left him alone in his new, upgraded cell, more confused than before.

Well, fuck.

Chapter Twenty-One

Maggie rubbed her eyes and pushed herself away from her desk. She stretched her arms above her and yawned. Damn, was she exhausted. Dana and Kurt had left not long ago to get some shut-eye, and even her dog had long abandoned her to go sleep upstairs. Maggie supposed she should try to do the same. As she wandered into the living room on her way upstairs, she yawned again and nearly jumped out of her skin when she saw someone sitting on the couch.

"Oh. Argus, I didn't know you were still here."

"Of course I am," he said, his attention never straying from the journal resting on his lap. "Why wouldn't I be?"

"I don't know…I'm not sure it's still worth your being here." She flopped onto the sofa next to him, sinking into the cushions.

Argus pulled his reading glasses off and set them on the journal before putting it on the coffee table in front of them. He focused on her. "And why not?"

"Let's see… We've spent the last two days pouring over journals and doing everything we can to find whatever it is we're looking for. We—I have a stolen body in my mother's basement that I need to get rid of somehow. Gene is MIA because he's probably freaking out about the whole monster thing again because he's a normal guy who didn't grow up around all this. And what do we have to show for it? Nothing."

She paused and caught her breath. "On top of that, we're not eating, we're not sleeping, we're spending all our energy on this. And yet, it seems pointless. We're not finding any answers; we have no clue where Jack is. It's...I don't know if—" She broke off with a sigh. "Dana and Kurt left to get some sleep. I think that's a good idea, so I'm going to turn in. You should too."

"Maggie..."

She determinedly avoided Argus's eyes, afraid he'd read her in a second.

"I have been friends with your family for quite some time. I'd like to think I understand you. Perhaps better than Dana... And of the people here, I believe I'm one of your closest and oldest friends. You know that you don't have to pretend in front of me. You can tell me the truth."

"You want to know how I'm feeling, Argus? I'm frustrated. And I'm scared."

"Fear can be powerful; frustration can be defeating—but only if we let those emotions drive us." He paused. "I know Jack and I don't always see eye to eye, but you know I love you and him as I would my own children. You know that, right?"

Maggie squeezed her fingers together. "I do...and although Jack doesn't show it, he knows it too."

"He doesn't have to show it. It's part of being family."

In the quiet, Maggie admitted, "I miss my mom."

"When was the last time you went to see her?"

"It's, uh, been a while, I have to admit. But I don't know... Every time I go, it gets harder and harder."

"She's not doing well?"

"No." Maggie shifted, pushing herself up straighter, and hugged herself. "I mean...well, you know."

"Yes. Yes, when I met her, she had recently started to...decline?" At Maggie's nod, he continued. "To my knowledge, her condition—if we should call it that—is genetic?"

"Yeah, but it skipped a generation. Jack and I don't have it."

"You're sure?" he asked.

"I'm positive." she said. Maggie had never been more disappointed in that fact than right now. "It usually starts in late puberty and develops as you age before..."

Argus winced.

Maggie cleared her throat. "Mom's case is a rare one anyway. Her mother didn't experience anything this advanced until she was much, much older."

"Do you remember that? You must have been so young when your grandmother died."

"I was. I don't think I ever met her. Mom and Granddaddy didn't let us near her toward the end because of...everything."

Argus hummed an understanding.

"I keep feeling that if it didn't skip me, I would be able to find him, but I—I can't."

"Well, lost people are found every day. And you are brilliant. I have no doubt you'll find him." Argus paused. "Can I ask you a question?"

"Shoot."

"You have Dana going through a different set of journals, seemingly unrelated... Why? Shouldn't we all be focusing our efforts?"

"Well, Gene brought something to me the other day, something he wanted to keep quiet." When Argus's expression conveyed nothing but confusion, she said, "Something about an old case of his that he's very protective of for some reason. I don't get all the secrecy. But he only wanted one other person working on it with me, so Dana and I are tackling it. This new information from the latest victim has overshadowed it. I *think* it's something, but..."

"What?"

"I mean..." Maggie knew Gene didn't want her talking about this with anyone else, but truth be told, the more she dug into it, the more she needed a new pair of eyes on it. "He wouldn't want me to ask you, but...you've been doing this for a while."

"No, I started last week. What are you talking about?"

"Okay, seriously."

"Yes. I've been *in the business* for a long time. Some might say since the dark ages."

"Yeah, yeah." Her smile faded. "So, in your experience...and this is hypothetical..."

"Why, of course."

Maggie hesitated, unsure how to phrase it. "Have you ever come across, like, a cultish religion of monsters?"

"A cultish religion of monsters," he repeated. "I'm sorry. What do you mean exactly?"

"Like a religion...for monsters...I guess."

Argus eyed her curiously. "Er...well, no. I have not, I'm afraid to say. Do you think that's what this is?"

"You remember that meeting when Jack suggested something outside the box, and it was a little too out there? And he got frustrated because we weren't pushing our limits, I guess, and he was right. We weren't thinking creatively enough." Maggie paused. "But sometimes, you just know. Right?"

"If you're thinking it's some religion or cult, whatever, of monsters—which again, would be quite unusual... I mean, we know that outside of some varieties of Weres, there aren't a lot of group-friendly monsters. It's weird to see them band together." He seemed to consider the idea. "It *would* be something different though."

Maggie let her head fall into her hands.

Argus put a hand on her shoulder, squeezing gently, reassuringly. "But I say, you've been doing this for a while now too. You know, I may have seventy years of experience whereas you have thirty—"

"Less than thirty, thank you," she said, sitting up some.

He gave her a level look, which she ignored. "At the end of the day, you still have a good amount of experience; you're an expert. And of all of us, you're the only one with a doctorate. You're very smart. If you think something is fishy, or if your intuition is telling you something...in my opinion, you should listen to it."

"I...I feel bad for Gene. I think he desperately wants an answer to this case he brought me. There are some coincidences that are hard to explain, but..."

"Like what?" Argus asked.

Maggie took a deep breath. "The cabin where I sent Jack when he was—" She broke off, overcome with emotion. "The cabin was involved in Gene's case too."

"That is an odd coincidence," he admitted. "But still, most likely, only a coincidence."

"Exactly. Besides, it was owned by a different person at the time. And the one other connection that's a bit firmer is still pretty slim. So...I can tell he wants an explanation, but I don't think I can give it to him."

"Well...I told Jack faeries are a myth, and while monster religions are not a myth, they might as well be. I can't say that with the same amount of certainty, of course. But...I'm afraid Gene is new to this. I would trust your instincts before you trust his."

"Well, he may be new to the whole monster hunting thing, but he's been a cop for ten years at this point."

"And what do you always say about cops?"

"There are no good ones."

"Exactly."

They laughed.

"All right," Argus said, tapping her shoulder and then pushing himself off the couch. "I think it's time I let you sleep. You need a nice, long rest. Can you promise me that?"

"I promise."

"Good," he said, smiling down at her. "I'm going to follow Dana and Kurt's lead and return to my hotel room as well. Try to get some sleep myself. You're right that we're not doing ourselves any favors here."

Argus headed toward the door but paused halfway there and turned. "But Maggie? Remember, there is no darkness that cannot be illuminated by the light. And though we're in dark times now, we'll soon find the light again. I promise."

His words, ever wise, made her smile pensively.

"Thank you, Argus."

He bowed his head as if to say, *of course*, and then, "All right, I'm gone. Sleep well."

As the door clicked shut, Maggie slumped into the couch. Maybe I'll sleep here, she thought as her eyes fluttered closed, exhaustion taking over.

Chapter Twenty-Two

A couple of days passed, and they were no closer to finding Jack. Gene hadn't been to see Maggie since their little illegal autopsy. He worked from home over the weekend, unable to do anything else. Because if he stopped to think, it was of Jack and Maggie and monsters and bodies cut open in makeshift morgues.

When Gene did return to work, the office was abuzz with news of a stolen body from the morgue. He'd thought it was odd the news was only now coming to light, but as he pieced together the story from his coworkers' gossip, it made sense. They had apparently discovered the body missing the day after Gene and Maggie had taken it, and then the burned remnants of it had been discovered this morning. *I guess Maggie figured out a way to get rid of it.*

Thankfully, none of the theories floating around implicated him or came close. Nor should they.

Gene took a seat at his desk, and Jack's journal sat right where he'd left it: in the center in front of his keyboard. He had tried reading it the other day, and as he'd found with the few entries he'd read of Maggie's, it was extremely personal. Jack and his sister didn't limit their observations to the case and their theories. They also wrote about their lives, their innermost thoughts on display, and Gene felt as if he was invading their privacy, Jack's especially. Although Jack used the same code for his crime notes, and Gene had been reading those for months, Jack's code, in that context, didn't hide much. But in his journal, the code seemed purposeful, a warning that clearly stated *KEEP OUT*. Needless to say, Gene had only gotten so far in his attempt before feeling as if he was reading something he shouldn't and stopped.

But he had spent the past two days attempting to come up with a reasonable explanation for all this—and he'd failed. If Maggie thought Jack's journal could reveal some clue they didn't already know, then he should give it a try.

Gene opened the journal to the middle of a recent entry, and after he got used to the encryption, he could read it easily.

...new body in the desert last night. Had to share a room with Gene, which was weird. Not because he was weird about it or anything, it was just weird. And I came out to him for some reason? I had never planned to do that. It just came out. (no pun intended)

Anyway, the new body is the same as the other one. Shredded to bits, looks like hell. I noticed something this time though. Something that won't be in the forensics report, MAGGIE. Something seems to be repelling animals and insects from eating on the bodies. Don't know if it's the lavender scent or something else. Need to follow-up with Maggie on this...

Well, that was something they didn't have before. Gene pulled out his own notebook and scribbled a note about it. He vaguely remembered Jack saying something about that at the crime scene, but he'd dismissed him at the time. *Or, I didn't understand him.* To be perfectly honest, he didn't remember much about that particular scene other than being annoyed they had to stay the night. When Gene finished making his own note, he continued to the next entry and kept reading.

Meeting with Argus was a shitshow. None of them are willing to THINK. To use their goddamn BRAINS. When I went to Maggie for help, I wanted HER help, not the fucking cavalry. We can do this without Argus. I don't know why she keeps insisting we need his "expertise" or whatever. The man's a dinosaur. We can do without him.

Then I come into the office, and we have to do a stupid TRACE stakeout? Seriously? What the fuck is this? I'm sick of this. Sick of being pulled in different directions. Sick of feeling I don't fit. Not here with my own freaking sister and people I grew up with. And certainly not with the fucking police force. Not even Gene—

Gene skipped to the next page. That one was too personal. The next one was the last entry he'd written before he disappeared.

I'm at a cabin in the middle of the woods, up in the mountains in Little Cottonwood, in the middle of the night. I'm probably going to die tonight. I don't know where Maggie gets off sending me on these things. She knows I don't like doing this shit at night.

The house is a bit run-down. The roof is caved in in some places, and the landscape around it is covered in undisturbed snow. I doubt the place has seen a human soul in years. Very creepy. I don't want to go in. I have to go in. But I don't want to.

So, I'll prolong the inevitable, shall I? I'm telling Gene tomorrow. Don't know if it's the right idea or not, but at least, I won't be lying to him anymore.

Gene almost stopped reading, but he saw his name multiple times down the page, and dammit, curiosity got the better of him.

I spent the evening with his family tonight, and damn, I thought my family had its mess. His is quite the piece of work. His niece was nice, maybe if she can get out, she'll be all right. Gene's mom? The epitome of a Mormon matriarch. She's Jeanne Triplehorn from Big Love IRL. I sure hope his dad doesn't have multiple wives...

Gene couldn't help a laugh.

...And that man is another story altogether. Reeked of pompous, arrogant asshole. Looked at me like I was a disappointment, and I'm not his son. Can't imagine Gene's thought process when we saw him. When I told his dad I was his partner and didn't explain away the double entendre, you could practically smell the homophobia. Funny how they're always the ones who assume something gay is going on, isn't it? Icing on the cake is he tried to get me to leave and not make a scene. I got to tell him "Oh, no, sir, you're confused. Gene's my partner at work. I'm a cop." His face was priceless. Only hope I didn't fuck up Gene's standing or something, but he didn't seem that close to his dad anyway.

All right, fuck. It's time to go into this creepy, scary, probably gross cabin in the woods. Hope I don't die.

The last four words were a punch to the gut. Gene closed the journal and started collecting his things. He'd be damned if that hope didn't come true.

*

It was late, close to three in the morning. Gene wasn't sure why he'd come here. He hadn't been able to sleep, tossing and turning for hours, until finally getting up and driving over to Maggie's in the middle of the night. Now, he sat in front of her house, thinking *it's way too late for this.*

Fuck it.

He got out of the car and stared up at the dark house. When he made it to the door, he held his hand up for a few seconds before finally knocking. He immediately regretted it.

"What the fuck am I thinking?" he said to himself.

Before he could withdraw, though, a light turned on inside, and Maggie poked her face in the window. She appeared unsurprised to see him and dipped behind the door to open it.

"Finally done sorting through it all?" she asked around a yawn.

"Yeah, not even close," he said.

She gave him a pitying look before stepping back and opening the door wider, gesturing him in.

"Sorry for coming by so late," he said as he entered. "I couldn't sleep."

"All good. Haven't been sleeping much myself. Come on. Let's talk in the kitchen. I'll put on some coffee."

She led him farther inside, and as she fiddled with the coffee maker, he made himself comfortable at the bar. Once the pot started brewing, Maggie turned around and leaned against the counter.

"So what's up?" she asked.

"Something in Jack's journal caught my eye, and I wanted to see if he ever mentioned it to you."

"Okay, what is it?"

"At the last crime scene in the desert, he noticed some fox tracks that approached the body, stopped, and then turned and went the other way. He said he thought something was repelling animals and insects from eating the body. In his journal, he said he'd follow up with you on it. Did he?"

"Nope. But that sounds vaguely familiar for some reason. Hold on," she said as she left the room.

Gene thought about following her, but the coffee maker beeped, and he rummaged around for a couple of mugs instead. He'd just finished pouring the second cup when Maggie returned with a ponderous expression.

"What?" he asked, offering her a mug.

She took it absentmindedly. "I can't find a journal."

"Is that odd?"

Maggie took a sip of the black coffee and screwed up her face in disgust. "*Blech.*" She opened the fridge and added some cream. She offered it to Gene before putting it away. "It's not odd, necessarily...Okay, yes, it's weird. I thought I'd grabbed all of Mom's journals from her house and brought them here."

"Maybe you missed one."

Maggie hummed as she took another sip of her coffee. "Maybe."

"Any luck with the case I brought you?" Gene asked as he took his seat again.

"Listen, I'm not sure it's anything."

"I get it. I'm new to all this, right?"

"It's not that..."

"No? Then what is it?"

Maggie hesitated.

"What?"

"I asked Argus about it, and he's never heard of a monster religion." She at least appeared to feel bad about going behind his back, though he saw through the facade.

"So that automatically means it's not real? I thought we were supposed to be thinking of things you haven't encountered before."

A muscle in Maggie's jaw jumped. "Argus has been around for—"

"Forever, yeah, I get it, but...but come on, Maggie. It's not like he's the end-all, be-all."

"The journals aren't showing anything. I'm sorry."

Gene grimaced. "Jack was right. You all refuse to use your brains on this." He gave a short laugh.

Maggie didn't say anything, only shifted her weight from foot to foot.

He took a deep breath. "There's no one else? No one else with his experience? Is that what you're saying?"

"Well—no. There's...there is someone else, but—"

"Great! Let's go ask them. Get their input on it."

"It's not that simple, Gene."

"Maggie, we're stuck here. You see that? You get that? We're stuck. We've been stuck since before Jack was taken. And now, we got to get our fucking asses in gear, or we may never find him." Gene attempted to regain some of his composure, zeroing in on his clenched hands resting on the counter.

"Please," he said. "Look, if there's someone else, someone who can shed some light on this, who was active around the time the sect was last here. Please, we have to try. We have to talk to them and see if they know something."

Maggie bit her bottom lip. "She's not— Fine. We'll have to go in the morning."

"Right." Of course. It was 3:00 a.m. They couldn't go barging in on someone now.

"Pick me up around eight? We'll want to get there right when they open. Gets crowded later in the day."

"Right when they open? Who's they?"

Maggie stared straight ahead, and the longer she remained silent, the more he thought she wouldn't respond. Then, her eyes still fixed in front of her, she said, "All Seasons Senior Living."

Gene winced before gently pressing on. "Right. And who are we seeing there?"

Maggie poured the rest of her coffee down the drain. "My mom."

Chapter Twenty-Three

At a glance, the assisted living home appeared to be a normal apartment complex, and to many degrees, that was exactly what it was. Gene parked, then turned to see Maggie recoiled into herself. He got the feeling that whatever lay waiting for them inside was anything but normal.

"Ready?"

Maggie unbuckled her seat belt and got out of the car. "As I'll ever be."

Gene followed her inside. The lobby smelled clean, exactly what you'd expect from an old folks' home. Early morning rays streamed in through east-facing windows, bathing the area in gentle, serene light. A calm, quiet melody of classical music played in the background, and the sounds of breakfast came from somewhere down the hall—knives and forks on plates, the dulled tones of conversation.

The middle-aged woman at the reception desk smiled kindly as they approached. All was as expected, yet Gene felt a chill creep up his spine the longer he was here, and he suspected it wouldn't leave him until they'd gone.

"Ah, Miss Cartwright, how nice to see you again," the receptionist said.

Maggie gave her a tight smile. "I called ahead. We're here to see my mother, Ilka Cartwright."

"Yes, of course. I'll page the nurse, and she'll show you to your mother's room. While we wait, here are some visitor badges. Please fill in your names." She handed them each a clip-on badge with a space to write a name. By the time they'd affixed them to their shirts, a woman in light gray scrubs adorned with the All Seasons logo stood waiting for them.

"You must be Ilka's daughter," she said, holding out her hand for Maggie to shake. "I'm Caroline. It's nice to finally meet you. I've heard so much about you from your brother."

Gene gave Maggie a sidelong glance, but she ignored it. She offered Caroline little more than a handshake and a smile.

Caroline didn't seem fazed as she offered her hand to Gene. "Are you another brother?"

"No, ma'am. I'm a friend of the family."

"Oh, how kind of you to come visit today. Ilka will be so pleased to see you—"

"I'm sure," Maggie said.

"Come on," Caroline finished, "we're this way."

Caroline led them down the left hallway, either not having heard Maggie's comment or choosing to ignore it. As they neared the end of the hall, Caroline slowed and faced them. Considering Maggie's nervous countenance, Gene guessed they'd stopped outside her mother's room.

"She's doing quite well. You caught her on a good day," Caroline said. "But she's still quite fragile. Try not to excite her, hmm?"

Maggie nodded.

Caroline gave her a sympathetic smile, inclined her head to Gene, and left them.

They stood there for a while before Maggie finally said, "Let me do the talking, okay?"

"Okay," Gene said.

"And don't—" She moved toward the closed door. "—don't touch her."

Before he had a chance to clarify, Maggie was entering her mother's room. He followed her in, swallowing his questions.

Maggie and Jack's mother sat on a small sofa chair next to a twin bed, a plate of half-eaten breakfast on the small end table next to her. She didn't appear that old; in fact, she looked younger than Gene's mom, and yet, something was off about her. Her posture was dejected, withdrawn—her hands folded loosely on her lap, her shoulders hunched forward. And her expression was eerily similar to Maggie's last night. Blank. Fixed on nothing.

"Mom?"

Ilka's eyes widened, and she straightened up. She smiled when she saw Maggie standing before her. "Oh," she gasped, "Magdalena! It's been so long."

"Yeah, uh, sorry about that." Maggie inched closer to her mother.

Ilka's gaze slithered past her to Gene. "Jack's not with you? Where is Jack?"

"Well, that's why we're—"

Ilka reached out and grasped Maggie's hand in a flash.

"Fuck, Mom, that hurts. Stop."

Ilka's stare was fixed on nothing again, her eyes wide, her breathing hitched. Then she stared at Maggie, still gripping her hand, her brow furrowing in fear, in worry. "How could you let this happen? You must find him. You must find him, Magda. You must."

"That's— Shit, let go of me!" Maggie finally wrenched her hand away. "That's why we're here."

"You let them take him. How could you?"

Maggie met Gene's eyes briefly before refocusing on her mother. Gene didn't know why; he was lost the second he stepped foot in this room.

"Them?" she asked.

Ilka started rocking slightly in her chair, her torso swaying back and forth, back and forth. "She'll use him."

Maggie squatted before her mother. "He's alive, then?"

"Oh yes," Ilka said, squinting down into Maggie's eyes. "Can't you feel it?"

"You know I can't."

Ilka took her hand again and closed her eyes. This time, Maggie didn't struggle. "Yes, you can. Think it. Feel it. He's there." Ilka smiled. "There, right there. Like light anew. Don't you feel it?"

Maggie didn't say anything, only stood and let her hand slip out of her mother's grasp. She took a step back. "We're hunting something."

Her mother's eyes opened and focused on her. "It's hunting you. You have to find it."

"Do you know what it is?"

Ilka stared.

Maggie pushed. "It's...it's killing people, leaving them in the desert. Their bodies are—shredded. Please, Mom, we've never dealt with something like this."

Ilka continued to rock. Back and forth. Back and forth.

Maggie shot a pleading look toward Gene.

"One of the bodies was shriveled," Gene said, stepping in. "Like her very essence had been sucked from it."

Ilka froze.

Maggie took a step forward. "I think she was immortal. Her bones didn't match her age."

Ilka didn't say anything but remained motionless.

Maggie glanced at Gene as if to say *what else?*

"Lavender," Gene said. "The bodies smell of lavender, animals and insects don't eat on them—"

Ilka gasped and started rocking again, this time with more fervor. "No," she said. "No, it can't be. They're back; they can't be. They can't be. He. Promised. Me."

"Mom, do you know what it is?" Maggie got close again, tried to calm her mother by placing a hand on her shoulder. If Ilka felt it, she didn't show it.

"He lied. He lied? He lied to me. Promised me. Lied to me."

Maggie bit her lip, squatted again, trying to get her mother to look at her. "Please, Mom. What is it? Argus doesn't—"

Ilka stopped, gripped Maggie's shoulders. "Argus?" Her voice chilled Gene to the bone.

"Yes, you know—Argus."

Ilka shook her head slowly.

"Our friend? Your friend?" Maggie added.

"No." Ilka tightened her grip and began rocking violently. "He's one of them, Magda! He's one of them. One of them. One of them, one of them, one of them! Lied to me! Lied to me! Promised me, promised me, promise, promise. Lied!" She screamed.

Gene pulled Maggie up and away as nurses swarmed the room. Ilka tried to follow them, but she was pushed down into her chair.

"One of them, one of them, one of them! Lied! Lied to me!"

The nurses put a needle in her arm, and as if in a movie, Ilka lost all fight. Within seconds, she was asleep.

*

They managed to make it out to Gene's car without causing too much more of a scene. Now, sitting in silence, Gene waited for Maggie to say something, anything. A deep-set contemplative expression wrinkled her features as she stared out the windshield. Her eyes darted around as if she were working through a problem in her mind.

The longer she remained silent, the more Gene thought he shouldn't push her into anything, so he turned forward to the beautiful day in Salt Lake City. It remained cool, but it was the first day of the year that was supposed to feel like Spring, and it looked like it too: sunny, bright, brimming with and radiating pure warmth, not a cloud in the sky. The view of the snowcapped mountains to the east wasn't hindered by smog—beautiful.

After several minutes of tense silence, Gene figured they ought to leave. He put the car in gear and drove toward his house as it was closer than Maggie's. Plus, he didn't want to run into any of the others. He felt he and Maggie should have this conversation alone. His home would be safe.

As Gene drove, a string of questions ran through his head, but he couldn't voice any of them. Was Argus...evil? Was that why Gene had judged him before he spoke? And could he take Ilka for her word? She certainly was not well. He didn't know what plagued her, but there was no doubt her mind wasn't what it used to be. What did she mean, anyway? *He's one of them...* It could mean anything.

He pulled into his driveway, and the feeling of the car stopping seemed to snap Maggie out of it.

"Where are we?" she asked.

"My house. Figured it'd be a good place to talk. Come on." He didn't wait for her to respond, just got out of the car and went inside, assuming she would follow.

His house was a little messy, but on the whole, it wasn't that bad. He kicked some shoes out of the way in the entry hall and gestured Maggie in. She walked in and stood in the living room, her hands in her pockets, seemingly unsure what to do with herself. She surveyed the room, taking it all in.

"Didn't know you could afford a place in the Avenues," she said.

Gene snorted as he took his coat off and hung it up. "Yeah, I bought it before prices went crazy." He threw his keys on a table near the door. "You can sit down, you know."

She dropped onto the couch, right on the edge of the cushion as if ready to spring into action at a moment's notice. Her right leg bounced incessantly, her eyes still darting about the room.

"Want something to drink? Coffee?"

"I'd take a whiskey if you have it."

He winced but went to get a bottle anyway. Who was he to judge? He placed the bottle and a glass on the coffee table and sat across from her. Maggie reached for the liquor, uncapped it, and sniffed. She poured herself half a shot, barely a sip, and knocked it back. Then, she set it on the table, pushed it away, and sank into the leather.

"So," Gene said.

"So."

They stared at each other.

Maggie sat up and rested her elbows on her knees. "Where do you want me to start?"

"Why not with the elephant in the room?"

"Oh, sure. Would that be my mom or Argus?"

"Honestly, either will do."

Maggie reclined on the couch once again. "It's simple enough with my mom, I mean she's…" She rubbed her eyes. "She's crazy. And I don't mean that hyperbolically. You saw her. You think she's sane?" She opened her eyes, focusing on him. "She's been on the decline since I was ten. Jack and I decided to put her in a home about…eight—nine years ago. She couldn't take care of herself any more, and Jack couldn't manage it on his own, so… Like I said, it's simple enough."

"Why did you tell me not to touch her? What was up with her gripping your hand?"

"The women in my family have a, uh, a gift. If you want to call it that. She's a little clairvoyant."

"She's psychic?"

"No. Psychics aren't real. No, she—she can tell things. It's hard to explain. She can't see the future or anything. But sometimes…sometimes she can feel things that others can't. Like my brother. Today, she felt him, felt his life force. It's of no use to us, really, but she felt it. It's usually nothing more. She can tell when people lie. She can feel people across the world if she's connected to them, but that's it. She can't—she's not a psychic."

Gene tried to process that. "Okay…"

"I know it's confusing, but it's hard to explain."

"Wait, you said women in your family have this trait. Do you?"

"No. Jack and I never showed any sign of it. My mom once said she thought it was because we were twins, but…I don't know."

Despite Gene finding a lot of this fascinating, it wasn't what he wanted to talk about. Unfortunately, Maggie seemed to be avoiding the other elephant in the room. So, he pushed her.

"Does that mean we should disregard what she said today?"

Maggie let out a singular laugh. "And what *did* she say today?"

Gene almost answered, but she beat him to it.

"I mean, seriously. What the fuck did that mean? He's one of them? One of who? He promised me? Who promised her? Lied to me? Who lied to her?"

Gene tilted his head as if to say, *You know the answer to those questions.*

"No. He can't be—" She blew out a long breath. "I can't believe this. I can't."

"Maggie..." Gene got up and sat next to her on the couch. "Can we take her word for it, or not?"

"She doesn't lie. Can't lie. Not in her state. It's...it's something that started a few years ago. She has no filter anymore. Everything that comes out of her mouth is the truth, or at least, what she thinks is the truth."

A wave of sympathy washed over Gene. He'd gotten the impression earlier she hadn't been to see her mother in a long time; now, he understood why. He let the silence linger, allowed her time to think, to process, and then he said, "So what do we do?"

She didn't speak for a long time as tension radiated off her. Gene waited, and eventually, she sat up as if literally shaking herself out of her thoughts.

"We start small. You run a background check on Argus; tell me what you find. Dig—and I mean *dig*—as deep as you can. Pull him apart."

Maggie stared straight ahead as she said it, her voice hard, distant. "I need to find that missing journal. It's from the early 2000s, I think it has something about bodies repelling scavenging animals in it. If I can't—" She rolled her shoulders. "I need to find it."

The plan seemed simple enough. "I can do that." Gene paused, unsure if he should say what was on his mind.

Something must have given him away because Maggie said, "What?"

"I hate to say it, but if we can't trust Argus, how can we be sure of..."

Maggie filled in the blanks. "I know."

Gene locked eyes with her.

"I trust Dana with my life," she said. "Kurt too. To think I can't trust them— I said the same thing about Argus though."

She gave Gene a hard look. "For now—and I can't believe I'm saying this—you're the only one I trust."

Gene tried not to squirm under her intense scrutiny. Instead, he said, "All right. Until we get Jack back."

Her eyes dimmed, softened, shifted to the bottle on the table. "Until Jack is back."

Chapter Twenty-Four

Jack squirmed in his sleep, under a heavy weight. He wiggled and pushed until the body shifted. His eyes flashed open as the person next to him shifted their weight off him, and an arm was thrown across his middle. The arm tightened as he attempted to roll away, and he was pulled flush against someone's chest. Warm lips lazily pressed against his nape. He went still.

"Not so fast," a familiar voice said, heavy-laden with sleep.

Tension ebbed from his bones as he relaxed into the comforting embrace.

Gene nuzzled into his neck, like a cat. "It's early. Stay in bed."

Jack huffed a small laugh and turned to face him, careful to stay within his embrace. Gene's eyes were still closed, but the lazy smile on his lips gave him away. "And you say I'm the lazy one."

Gene's smile widened as he cracked one eye open. "It sure as hell ain't me."

Jack gave him a playful push, making him laugh. "You're the one who wants to waste the day in bed!"

Gene pulled him closer, both eyes open now, looking serious.

"You're saying you don't want to?"

Jack zeroed in on his partner's lips, soft and inviting. "I think we should get up. Be on time to work for once."

Gene narrowed his eyes playfully. "Where did all this initiative come from all of a sudden?"

"Must be your bad influence."

"Hmm, must be... And what can I do to convince you?"

"They're your dumb rules."

"And aren't you always saying rules are meant to be broken?" The heat in Gene's voice made Jack's stomach coil in warmth.

"This one has its merits."

"Uh-huh." Gene's fingers trailed down his back light as a feather, leaving goosebumps in their wake.

"We're going to be late, Mr. Punctual." To his own ears, his voice sounded weak.

"Maybe," Gene said, his hand slipping lower.

"We should get up." Jack made no effort to do so, to pull away. If anything, he let himself be pulled closer as Gene's hand settled on the small of his back.

"We probably should..." This time, it was Gene's brown eyes that darted down to Jack's lips, then danced back up to meet his steady gaze. "But where's the fun in that?"

Jack grinned, was pulled closer, closer, closer—

And then he was sitting up straight, breathing heavily, dazed and confused, as he took in unfamiliar surroundings. Soon enough, he recognized his new cell, and then reality came crashing into him in such force he thought he might throw up. His chest ached as though his heart had been pulled straight out of it.

He swung his legs over the side of the cot and put his head between his knees as his mom had taught him when he would get carsick as a kid. Except the feeling inside him now wasn't as simple as nausea. No amount of ginger ale would make him feel better.

Jack wasn't sure how long he sat like that, but after a while, the feeling subsided, leaving only the ache in his chest.

He sat up straighter. It was dark out, though he wasn't sure if it was night or early morning. He had no idea which side of the sunrise he was on, just knew he could barely see a goddamn thing. The room was brighter than the one he'd been in before, but not by much.

God, he had to get out of here. He couldn't stand another minute of this place. Alone. He knew, he *knew*, if he could get out of here, the dreams would stop. They would. Because he hadn't had them before. They had to stop.

He lay back down, pulling the thin blanket over him. He had to get out of here. He had to. Whatever plans she had for him… He didn't want to think about it. Couldn't think about it. Tomorrow, he thought as his eyes grew heavy. I'll find a way out tomorrow, and he drifted off to sleep.

*

With warnings and placations of being careful, Gene dropped Maggie off at her house in Provo. It was early still, and no one else was there. Gene tried not to worry too much as he drove back to Salt Lake. She could lie; he knew because Jack was an expert at it, and it only made sense that Maggie would be too. The thought bothered Gene, but he pushed it aside. Focusing on how to find Jack was what was important right now. He could think about his shortcomings later.

Gene had never been more relieved to be working on a Saturday than he was today. The office was deserted, save for a few rookies working the weekend shift, and no one paid him much mind as he settled at his desk.

It didn't take him long to run the background on Argus Vasil. Normally, he'd export the job to one of said rookies, but today, he kept it close. For obvious reasons. Born in Dingwall, Scotland in 1945— *Shit, that made Argus close to 80*. Immigrated to the US in the late nineties, moved to Utah in 2000. All in all, it appeared legitimate. All his immigration papers were in order—he'd become a citizen a few years ago—and his birth certificate on file seemed real. Though if Gene were honest, he wasn't an expert on Scottish birth certificates from the 1940s. Time to dig further; Maggie *had* said to pull him apart.

There was only one school in the town, Dingwall Academy, and Gene searched its history until he came up with a class picture that would have included Argus. The children's names were listed next to the picture in order of appearance, and he found Argus's picture easily. *Why did I think a picture of him as a teenager would help?* He couldn't tell if it was the same person as the man he knew. Not only was the person in the photo much younger, but it was also from the late fifties, faded, grainy, black and white. He kept sifting.

He needed something more recent. gene did a basic, wide search for the name, "Argus Vasil," and he found an article from the *Ross-Shire Journal*, published in 1994—a few years before Argus moved to the US.

Local Man Spends Weekend Off Cleaning Up Dingwall Castle—19 June 1994.

Local Dingwall man, Argus Vasil, thought he would spend his first weekend off from work with a leisurely trip to Dingwall Castle. "I've lived here all my life, but I've never been," he said. He was surprised to see it over-run with weeds and dead vines. "I thought to myself, well, this won't do."

After a quick jaunt home, he came back with some gardening supplies: gloves, pruning shears, and a till. In a few short hours, he had cleaned up the castle. "Was good as new," he said cheekily.

Dingwall Castle is one of the prides of our town, but due to recent budget concerns, park maintenance has fallen to the wayside, leaving the job to upstanding citizens like Mr. Vasil.

"It's nothing," he says. "I saw a job that needed doing. So, I did it."

Well, I think I speak for all of Dingwall when I say thank you…

Gene stopped reading and skimmed for pictures. There were two included with the article, one of the castle, all cleaned up, and another of a pile of dug-up weeds and vines. This was becoming pointless. He could only dig so far into someone from another country. He needed a breather, so he stood, stretched, and went to the break room for some coffee.

As he waited for the pot to brew—wishing the department would invest in a Keurig already—his thoughts drifted to Jack. As they so often did lately. And not in the oh-shit-he's-missing-we-need-to-find-him type of way. No. In the oh-God-I-miss-him type of way. It was weird. If someone had told him a month ago that Jack wouldn't be around, Gene would have made a joke about how he wasn't around all that much to begin with. He'd have made some dig at his laziness or not contributing enough to investigations. Gene would have secretly been happy to hear it. But now? Now, he felt… He didn't know how to put it to words, if he were being honest. Gene came to work and saw Jack's empty desk, and his stomach lurched. He went home and saw the empty airplane whiskeys in the trash, the ones from Prue's party, and his chest twinged. He went to sleep and dreamt—

"No," he said to himself. He slapped his cheeks to knock himself out of his trance.

It didn't work.

And his thoughts drifted to the dream he'd been torn from in the middle of the night. Though fuzzy, he remembered enough of it. Jack's hands tangled in his hair, his fingers rubbing circles into Gene's scalp and sending goosebumps down his spine. Lips against his neck. The sound of his laugh, the brightness of his smile.

The phantom touches lingered as if they'd been real.

His dreams about Jack had changed recently, even before he went missing. The fantasies of Jack as a helpful work partner were replaced with domestic fantasies of lazing around in bed with him, of dancing with him, of simply *being* with him. Sometimes, Gene would wake up and have to remind himself it wasn't real. That he and Jack were only coworkers, not friends. He had to remind himself he didn't even like him.

But then he'd remember the feel of Jack's hands on him, the ghost of his lips. All fake, all a fantasy, yet so, *so* real. Gene wished he could sleep forever as long as those were the dreams occupying his mind.

The nightmares, he could do without. The ones where he screamed himself raw, searching for Jack in a never-ending void. Worse were the ones when Jack's voice answered back, but Gene still couldn't find him. He'd jolt awake, covered in a cold sweat, his heart racing, his soul aching.

The coffee pot beeped.

Suddenly no longer thirsty, Gene turned and went back to the bullpen.

By the time he settled at his desk again, the office had thinned out. Most of the on-duty officers were probably out on patrol if they hadn't gone home. Gene liked the quiet. It wasn't all that unusual for him to work on a weekend. Sundays were usually the best day. No one was there, everyone either asleep or at church (mostly at church). Which was why he always got the most work done on the weekends.

He stared at his computer, trying to think of what else to do, what else to search for. Eventually, he thought maybe he could track down a relative. Get some insight into Argus from a third party. Unfortunately, because Argus was so old, most of his family was dead. Gene did manage to find a cousin who was alive and lived in Dingwall. Clydell MacCallan was only eight years younger than Argus, but he still worked as a professor of Gaelic poetry at a university in Inverness. Gene found a phone number for the professor on the university's website, and after a quick Google search to check the time in Scotland, he called him. As the phone rang, it dawned on Gene that the number was likely an office phone, and the chances of catching him this late were slim to none.

Luck seemed to be on his side, though, because a gruff, thickly accented voice answered on the sixth ring.

"Hello?"

"Uh, hello, is this Mr. Clydell MacCallan?"

"That's Doctor MacCallan if it pleases you," he said. "Who's this?"

"My name is Eugene Bradshaw. I'm a detective with the Utah State Bureau of Investigation—"

"Utah?" MacCallan interrupted. "Why would someone from all the way over there be calling me?"

"Well, I'm trying to gather some information for an investigation. I was wondering if you would be willing to help me."

"Your investigation. It have anything to do with Gaelic poetry? Or Gaelic literature?"

"Er, no, but—"

"Then, I'm afraid I won't be of much help."

"Sir, I have a couple of questions about your cousin."

"My cousin?" He sounded confused.

"Yes, Argus Vasil. I was—"

"Argus died in '98."

Gene blinked. A death certificate hadn't come up in his background. "He did?"

"You think I'm daft?"

"Of course not... Sir, I think someone may have stolen his identity. Could you—"

"Stolen Argus's identity? Who would want to do that? The man was a gowk."

Gowk? "It's actually quite common if someone dies young like he did."

"He wasn't young! Nearly fifty-three. My dad only lived to sixty."

"Yes, well...would you happen to have a copy of his death certificate, or a picture of him around the time of his death?"

"A copy of his death certificate? Who do you think I am, his mum?"

Gene pulled the phone from his ear and rubbed his eyes with his free hand as MacCallan ranted. Eventually, he put the phone back up.

"...think I have a picture, though," he was saying. "Can I fax it?"

Gene almost laughed. "You think you could email it?"

"'Course!" he said. "I'm no rocket."

Gene didn't ask and instead gave him his address to send the picture along. He had to coach him through how to attach a file to the email. Then, after learning MacCallan only had a hard copy of the photo, he walked him through taking a picture of it with his phone and sending it from there (which was another twenty minutes). Once his computer *dinged* with an email notification, he couldn't hang up fast enough. *God, I hope this image is good enough.* He did not want to call him back.

Gene clicked open the attachment and waited for it to load. Once it had, he slumped in relief at the quality and printed it out. One thing was for sure, it wasn't Argus. Not the man he knew anyway. This was the real Argus Vasil. Thinning, graying hair, brown eyes, and a long nose—markedly different from the person he'd met. Gene pulled up the DMV photo of the person masquerading as Argus and compared them side by side to be sure. He sent the pictures to the printer, too, and on his way from picking them up, he cut through the fraud division. Not used to working fraud cases, Gene felt out of his depth there. He caught sight of an old colleague's desk and paused. He checked his watch and jogged to his desk.

Gene only felt a little bad when the phone started ringing.

It took till the fifth ring for her to answer. "Detective Miller."

"Hey, Laura," Gene said.

"What're you doing calling me on a Saturday, Bradshaw? You working?"

"You know me."

She snorted. "Yeah. Stuck with a lousy partner."

Gene pushed the comment aside; it was nothing he hadn't heard—or thought—before. "I was hoping I could ask you a question."

"If you make it quick." A pause followed and then muffled talking.

"*But Mommy!*"

Gene winced.

Her patience seemingly thin, Laura said, "What did you need?"

"Where do you start when you look for someone's previous identity?"

"You mean for someone who's stolen someone else's identity?"

"Yes."

"Well. That depends. Are you trying to find their real identity or the one they had before the one they're currently using?"

"Both?"

She laughed. "Right. Well, in that case, it can be difficult to trace someone's steps, but it's not impossible... How is your guy stealing identities?"

"Picking it up after someone dies—I think, anyway."

Laura hummed in thought. "Then, I'd go back to when they assumed their new identity and look through other deaths in the same area around the same time. See if you can figure out which one he shed. It's likely if he's picking up identities that way, he's shedding them that way too."

Gene paused, a plan formulating in his mind. "Right. That makes sense. Thanks. And, uh, sorry for calling on the weekend."

"Hey, no problem," she said. "Good luck."

Feeling rejuvenated, Gene scooted closer to his desk and got to work.

It wasn't easy searching through death records this way, but it'd be worse if he'd been looking somewhere bigger than Dingwall. He worked well into the night, sifting through the small town's death records. The hours ticked by without much fanfare.

Gene's eyes were drying out from staring at the blue light of his computer screen. Right when he thought about calling it for the night, he found an obituary for a man who died in 1998, two days before the real Argus. Lewis Thomson. *Please have a picture, please have a picture, please have a picture.*

None with the obituary, but after a cursory search with the new name, he found a website for St. Clements Parish Church, which listed Thomson as an old minister. With a commemorative picture.

This time, the resemblance was unmistakable. *This* was the person Gene had met. He even had the scar, running down the side of his face. Although, he somehow appeared older in the photo than he did now, his hair thinner, his skin more wrinkled. Gene couldn't exactly run a background on Lewis Thomson since he'd been a Scottish citizen, so he worked with what he had and read the obituary.

> *Lewis Thomson, Dingwall native, passed away in his sleep at the age of 86. Mr. Thomson never married and leaves no children behind. He dedicated his life to this town and served its residents for over sixty years as a minister at St. Clements Parish Church. Services will be held at the church on Sunday at 11.30 a.m. All are welcome.*

"Eighty-six?" Gene said aloud. Impossible. That would mean... If he had that identity for the whole time, that would mean Argus—Lewis—whoever the hell he was...That would mean he was over a hundred years old. And still walking around and fighting *monsters*. Impossible.

"He's one of them!" Ilka's voice rang in his head, and a light bulb went off.

Hours later, Gene leaned back in his chair, eyes wide, as he tried to process what he'd learned. Unlike Argus-Lewis, Harriet Sparrow, their latest victim, was an American citizen. Gene could go back as far as he wanted, and he'd gone back very far. He traced three other identities to her before losing track of her somewhere in the late 1880s. She'd shed identities more often than Argus. But similarly, Gene had a hard time finding any pictures of her.

Immortal. Isn't that what Maggie had said?

The thought was hard to fathom, but at this point, Gene could hardly deny it. He couldn't come up with any explanation that would make any of this make sense. Was that what Ilka had meant? He's one of them—a monster? An *immortal* monster?

Gene shut down his computer and compiled all his printed research into a folder. The office was completely empty now. Dark, too, save for the lamp on his desk, and a little eerier than usual now that he knew things could be lurking in the dark, waiting to strike. He pushed the feeling aside, though, as he gathered his belongings and made his way out. He dialed Maggie as he got in his car.

When she answered, he said, "You'll never guess what I found."

"Tell me."

Chapter Twenty-Five

Up late, with her dog curled up in her lap, Maggie poured over the case files from Ohio and Kansas hoping to find some similarity that would point them in the right direction. But as with so many other things lately, it felt pointless. Worse, her mind kept drifting, unable to stay focused on the task at hand for long.

Argus. Evil? Nearly confirmed to be immortal? How was that possible? And Jack had been gone for *four days*. Did Argus know something about it, something he was withholding which could help them find him?

Maggie felt completely and utterly lost.

Pushing the folders and journals away from her, she sank into the couch cushions. It was almost five in the morning and too late to go to bed now. She might as well put on some coffee—

The garage door opened, making her jump out of her skin. The dog stirred beside her and let out a singular bark—so much for being a ruthless watchdog.

She pulled the stashed gun from under the table and inched toward the back door, waiting in the shadows.

When the door creaked open, Maggie raised the weapon...and nearly let out a string of grade-A swears when Elliot's face emerged.

"Elliot!" Maggie said, making him jump. "You scared the shit out of me."

"I thought you'd be asleep." His dark brown eyes zeroed in on the gun, now held at her side. "Jesus, Maggie, what's that for?"

"To shoot the intruder! I didn't know you were coming home to-day."

Elliot gave a small *hmpf* as he dropped his bag by the door, and their dog ran up to greet him, whining and wiggling her entire body. His dark curls were messy, oily. He needed a shower, as anyone would after a long flight—his clothes wrinkled, his skin smelling faintly of airplanes and airports and sweat. Wordlessly, he stepped into Maggie's space, his taller, more muscular frame towering over her, and gently eased the gun from her grasp. He placed it on the counter before pulling her into a warm embrace.

Maggie let herself sink into it, but before she knew it, he was step-ping out of her arms and stuffing his hands in his pockets. An awkward beat passed between them.

"I was about to make some coffee. Want some?" Maggie asked.

Elliot seemed to weigh the offer before he nodded.

As Maggie busied herself with the coffeemaker, she had a sudden onset of self-consciousness. The kitchen was a mess—she hadn't cleaned it in three days. Unfinished, rotting dinners congealed in their dishes; half-full takeout containers sat without lids, gathering fruit flies; dregs of days-old coffee lingered in the bottom of mugs. Elliot would have words about it later. He was probably too tired to pick a fight about it now, but it would come.

"Hey, what's all this?" Elliot asked from the living room. Appar-ently, he'd wandered in there while she was busy with the coffee.

She rushed over, coffee pot still in hand, faucet still running. "Oh. That's, uh. That's nothing. Some old books my mom had."

Elliot reached for one.

Maggie snatched it before his fingers could grasp it. "Honestly, it's boring." She set the quarter-full coffee pot down, quickly closed the other journals lying about, and stacked them on the corner of the table. When she stood and faced Elliot again, he seemed perplexed. "What?"

"If you don't want to tell me about...whatever that is, fine. But you don't have to lie to me."

"Lying? Elliot, I'm not—"

He held up a hand. "Don't."

The words died in her throat, and she shifted her weight from foot to foot. With little better to do, she grabbed the coffee pot and returned to the kitchen to finish what she was doing. As she put two scoops of grounds into the filter, Elliot drifted back in. He stepped up behind her, wrapped his arms around her middle, and pressed a soft kiss to the base of her neck. Goosebumps rose over her arms.

"I'm tired," he said. "I'm sorry."

Before she had a chance to respond, the doorbell rang, and Maggie froze. Distantly, she heard Elliot mutter, "Who the hell is that?"

She closed her eyes. *No, no, no. Not now.* "I'll go see." Maggie disentangled herself from her husband and went to answer the door.

On the trek from the kitchen to the front hall, she longed to live in a normal world, in which her brother had not been kidnapped by a crazy monster, in which she did not hunt and track and kill monsters, in which she lived a nice, peaceful life with her normal husband.

Reality had other plans, though, currently demonstrated by Gene standing on her front porch.

She took a deep breath and opened the door. "Gene, hey, now's not—"

Gene scooted in past her, as if this was his goddamn house, and headed for the kitchen. "Sorry for swinging by so early, I thought we should talk in person."

"Gene, no, wait—" Maggie said as she followed.

Gene came to a halt when he reached the kitchen, and Maggie rushed up beside him. Filling the coffee pot with water, Elliot was clearly shocked to see a stranger in his house because the pot began overflowing. Gene, stuck to his spot like glue, appeared to be trying to figure out who Elliot was too.

Elliot turned off the faucet and tilted out the excess water. He set the pot on the counter and stared expectantly at Maggie, but words escaped her. She opened and closed her mouth a number of times without saying anything. Finally, after a few dreadful infinite seconds passed, Elliot shifted his attention to Gene.

"I'm Elliot. You are?"

Gene glanced at Maggie before answering. "Um, I'm Sergeant Gene Bradshaw, Salt Lake Bureau of Investigation. I'm Maggie's brother's partner, and we're—"

"I'm sorry—her brother?" Elliot's eyes aflame, he focused solely on her. "You have a brother?"

Gene pressed his lips into a line. "I'll go."

Maggie grabbed his wrist before he had the chance. "No. We need to talk. Go wait in the study. I'll be there in a minute."

Gene met her gaze briefly before disappearing down the hall. For a few moments, she stared at the space where Gene had been standing.

"Maggie?" Elliot's hard, angry voice made her wince.

She turned to face him head-on. "I'm sorry."

A cynical laugh escaped his lips. "Right. Heard that before." He put one hand on the counter, one on his hip and looked her in the eyes. "You gonna tell me the truth, or should I go to bed?"

"What? Elliot—"

"No, Maggie. I'm sick of this. We've been married for almost four years, and you still can't tell me shit about your life. I thought we'd gotten past this. I thought you'd at least have answered honestly when I asked if you had a fucking brother. What, did you think I'd never find out?"

"Honestly, when we first met, I didn't—he and I were— It doesn't matter; I was stupid not to tell you, okay? You know I'm bad at talking about my family—"

"No, I don't, Maggie! Because all you told me is that you have a mother in assisted living. I figured that was it. But now—" He released a heavy breath. "I love you, but relationships—*marriages*—don't work this way. You can't just not tell me about your life."

"I'm sorry, El," she said, not knowing what else she could say. "I'm sorry. I should have told you."

Elliot's jaw pulsed.

Doesn't it get to you, lying to him every day? Jack's words haunted her. Because it did get to her, and at times like this, she itched to tell him, yet she couldn't bring herself to do it.

Elliot surprised her when he squared his shoulders, a hint of challenge behind his eyes. "Are you going to tell me what's really going on?"

Maggie was too shocked by the blunt question to respond. Seconds dragged by as she tried to shift her brain into gear, but it was already too late.

"That's a no, then." Elliot grabbed the coffee pot, poured the water into the machine, and replaced it. As he pressed the start button, he said, "I'm going to go take a shower, and then I'm going to have a nice, long nap. We can talk about this later. If you're still here."

And then he was gone, disappearing upstairs. Maggie watched him go before collapsing against the counter. All her strength, any last remnants keeping her façade from slipping, bled out of her.

*

Gene was reading over his notes on Argus when Maggie came in. He watched as she deflated in front of him, dropping onto the edge of a chair near the door.

"You okay?" Gene asked.

She let out a long breath. "Peachy. What'd you want to talk to me about?"

Straight to business. Right. "Any luck finding that journal?"

"No, it's not here. Or at my mom's house. I don't know where else it could be."

"You think Argus would take it?"

She seemed to stare through him, her jaw set, disbelief rolling off her. "I guess it's possible."

"We didn't talk about this last night, but is it possible he's a…"

Gene couldn't quite bring himself to say *monster*—he'd only been at this for a few days after all.

Maggie pushed off her chair and paced before him. "What? A monster?" She gave a half-crazed cackle. "I don't know. I don't know what to think."

She stopped and leaned against a wall. "I was ten when my mom started losing it. She could only raise us so much. My grandfather, he was pretty old, he could only do so much. Argus…Argus stepped in. Helped raise us. He—he took us to school, helped us with our homework, took us to fucking soccer practice. He taught me—" She turned her head away as if hiding tears. "I'm so stupid!"

Next thing Gene knew, she crumpled to the floor and pulled her knees close to her chest. He felt helpless as he watched her break down.

"Jack never liked him, you know. They've always butted heads. I thought it was Jack being Jack, being his angsty self. I thought they were too similar to get along, but maybe…maybe he felt something, saw something I didn't."

"Hey." Gene squatted next to her. "You were a kid. A kid in a pretty tough situation. You're not stupid for trusting Argus. That's on him, not you."

She didn't seem convinced, and when she continued her rant, it was almost as if she hadn't heard a word he said. "All these years…my whole life, the saving grace has been that they can't blend in. They can't look like us; they don't act like us! You catch the tail of a vampire? It's a string of bodies until you kill it. Werewolves? Same thing. They can't control themselves, can't blend into society. Even when they're not transformed, they can't act human. Ghosts? They're ghosts. Goblins? Ghouls? That's a given. But if Argus can blend in, if he's not human, how the hell are we supposed to fight that, Gene? Monsters are evil. They kill people mercilessly, unable to control themselves. But what if that's not true, what if there are more of them, more than we could fathom, existing under our noses. What is the point of fighting if they outnumber us? What the fuck is the point?"

Gene readjusted himself and sat opposite her. "I haven't been doing this for very long, this whole monster hunting thing. Been at it for barely three days, and I'm in way over my head. But I've been a cop for close to ten years now. And no matter how you feel about cops, believe me when I tell you I've seen some shit. Before I knew that all the fictional beasts I've only ever read about were real, I knew monsters were real. Humans can do some horrible things. I've seen children murdered by their parents. I've seen murderers and rapists walk free. I've seen people hide behind the church, expecting it to cover up their disgusting behavior. The list is endless. And the worst part? They're your neighbors, your relatives, the kid sitting next to you in class. Blending in, acting normal is what they're good at. And you're right. Sometimes it all seems hopeless. I think to myself, this is pointless. It's one bad guy after the other; there's always something else. And I think about quitting, seriously consider it, before I decide not to."

"How?"

"You see, Maggie, it's not about fixing everything. It's not about ridding the world of all the bad guys because, as much as that would be nice, it's impossible for one person to do. It's about doing what you can with the time you have. As long as I leave the world a little bit better than how I found it, it's worth it. That's the point."

Something shifted in Maggie's gaze, and he resisted the urge to look away. It was as though she was seeing him for the first time, and then she smirked. "Maybe there's one good cop, after all."

Gene snorted. "What about Jack?"

She regarded him levelly. "Look me in the eyes and tell me he's a good cop."

A laugh ripped out of him.

"Exactly."

As the weight of everything settled over him again, he sobered a bit. "Everything will be okay," he said, like a prayer.

She nudged him with her foot, a gesture far too comforting coming from someone he barely knew. "I hope so."

They stewed silently, and then Gene cleared his throat and stood. He offered a hand to Maggie.

"Come on. We've got work to do."

Accepting his hand, she pulled herself up. "Work, work, work," she joked. "You ever think about anything else?"

Nice to have you back. "The real question now is, do we confront him?"

Maggie seemed to consider that. "No. It stays between us. We still need to find that journal."

"Did you check Jack's place?"

"I haven't had a chance. Why don't you go check it out?"

"Okay...and what are you going to do?"

"I'll keep Argus occupied."

Chapter Twenty-Six

It was embarrassing to admit that he didn't know where Jack lived. Gene had to get the address from his HR file at work—which he wasn't technically allowed to access, but it was better than pulling Jack's DMV record. At least, that was what he told himself.

Jack's apartment was in downtown Salt Lake, a block south of Temple Square. The building, though nice, didn't have much by way of security, only a locked front entrance, which Gene bypassed by simply letting someone hold the door for him. Easy enough. It wasn't until he stood in front of Jack's door that he realized he had a problem. No key.

Gene knew how to pick the lock. The problem was he didn't want to. Couldn't. It was breaking and entering. He didn't have a warrant, didn't have probable cause, or any legally justifiable reason for going in. And yes, he *stole* a body from the morgue, but this—this felt different somehow.

Gene surveyed the empty hallway. No cameras that he could see. He squatted in front of the lock and picked it. A few minutes passed before he heard a subtle *click*, and the doorknob turned in his hand. Casting another guilty glance over his shoulder, he pushed the door open and entered the apartment.

As far as city apartments went, it wasn't all that special. The walls were a light shade of gray, the kitchen a bit simple, and the windows a bit sparse. The soul of the apartment was in the decoration—the mix of modern and vintage-style furniture, the abstract art and personal photos on the walls, the Thai takeout menus on the fridge. That was all clearly *Jack*. And as tempting as it was to study the space as a gateway into Jack's mind, Gene forced himself to focus on the journal.

A large bookcase stood along one wall in the living room, stuffed full of books, so he started there. Unlike those in Maggie and Jack's mom's house, these shelves held a vast array, from modern fiction to tattered journals. Gene's fingers itched to take a peek at the novels with cracked spines and faded titles, wanting to see which Jack read most often. Instead, he pulled journal after journal off the shelves and made a small pile on the floor. When he was finished a few minutes later, he counted ten journals. He sorted through them easily enough—and deflated. They were all Jack's. If his partner was one thing, he was organized—and maybe a little anal—and always wrote his name on the inside cover of his journals, including start and end dates. Of course, the lost journal wasn't in the most obvious place. Nothing was ever so easy.

Gene searched elsewhere. Magazines and mail littered the coffee table, but no luck there either. He checked the kitchen but only found days' old dishes piling up in the sink. He forced the neat freak in him to turn away—he wasn't here to clean Jack's apartment.

He headed to the bedroom down the hall. This room had the most personality of the entire apartment, and that was saying something. Patterned gray sheets covered the unmade bed, still wrinkled and ruffled from where Jack had rolled out of them days ago. An old-timey alarm clock sat on the nightstand, tilted slightly toward the bed. Dark blackout curtains, pulled open on one side, allowed light to pass through half the window above the bed. Gene pulled the other side open. On the nightstand, he noticed a "fresh cotton" scented candle and a picture of Jack's family. He couldn't help but pick it up to take a closer look. They stood before a rock formation in a national park, Capitol Reef if Gene had to guess. Dana stood in the middle, their arms around the twins' shoulders. They were all laughing, sun streaming down on them, packs at their feet. It must have been a good time. Gene set the frame back, careful to place it in the same position he'd found it.

He turned about the room. Going through Jack's closets and drawers felt odd, but what choice did he have? Shaking off the guilt, he started pulling open drawers and rifling through them, trying not to linger too long if there was no sign of a journal.

Running out of drawers to go through, he pulled open the bottom one of the dresser. Inside, he found a couple of old, ratty sweatshirts but nothing else. It wasn't intrinsically odd, but there seemed to be a lot of wasted space. Gene moved the clothes aside, checking for anything underneath them, and noticed a small hole in the back. Barely big enough for him to fit his index finger through, the bottom of the drawer popped open.

The secret compartment wasn't exactly what he was expecting. Velvet cloth lined the bottom on which lay a set of knives, ranging in blade length and versatility. Some folded while others had intricate handles with hilts, and all of them appeared well taken care of, each one sharp and shiny. Interesting...

But not what he was here for. So, Gene replaced the false bottom and the sweatshirts. He stood and turned to the closet, tried to open the double doors. Locked. The handles had been replaced with something more sophisticated. Gene hadn't found a key in all his snooping, so instead of searching the room again, he squatted to pick the lock. This one was a bit trickier than the front door deadbolt, so it took him a few minutes. At a soft click, the door popped open, and he released a breath of relief. As he pulled open the doors, a light kicked on.

He shouldn't have been surprised to find there wasn't a single piece of clothing inside. Weapons lined the rear wall of the closet: handguns, rifles, shotguns, *more* knives, a— *Is that a machete?* He did a double-take at that one. Maps covered the side walls, one of Utah on the right and one of the US on the left. Thumbtacks marked seemingly random places on both maps, along with little notes made in red ink. Gene examined them more closely. The thumbtacks on the Utah map were placed where the three bodies had been found. And the other map had three tacks pushed into Utah, with another one in Ohio and one in Kansas.

A workbench, such as one found in a woodsman's tool shop, sat against the back wall, full of papers, notebooks, and more journals. Content descriptions labeled the drawers, most of which Gene didn't understand. He didn't bother with anything else and zeroed in on the notebooks. He could tell they were Jack's without reading the inside cover—they all had Jack's handwriting. As he moved things around on the cluttered worktable, though, Gene found another journal under the heap. This one was little different than the others. All of Jack's journals were leather-bound, classic-looking. This one was hard-back, more like a legitimate book. He turned it over in his hands and opened the inside cover.

Ilka Cartwright / Jun. 1998 – Sept. 2001

This was it. Jack had had it the whole time. Gene flipped through the pages, but he couldn't read any of it. As with Jack's journals, it was written in code. He bet Maggie could read it though—

Gene froze, the hairs on the back of his neck standing on end. Slowly, quietly, he turned and made his way to the living room, drawing his gun.

When he made it to the bedroom door, he saw the front door was open. *Shit.* He edged into the hallway, keeping his back to the wall.

As he reached the bathroom, a few feet away, his hearing went. All sound around him went silent; he couldn't hear his own breathing. That couldn't be good.

The bathroom door was closed, as it had been earlier, so he kept moving toward the living room. He stepped into the open space and swept the room, checking each corner and up to the ceiling as he made his way to the door. He stayed behind it, and once he made sure no one was in the living room, he stepped out and checked the open doorway.

The hall was clear. Gene lowered his weapon slightly, closed the door.

Then something crashed behind him, his hearing returning in full force. He ran to the kitchen, his gun held high. Taking in the sight before him, he holstered his weapon and dialed 911.

Jack lay moaning in pain on the floor, his eyes closed. As the operator answered, Jack's head lolled to the side. And the moaning stopped.

Chapter Twenty-Seven

Someone shook Jack awake, and he blinked his eyes open. Bright lights blinded him. Something in the distance sounded like yelling...someone yelling his name? Maybe. He wasn't sure. He tried to force his eyes to focus, to open fully. Who was it? Who was holding him? Where...where was he? He willed himself to stay awake, to keep his eyes open. He *willed* it. But his body didn't listen.

And he succumbed to the darkness.

Next Jack woke, he was in a hospital room. He sat up in a panic, breathing heavily until he processed his surroundings. He barely registered the incessant beeping of some alarm before Maggie burst through the door.

"You're awake!" She crushed him in a hug. It amazed him that she was able to do so, with the way he was situated in the bed. She ran her eyes over him frantically. "Started to think you'd never wake up."

Jack sat up straighter. He winced.

"Something hurt?"

"No, not exactly..." he said, unsure how to describe the feeling pulsing through his bones. The ache, a soreness, was similar to what he might have felt after a tough workout, but—different. "I'm fine. What am I doing here?"

"Gene brought you—"

"Gene?"

"Yeah, he said he found you passed out in your apartment... Where have you been?"

Jack stared at her. "What do you mean? I saw you yesterday."

"No—Jack, you've been missing for four days."

He laughed. "No. No, I saw you yesterday. At your place. We were going over the case. Then, I went over to Gene's...sister's? Parents'? House? I don't know, someone's house...and then—then, I..." A couple of memories came to him. "Oh, shit, I stood him up for breakfast, didn't I?"

Maggie seemed concerned and exasperated at the same time. "Jack, don't you remember going to the cabin?"

"The cabin?" An image of a dilapidated house in the middle of the woods flashed in his mind's eye. "Yeah, yeah, the cabin. You called me, and I was checking out the cabin, and then I—" He touched the crown of his head, felt around for a knot. There was none. "I got hit on the head," he said, his voice quiet. "There's no wound."

"You don't appear to have any injuries," Maggie said gently.

Jack swallowed and focused on the sheets, his fingers still searching for an invisible wound. "I was hit. I know it."

"Maybe it healed."

A quiet beat passed, and then Maggie pressed him for more. "You don't remember anything? Where you were, who took you...?"

Jack started to shake his head, and then memories of the cold, damp, darkness washed in like sea debris. And then came memories that couldn't be real. Memories clouded in a shine, a hue, a fuzziness only present in dreams. Fantasies. A lump lodged in his throat, and pain hit his chest, nearly knocking the wind out of him. "No, only...only darkness." It was all he could say, his voice sounding much stronger than he felt.

"Are you sure?"

"Nothing that will help."

Maggie shifted in his periphery. She touched his arm gently. "*Anything* might help." She was pushing, he knew, because she wanted to help. She wanted to find whatever—whoever—had taken him, but what he remembered wouldn't help.

"It won't," he said firmly. When it seemed she might keep pushing, he cut her off. "It's not real. It's—fantasy. That's it. It won't help."

He must have been convincing enough because she let the subject drop.

Jack rolled his bottom lip between his teeth before asking, "You said Gene found me? Is he here?"

"No, he's—"

"Of course not," he said, defeated. He rested his head back on the flat hospital bed pillow.

"He's trying to keep Missing Persons off your back," she finished. "I can go get him though. He's probably nearby, if not in the hospital somewhere. He's been—"

"No. I can't—" His throat started closing up, so he cleared it. "I'm not ready to see him, uh...not yet."

"Okay..." She seemed surprised.

"Can you, uh, get the nurse? Maybe I won't have to stay here too long." Jack tried putting as much of himself into his voice as he could, but it didn't work. To his own ears, he sounded off.

"Sure. I'll be right back. We can talk about all this later."

He watched as she left the room, his eyes unfocused, fake memories playing like a movie reel. "It's not real," he told himself. "It's not real."

*

Gene blocked the other detectives' paths into the hospital. "I told you to get out of here."

Gomez huffed and put his hands on his hips like an angry school teacher. "You're the one who reported him missing, don't you remember? We're trying to do our jobs."

Daniels gave a derisive laugh. "He doesn't care."

"I told you," Gene said. "He's asleep. I'll call you when he's awake."

"Uh-huh, sure you will," said Daniels, the calmer of the two. He stepped forward as his partner stepped back. He was taller than Gene, only by an inch or two, but it was enough to notice, and he crowded in on him. Peered down his nose at him and stared.

Gene squared his shoulders, unfazed.

Daniels squinted slightly, the edges of his mouth curling upward into a small smirk. He stepped back. "We'll be back," he promised.

Gene watched them go before returning inside. The ER bustled with activity, but he made his way through to the other side easily enough. As he reached Jack's room on the third floor, Maggie emerged, a mix of relief and confusion etched on her face.

He's awake.

She spotted Gene, and her eyes darkened.

"Hey," he said, "is he—"

"Yeah…um. He's still resting, and well—"

"What?"

Sympathy was written on her face. "He said he didn't want to see you…"

Something broke inside Gene—as if a wooden post propping open a door had snapped, making it slam shut. "Right. No. That's—" He tried to swallow the sudden lump in his throat. "I probably need to head back to the office anyway. Uh—" He turned to leave, barely sparing Maggie a glance.

She grabbed his elbow, stopping him. "Gene, don't be an idiot."

Unfortunately for him, she didn't elaborate and left him standing there, utterly dumbfounded. A nurse walked past him and into Jack's room, snapping him out of it, and Gene found his way to the chairs in the nearby waiting area. He sat in one and put his head in his hands.

When someone slid into the chair next to him, Gene was surprised to see Elliot. He hadn't thought Maggie's husband had come.

"I'd listen to her, by the way," Elliot said with sympathy.

Gene hadn't missed Maggie, pacing outside Jack's room. Chewing his bottom lip, he shifted the conversation away from himself.

"Gotta say I'm surprised to see you here. I got the impression you didn't...that Maggie hadn't exactly told you..." He was unsure how to phrase it kindly.

Elliot sighed. "What? That she had a brother? No, she failed to mention it...but she asked me to be here, so. Here I am."

Gene felt as if Elliot might be prying for information, but in truth, he didn't need to pry. It was written plain on his sleeve.

"They a lot alike?" Elliot asked.

"Who, Jack and Maggie? I guess...I mean, they're identical, but...different, at the same time...Jack's eyes have these specks of gold in them, and his crow's feet are a little more pronounced, and his jawline is sharper and more stubbled. He's stubborn and annoying and a freaking know-it-all who always has to be right. And he can get so wrapped up in the work that he forgets about me, but—" He chuckled.

Elliot gave a laugh of his own. "Yeah, that's Maggie. She always has to be right."

"Exactly! And it's infuriating, right? And not because it truly is infuriating. They're so— It's so—" He looked at Jack's room again. "—endearing." The quieter admission was meant only for himself. "When he gets all wrapped up in his own head, I want to shake him. But he gets so passionate...it's hard not to get wrapped up with him." Gene let out a deep breath and focused on nothing as his mind raced a mile a minute through his interactions with Jack.

"Yeah," Elliot said as if he understood something Gene didn't. "Maggie can be that way too. I'll say it again; you should listen to her."

Gene stared at him.

"Don't be an idiot."

He opened his mouth to say something, but Elliot continued before he had the chance.

"I'm not telling you what to do, and I've barely met you, but—" Elliot paused, and then, "When Maggie and I first met, I couldn't stand her. She and I were total opposites, and nearly everything she did annoyed me. Until one day, none of it did. I didn't realize it at first. But suddenly, all those little quirks and irritants were what made her *her*. They made me love her."

He paused again, his eyes drifting to Maggie and sadness flashed in them. "And even now, knowing she's never been fully truthful with me, I can't help it. She could do almost anything, and I don't think I'd be able to stop loving her."

Gene shifted in his chair, his stomach suddenly feeling as if his intestines were weaving themselves together. "What's your point?"

Elliot refocused on him and gave him a small smile. He opened his mouth to speak but never got the words out because Maggie approached them so abruptly that Gene nearly had whiplash.

"Elliot," she said, "can you give us a minute?"

Elliot patted Gene on the arm before vacating his seat.

Maggie took his place. "Jack's having trouble with his memory."

"Like amnesia?"

"I honestly don't know," she said with a grimace. "I get the sense he remembers more than he says but won't tell me for some reason."

A slew of reasons occurred to Gene's from as benign as Jack being stubborn to his wanting to protect Maggie from some horrific torture he'd endured over the past four days.

"So, I need you to talk to him."

"Maggie, he said he didn't want to talk to me—"

"He's holding something back, Gene, I know it. I can't force it out of him. Maybe you can."

"Force it out of him? No, I'm not interrogating him."

"Why not? We need to know who took him and why they let him go, apparently without hurting him. You're a cop; you've trained for this. Treat him the way you would a witness."

"He's a victim, Maggie. No. I'm not doing that."

Maggie let out an annoyed huff. "Look, he has a soft spot for you—"

"A soft spot for me?" Gene laughed.

"He does. It should be easy to get him to talk to you."

Gene wrung his hands between his knees.

She placed a hand on his forearm. "Please. Would you please go talk to him? That's all I'm asking." She paused, then added, "God knows you two need to air some shit out."

"What's that supposed to mean?"

"You know exactly what I mean."

Gene swallowed, suddenly losing humor, and shook his head. "No, that's not—he doesn't— Airing any of that would only complicate things. It has nothing to do with what's going on. Besides, he doesn't—"

Gene didn't want to have this conversation with Maggie. In truth, he didn't want to have it at all. "He doesn't feel...that way. About me."

"Fucking idiots, the both of you," she said, though her eyes were soft.

Elliot returned with two cups of coffee and handed one to Maggie, their gazes narrowly avoiding the other's. Gene wondered what else she hadn't told her husband—and whether he was as ignorant to it all as she seemed to think.

When they both turned to Gene, delivering a stern look, he stood. "Fine."

He walked up to Jack's door and paused before it. A small, slender window allowed him a view into the room. Jack lay in bed, his eyes closed, but seemed too tense to be asleep. Gene knocked softly as he opened the door.

As it shushed closed behind him, he came to a stop a few feet away from the foot of the bed. Gene had been so worried about Jack the last four days that he'd forgotten how angry he was at him. Now that the adrenaline from finding Jack had faded, the anger returned in full force.

Jack's eyes opened, locked with his, and darted away. He pushed himself up a little, grimacing as he did. "I told Maggie I didn't—"

"I don't care." Gene stepped closer to the bed, balling his hands up tight into fists.

Jack picked at the thin hospital blanket lying across his lap, still avoiding Gene's eyes. He didn't say anything.

The silence stretched between them. Gene's heart raced. In the last four days, he'd barely slept, barely ate, and now Jack was back. Safe, unharmed. But something was off, something different. And he knew he should steer them to the case, that he should put his cop hat on and interrogate him as Maggie wanted.

"I've been scared shitless the past few days," Gene said. The words, nothing but the truth, came out rough.

Jack's hands stilled on the blanket.

Gene took the last few steps to the foot of the bed and gripped the rails, his knuckles white. "I thought I'd be more relieved when we found you, but I'm still scared. Still have this knot making my insides feel like they're boiling."

Jack's jaw pulsed, and something flashed in his eyes when he finally lifted them to meet Gene's, albeit briefly, some flicker of an emotion in them. He shrugged. "Well, the docs say I don't have any injuries. I'm fine, so no need to worry."

Gene shoved away from the bed and paced. "Why do you do that?"

"Do what?"

"Lie. Pretend everything's fine when it's not."

"I'm not lying, I feel fine—"

"Right, so that's why you winced when you sat up."

"I'm over thirty, dude, my back hurts, like, all the time."

Gene stopped pacing and put his hands on his hips.

"What? It's true."

Gene stepped toward the bed. "Right. So then why can't you remember anything from the past four days?"

Jack's defiance vanished in an instant. "Maggie told you?"

"Actually, she told me everything."

Jack frowned before realization dawned, and his mouth dropped open. "I...I was going to tell you when we got breakfast, but I..."

"You got kidnapped. I get it."

Jack's lips quirked up slightly, but Gene was still mad.

"You know," he said. "I always thought there was something you weren't telling me. And when you came out to me, I thought maybe that was it, but then that night at Prue's party? You lied with such ease—if I hadn't been in on it, I would have believed you." Gene let out a rough breath. "And yet, I could never bring myself not to trust you."

"I didn't think you would believe me."

"Yeah, well."

Gene zeroed in on Jack's tensed muscles under the blankets, how darkness underlined his eyes, his skin pale and clammy. And the anger seeped out of him like water through a crack in a dam. Suddenly, it didn't matter anymore what Jack had or hadn't told him. They were on the same page now, and that was all that mattered.

"You don't remember anything?"

Jack's face darkened, and he pushed himself into the pillows piled behind him, as if trying to distance himself from Gene.

"Come on, Jack, any detail, no matter how small, might help."

Jack closed his eyes. "What I remember is a lie. They're—fantasies. Dreams. They're not real."

Gene rounded the bed. He hesitated before placing a hand on Jack's shin. Jack jerked away, and Gene lifted his hand immediately.

"Sorry, I—"

"No," Gene said, "it's okay."

After an awkward beat, Jack pressed the heels of his hands into his eyes.

"Dreams, huh?" Gene asked.

Jack's silence spoke for itself.

Gene reconsidered his approach. "Mind if I sit?" He gestured to the side of the bed. At Jack's noncommittal grunt, he situated himself and said, "You know, you're a frequent fixture in my dreams. They're usually about a better world where you answer your phone and come into the office—"

Jack swatted him on the arm.

Gene laughed softly. As his smile faded, he turned his attention to the bed. It was his turn to pick at the blanket.

"It wasn't until Prue's party that I realized—I didn't hate you... And then, I thought we were going to talk about it, but you stood me up. And I was so, so mad at you. So mad that when Maggie showed up at the station, I didn't believe her at first when she said you were missing. But soon enough, that was all I could think about. And I got swept up in a world I couldn't even fathom a week ago. Next thing I know, I'm digging into monster journals and seeing and doing things I never thought I'd do or see. All because I was getting more and more desperate to find you. And suddenly, you're back. But the nerves are still there. They won't go away, and it's annoying me to no end. Kind of like you sometimes."

Feeling Jack's stare, he looked up and met it head on. "You know, I'm pretty sure I fell for you before I even liked you."

Jack blinked as if he didn't understand what Gene said, and then he opened his mouth to speak, but no words came out.

"Don't worry," Gene said. "I don't expect anything. We're partners; nothing has to change. I..." He trailed off when Jack started pushing himself up.

"Wait, wait, wait," Jack said, leaning forward. "Let me get this straight. You're saying that you—what, that you love me?"

Gene tried not to look away from him as he nodded. "Well, if you need me to spell it out for you."

Jack let out a small laugh. "I never thought you'd— I spent the past four days, I guess, waking up from dreams that felt so real I couldn't tell the difference between them and reality. And you were the only common element."

"So, wait, you—"

Gene didn't get to finish his thought as Jack grabbed a hold of his lapels and pulled him in for a brief, soft kiss. For a moment, the world deafened, and all he was aware of was Jack, fingers clinging to his shirt, puffs of breath against his nose, lips pressed ever so gently against his own. When they parted, Gene briefly felt respite as bright, happy, sweet relief surged through him. It lifted him high enough that the crash angered him more than it should have.

"Well, shit!" he said.

Jack pulled back. "Damn, I know it's been a minute since I kissed someone, but come on. It couldn't have been that bad."

"No, no, it's not that. I mean, it's great we're on the same page, woo!" He tossed his hands up in mock victory. "It's only... Maggie's right."

"Oh, shit, about what?"

"She called us, quote, fucking idiots."

"Damn," Jack said, clearly disappointed. "I mean, it tracks, unfortunately."

Gene hummed an affirmative. He let himself stew in the annoyance of proving a Cartwright sibling right, but then Jack was looping a finger in the collar of his shirt, drawing him closer.

Gene pressed his forehead against Jack's. "Wait," he said. "I need to catch you up."

Jack smiled wryly. "It can wait five minutes."

And, *dammit*, it could.

Chapter Twenty-Eight

By the time Jack was fully caught up on all he'd missed, he could hardly believe he'd only been gone for four days.

"You stole a body from the morgue?" *Who the hell are you and what have you done with Gene Bradshaw?*

"You're focusing on the wrong thing," Gene said, a hint of his usual irritation lacing his tone. Somehow, though, it felt affectionate.

"No, no, I think we're going to be talking about this for a long time."

"If you're so smart, what would you have done?"

"Hell, I don't know. I don't think I would have stolen a body. That's like. Gene, that's a felony. Is that a felony?"

Gene gave him a deadpan look. "You're a cop, you should know the answer to that one."

"Man, three days with my sister, and she turned you into a criminal."

"Jack."

He blinked at him.

"Argus? The whole immortal thing? Any comments?"

Jack rubbed his neck. See, this was what he didn't want to talk about. "Argus and I don't get along, and he's old as all hell. Don't get me wrong, but...I don't know... Immortal?"

"I know it's hard to believe he could be evil, but—"

"Oh, that's not what I'm struggling with here."

Gene gave a small laugh.

"But hey, you say it's true, and I believe you. How's Maggie handling it?"

Gene tilted his head side to side. "Not great."

That sounded about right. She and Argus had always been close, especially since their mom took a turn for the worse. It hadn't been long after they met him, and by that point, their grandfather couldn't quite take care of them as much as he could before. Their mom was in that weird place between being totally fine and totally insane. Jack had pushed through, come out more independent than any eleven-year-old should be, and Maggie had leaned on him and Argus for support.

"I'm not sure how much longer we can avoid confronting him," Gene continued.

Jack grunted in agreement as he thought about everything Gene had told him, attempting to sort through it all. Something tickled at the back of his mind. "You said something about a theory you had?"

"Huh? Oh, yeah. I'm having Maggie and Dana dig into this religion angle, but I'm not very confident it'll lead anywhere."

Flashes of a memory flitted across his mind's eye. "Wait." Jack tried to force them to the forefront, and then he heard a ghostly voice in his ear.

I'm just a naive disciple.

"A disciple. That's what she called herself."

"Anything else?" Gene asked, capitalizing on this brief window of clarity. "Hair color, eye color, anything?"

Jack tried to remember her face. The distant shape of it would be a start, but all that came was a pale hand reaching out through blinding lights. "She was pale. Young, I think."

Gene deflated. "It'll come to you," he said, though he didn't sound particularly convinced.

"Maybe."

A look of uncertainty and fear passed between them before a nurse came in to tell them Jack needed to rest.

Gene stood to leave, but Jack grabbed hold of his wrist.

"Can he stay?" he asked.

"As long as you take some time to rest." She said to Gene, "It's lights out."

Gene saluted her. Being the goody-two-shoes he was, he probably had no intention of disobeying her orders. Though, in truth, Jack didn't think he'd have any trouble falling asleep, his eyes drooping already.

After the nurse had taken some vitals and checked on a few things, she left them, dimming the lights on her way out.

Gene settled into the chair to the right of the bed. "We can talk more when you wake up."

Jack yawned, slinking further into the sheets. Before he knew it, he was out.

*

Jack stirred, his eyes still closed. At first, it wasn't clear why he had woken up. Then he heard footsteps. He jolted awake.

"Good to see you're recovering," Argus greeted him.

"Gene—"

"Ah, ah, ah." Argus's tone was as condescending as ever. "I'm afraid he can't hear you."

Jack's eyes darted to Gene, still sound asleep in the chair. "What did you do to him?"

Argus chuckled. "I assure you. I did not touch him."

He didn't believe him. Jack tossed his blanket aside and tried to get out of bed when a familiar sensation struck him. It wrapped around every fiber of his being as Argus forced him to sit down, his legs stretching out as straight as they were before. Jack couldn't move.

"Not so fast," Argus said.

"You're like her, aren't you?"

Argus smiled but didn't say anything. Instead, he rounded the bed to Gene's chair and raked his eyes over him as if he were an impossible phenomenon. Jack's fingers itched with his desire to move, to protect Gene— *Why isn't he waking up?*

Without turning to face him, Argus asked, "Where is she?"

"You think if I knew I'd be here?"

That earned him a glare from Argus, the corner of his mouth twitching. "You always have to talk back, don't you? Nothing is ever easy." He inched closer to Gene, reached out, and ran his middle finger along Gene's forehead. Gene didn't wake up, didn't even flinch.

"You hurt him, and I swear—"

"He is only sleeping, Jack." Argus's hand traveled up and rested on the back of Gene's cranium. "For now." He drummed his fingers atop Gene's head. "I'll ask you again. Where is she?"

"I don't know. I don't remember anything."

Argus's fingers went still on Gene's head and burrowed deep into his scalp. "Tell me what I want to know, Jack."

"I told you! I don't know anything. Don't hurt him." His voice came out weaker than he wanted.

Any kindness Argus had for Jack was completely gone now. They'd never gotten along, but Jack had never seen Argus look at him this way— as if he was a predator and Jack was the prey.

"Please, Argus. Please don't hurt him."

"You know that what we do doesn't hurt," Argus said with a tilt of his head. "It shouldn't, anyway."

"I remember enough to know that it can."

Argus dropped his hand from Gene's head. "Interesting. There were rumors she was using forbidden...tactics." His gaze met Jack's and pierced through him. He touched Jack's wrist, and a pulse of energy surged through him, making him lightheaded at the rush.

As quick as it came, the energy was sucked out of him, and Jack was left feeling drained and empty. But there was no pain.

"*Hmm.*" Argus released Jack's wrist. "How old was she?"

Unable to stop himself, Jack said, "How should I know? You look eighty, but Gene tells me you're over a hundred."

Argus laughed, though it wasn't a cheerful sound. "Oh, Eugene." He moved behind Gene's chair and caressed his forehead once again. "Such a clever one. He was so quick to catch on... Makes me want to crack open his skull and eat his brains."

He buried his fingers in Gene's hair again, and Gene seized up, his entire body tensing as if experiencing a shock.

"Stop! Stop, please. I don't remember. I can't—"

"Think, Jack. How old?"

A brief flash of a face. "I don't know. Twenties."

Argus released Gene, and his body relaxed, returning to sleeping peacefully. "Impossible." He backed away from the chair and walked to the foot of the bed, muttering to himself. "She couldn't possibly be... no."

While Argus worked through whatever he needed to work through, Jack noted that Gene appeared to be okay, his breathing soft and regular, everything seemingly normal again.

"What else did she tell you?"

"What part of I don't fucking remember, don't you understand?" Jack said.

Argus's eyes went cold. "Then perhaps you are of no use to me. Unless...you're holding out on me."

The sensation in Jack's body flared up again, growing tauter until he broke into a cold sweat.

"What is she planning?"

"I don't know, okay? I don't know."

Energy rushed through him again, making him dizzy, as if he was becoming pure light.

"You can do better than that," Argus said.

As the light within him diminished, Jack crashed back to the ground as if he'd fallen twenty stories, but he hadn't moved an inch. He could barely breathe.

"You remembered something, didn't you. Something she said, perhaps? Tell me."

"She...she called herself a disciple. I swear—that's all I—I remember." Jack gasped.

He was so out of it, he barely heard Argus mutter something about "the Collective," but he had no idea what it was or what it meant.

As Jack's breathing leveled again, he noticed Argus staring at him as if trying to decide what to do with him.

"Let's say I believe you," Argus said, "and that's a big assumption, but let's say I do. What use could you possibly have to me now?" Not waiting for an answer, he continued. "None, it seems." He turned to leave the room. "Unfortunately, the only one who might be helpful has already lost her mind—well, most of it, anyway." He took two steps toward the door.

"You touch a hair on her head, and I swear to God, I'll kill you myself."

Argus shook with laughter. When he faced him again, Jack wondered how he'd ever thought he was human. "What makes you think I haven't already?"

Jack tried to push himself up despite knowing he was under Argus's control, and he was suddenly struck with a stronger paralyzing force. And when the pain inevitably followed, he barely felt it.

Before he blacked out, he heard Argus chuckle again.

"Oh, my sweet Jack. I think I'll enjoy killing you most."

Chapter Twenty-Nine

EMERY COUNTY, UTAH
About 70 miles west of Moab

The sun was still half above the horizon, and we'd made it deep into the desert when Ilka finally woke. As expected, she was disoriented and a little combative, as fruitless as her efforts were.

"No!" Ilka screamed, trying to run. But in her weakened condition, she didn't get very far before she tripped and fell to the rocky desert floor. Flailing, she rolled to her back and let out a deafening scream.

I flinched. This was one of the reasons I'd chosen such a remote location. I placed a hand on her ankle and brought her under my control, freezing her movements. "There," I said. "Isn't that better?"

Her terrified eyes stared up at me. "One of them! One of them! One of them!" she screamed. "Lied to me! All of you. *Lied.*"

"I didn't lie to you. Argus and the others lied to you."

"Promised you would leave!"

"And Argus never left, did he? He's been here the whole time...toying with you."

"Promised me, promised…Lied." She muttered to herself, her eyes glassy, gazing in front of her into the vast expanse of nothingness. It was an expression I recognized all too well.

"He messed with your mind, didn't he?"

She didn't say anything. How could she? She didn't know what he'd done. They never remembered.

"And they say I'm the one using forbidden magic." I *tsk*ed. "Even I don't do that."

"Before Argus."

"Yes, but people with your abilities don't usually experience symptoms this severe until they're in their seventies. You're how old?"

Ilka remained silent, only stared up at me, terror still plain in her eyes.

"He should have at least had the decency to put you out of your misery. You're practically useless in this…state."

Ilka went still at that, her eyes taking on an intrigued gleam.

"You know they lied to me too?" I asked. "Made me promises? My whole life, strung me along like a fish on a hook. Fed me lies about what it meant to be good…to be pure. Promised me a life superior to others. All I had to do was follow the rules, do as I was told, and trust in them. In the Collective." I clenched my fists, my knuckles turning white. "But it was all a lie."

"Need me," she said.

"Yes." Maybe I could get through to her.

"One of them!" she screamed again.

Well, so much for that. "Yes. We've established that, haven't we?" I regarded her, studying her. "How did you discover us all those years ago?"

A wry glint appeared in her eyes, similar to one I'd seen in her son's. "Not as discrete as you think you are."

I cracked a small smile at that before tightening my hold on her, and she let out another scream. "You started all this. You found them out; you were going to hunt them. Why didn't you finish?"

"Promised me," she gasped.

"Yes. They lied to you. I know. Why take the deal though? Why not wipe them out then and there?"

To that, she didn't answer.

"Isn't it nice that life has presented you with a second chance?" I smiled down at her. "Help me, and you'll finish what you started."

I cinched my hold on her the slightest bit, and she tensed—but didn't scream.

"Don't you want to be set free? As I have been set free?" I paused. "Do you know what it does to you? Your *gift*, as your mother called it? It eats away at your brain until it's nothing but fried eggs."

Ilka's expression took on a new terror, one that had nothing to do with the hold I had over her.

"It makes you forget who you are, who your family is. It makes you forget how to eat, how to drink, how to *breathe*. You're halfway there already. What do you think will happen when you start developing the real symptoms?"

"What do you want from me?" The words were breathed into the air, like a prayer, like a curse.

"Help me, and I'll help you."

"How?"

"I can end it. Set you free. Don't you want that?" I paused and added, "Help me, and your children may make it out of this alive."

Somehow, still, she seemed unconvinced. *Fine, enough. This oughta do it.*

I closed my fist, wringing her essence out like a wet towel. She didn't scream, but my guess was it wasn't from lack of trying.

"You will help me," I said. I opened my fist and released her.

She panted, her eyes wide. She nodded.

"Good," I said. "Now. Let's get to work."

Chapter Thirty

Gene stood in a meadow, the lush, green grass brushing his knees. The sun shone overhead, but it wasn't hot, rather a perfect temperature. So perfect he couldn't tell where his skin ended and the air began. A gentle breeze blew in from the south, rustling his hair, tilting the grass, and he breathed in the scent wafting after it—dewy and sharp like unshed rain. Hints of lavender underneath it all.

Suddenly, he plunged into darkness, and he fell down, down, down, endlessly. Dread filled him, and his heart lodged in his throat, but he didn't wake up, couldn't wake up. He could only fall. He lost track of time, how far he crashed, surrounded by a never-ending blackness.

And then he was back in the meadow. Cool breeze in his hair, sun shining, the scent of rain and lavender swirling in the air. This time, he stayed there, enveloped in peace, until slowly, the scenery began to fade...

"Gene!"

Jack startled him awake, cradling his face, as his worried eyes roamed over him. He released a soft puff of breath when Gene met his gaze and then pressed a soft kiss to his forehead.

Gene took in his surroundings, the meadow now Jack's hospital room. "What is it? What happened?"

"Argus was here." Jack stepped back, his hands dropping from Gene's face. "We need to get Maggie and get out of here. He's going after our mom."

*

When they made it to the assisted living center, it was too late. Ilka was gone. Jack and Maggie were distraught. The whole situation oddly made Gene want to call his own mother, despite knowing she wouldn't have a kind thing to say to him. She'd be polite, maybe, but that wasn't the same as kind.

"I'm going to kill him," Maggie said. "He's dead."

Gene watched, leaning against his car, as the twins paced in front of him in the center's parking lot, walking in opposite directions, the same stormy expression on their faces.

"I have some silver bullets in my trunk," Maggie continued as if this were a normal conversation and she wasn't seething with rage. She flicked her chin toward Jack. "You?"

"You know me—" He lifted his shirt, flashing his sidearm and a knife strapped to his hip.

Gene pinched the bridge of his nose and pushed himself off his car. "We don't know for sure Argus took her—if she was taken at all. Besides, you can't go off killing people!"

Jack and Maggie stopped in their tracks and turned to him, as if they'd forgotten he was there.

"I know you're new to this," Maggie said, "but this is how it works. This is the hunting part of *tracking and hunting* monsters. We find a monster, and we kill it." She paused, challenge in her stance. "What did you think we did once we found them?"

Gene ground his teeth. "And what if he's not the one who took her? What if she simply wandered off? Killing him won't help you find her."

Jack regarded him curiously. Maggie, on the other hand, crossed her arms and lifted her chin proudly.

"Then what do you suggest, genius?" she asked.

Gene pulled his badge from his hip. "How about some good old-fashioned police work?"

*

Alone, Gene entered the lobby and scanned the space. The city police had already come and gone, but a sense of anxious tension lingered among the staff. Although it wasn't unusual for someone in Ilka's condition to wander off, it certainly wasn't good for the center's reputation.

A young red-headed woman sat at the welcome desk, clearly distracted with worry. When she saw him, she forced a smile.

"Hi! How may I help you today?"

Turning up his charm, Gene walked over and gave her a smile of his own. She relaxed a bit. Her nametag said her name was Sarah.

"Hi, Sarah. I'm Sergeant Bradshaw with the Utah State Bureau of Investigation."

Her anxiety returned in full force as he showed her his badge, her eyes growing impossibly large.

"I'm investigating a missing person—nothing official quite yet—and I was hoping you could help me out."

"We, uh, we already filed a missing persons report with the city earlier this morning..."

Gene did his best to ooze confidence. "Like I said, my investigation isn't exactly official yet. And we often work overlapping cases."

Sarah seemed to buy it but said, "I don't know how I could help."

"Oh, I'm sure you can. You practically run this place if I had to bet." Gene continued as she lost some tension in her shoulders. "I need to know who's visited this facility in the past, let's say, thirty-six hours. Employees and guests. Surely, that's something you can help me with, right?"

Sarah turned sheepish. "No—I mean, yes. Yes, I can get that information. But...I don't think I can give it away..."

Come on, come on. Say the magic words.

"...maybe you need a warrant? I don't know."

There you go. "Well, we could go that route. I can talk to your supervisor, and we could certainly work something out. Although..." He pulled the guest book lying on the desk toward him. "This has pretty much everything I need, doesn't it?"

"Um—well. It doesn't include employees."

Gene hummed contemplatively and began leafing through the book absentmindedly, letting the silence drag.

"Y-you don't need a warrant?"

"It isn't required by law as long as I have consent to conduct a search. Besides—I'm not performing a search. I only need a quick peek at your visitor records. Copies would be fine."

Sarah folded her lips together, her eyes dancing around nervously. "I won't get in trouble if I give them to you?"

Gene closed the book and leaned forward in one smooth motion. He gave her a wink. "It'll be our little secret."

Sarah hesitated for half a second longer before she began typing on her computer, and a few minutes later, the printer was running. She pulled the pages off and passed them to him.

"This is a list of our employees and their schedules for the last month. You can take a picture of the guest book."

Gene gave her an appreciative smile as he did. "Thank you." He folded the employee list and stuffed the papers in his back pocket. "And Sarah? Where's the bathroom?"

"Oh, um. Go down the hall behind you all the way to the end and turn right. You can't miss it."

He smiled and winked again. "Thanks for your help today, Sarah. You have a good day now."

She flushed and gave him a small wave when he backed away.

As he turned and headed down the hall, Gene fought off the feeling of guilt churning inside him. He cast a quick glance over his shoulder as he made it to the end. Sarah was out of his eyeline. Instead of going right as she indicated, he turned left toward Ilka's room.

It looked the same as it had when he'd come with Maggie. The bed was unmade, and a few shirts and socks were thrown about here and there, but nothing suggested a struggle. As he turned to leave, he caught whiff of a faint scent.

Lavender.

He needed to see the security footage. Wracking his brain for where the security room might be, Gene figured it would be nearer to the facility's lobby and office space. He retraced his steps to the lobby. At the end of the hall, he found a door labeled "Staff Only." He tried the handle but needed a keycard to get in. Gene cursed under his breath and headed out to the lobby.

Sarah wasn't at her desk when he returned. A bad, stupid plan started forming in his mind.

It took a few minutes, but eventually, a staff member passed him, wheeling a cart full of food toward the patient rooms. He followed a hundred feet behind her. When she stopped to make a delivery, he swiped her badge from the cart and used it to unlock the staff-only area. Once he had the door cracked, he tossed the badge back in her direction.

The door led to a short hallway lined with half a dozen closets and rooms. The closets were mostly used for supplies, and one of the rooms at the end of the hall appeared to be the break room.

A few feet into the hallway, though, Gene found what he needed: the security room. The handle gave when he tried it, and he released a breath of relief. Closing the door after him, he found an empty desk and chair inside. Three computer monitors sat all lit up and divided into four camera feeds. It didn't take him long to find the on-duty security guard taking a smoke break at the side of the facility. Gene would have to be quick.

"Come on, come on," he muttered, clicking through the camera feeds. It took him a minute to find the one monitoring the corridor outside Ilka's room. Scanning backward in the recording, he tried to see when she left but didn't find anything. *Exterior cameras, then.*

Not sure which angle he should check first, Gene clicked through them all, going back at least fifteen hours. He checked between the old footage and the current view of the guard on break. The front camera was clean, as was the rear. It wasn't until he scanned the west-side feed that he came across anything of note.

Gene moved quickly through the file, so on the first watch, it looked like a camera flash, it was so quick. He stopped, rewound, and played the recording at three-quarter speed. A bright, blinding light flashed at 07:02, and it lasted for twenty seconds. Once the light was gone, Gene saw nothing out of the ordinary.

He pulled up the parking lot camera and scanned to 07:02:20. After a few seconds, he noticed a wheelchair seemingly pushing itself toward the rear of the lot. He zoomed in on Ilka sitting in it, passed out. The passenger side door to a silver sedan opened on its own, and Ilka was lifted into the passenger seat. Six seconds later, the driver's side door opened, and the car started up and pulled out of the lot.

Who the hell is driving?

Gene managed to get a plate number, and he scribbled it down.

Suddenly, he heard footsteps and voices approaching the room. He glanced over to the live feed of the security guard—but he was no longer there.

"Shit."

Gene scrambled to copy the recording to a flash drive before the door to the security room opened.

"Excuse me, you can't be in here. Who are you?" The burly guard put his hands on his hips.

Sarah stood behind him, and she seemed on the verge of a panic attack.

"Sergeant Gene Bradshaw. I was waiting for you to get back. The door was unlocked."

The guard grunted. "Well, it shouldn't have been, and *you* should have waited outside. Do you have a warrant?"

Gene licked his lips, trying to come up with a way to get out of this. Out of sheer dumb luck, his phone rang. He flipped it open and said, "Hello? Yes, I'll be right there."

"Uh, Uncle Gene?" Prue said on the other line.

"Yeah, uh-huh. Copy that."

Prue giggled. "Do you need to call me later?"

"Sounds good," he said.

She laughed again before hanging up.

He closed his phone and turned to the security guard. "That was my CO. I'll have to get what I need from you later. Thank you." He squeezed past the guard and escaped the room.

As he exited into the parking lot, Gene let out a hysterical laugh. *Holy shit.*

*

When he returned to his car, the twins were arguing.

"It's like you don't care!" Maggie said.

"Seriously, Mags?"

"Well, why are we waiting around for Gene to—"

"Gene has a lead, thank you very much," Gene said, coming to a stop next to them.

Maggie had the decency to at least look embarrassed for whatever she was about to say—for a little while, anyway.

Jack turned to him. "What'd you find?"

Gene relayed what he'd seen on the security cam footage, and both of their frowns deepened. Having met them separately, Gene hadn't given it much thought, but with them standing next to each other, it was uncanny. They had the same exact eyes—a light green that could almost be blue in the right light. They even had the same freckles dotting their cheeks, the same crow's feet at the corners of their eyes. And yet, Gene could spot the differences too—Jack's slightly more pronounced jawline, Maggie's curlier hair, Jack's longer and skinnier nose. All differences so subtle he might not have noticed ordinarily, but after having spent so much time with each of them, he could see them clearly.

"Only a handful of creatures don't show up on camera," Jack said, pulling Gene from his thoughts. "And it can't be any of them. She's not a vampire, not a ghost, not a goblin—"

"I'm sorry—a goblin?" Gene cut in.

"They're too small and fast. Cameras simply don't pick them up."

"Yeah, that's not what caught me off guard there."

Maggie huffed. "Great. So, we know what it isn't. Still." She threw her hands up and slammed them against her thighs. "Back to zero."

"Well." Gene held up his notebook. "Not exactly. We do have a plate number."

Maggie seemed to accept that as positive, if only barely. "How long will it take to run it?"

"Shouldn't take long. Let me call the office, and I'll have someone check on it."

As he stepped away to make his call, Jack and Maggie returned to bouncing theories off each other. Gene had a budding theory himself, but he wasn't sure he should share it. He was still new to all this, after all.

It didn't take long for the officer to give him a name. He thanked them and turned back to the others.

"Well?" Jack said.

Gene hesitated, staring at his phone.

"What is it?"

He looked up, meeting Jack's eyes, then shifted to Maggie, who watched him curiously.

"You got an ID." It wasn't a question.

"Yeah, the car was registered to..."

"Spit it out," Maggie said.

"It's registered to Dana Martin."

Maggie's lips pressed together in a thin line. And then she was moving, too quick for them to stop her as she hopped in her car and sped away.

Jack and Gene rushed to his SUV and did their best to follow her.

"Where do you think she's going?" Gene asked.

"Probably to go strangle Dana; that'd be my guess."

"That's not what I meant, smartass."

"Far as I know, Dana and Kurt were at Maggie's house. Although, if her husband's around, they probably moved over to my mom's house in Sandy."

Gene merged onto I-15, heading south. After a few miles, he

spotted Maggie's car and cut around traffic to get in the lane behind her. She didn't try to shake him, so he let himself relax a bit, and his mind turned to this new evidence.

It didn't sit right with him. Something felt wrong, off, too easy.

"What do you think the chances are that both Dana and Argus were lying to you about who they are?" Gene asked.

Jack turned toward the window. "I don't want to believe it. It's harder for me to swallow. Argus was one thing, but Dana? I've known them my whole life. We grew up together. They're the extra sibling I never asked for." He faced forward again. "What type of car did you say it was?"

"Silver sedan, pretty nondescript."

"Hmm…Dana drives a green Mustang, and as far as I know, that's their only car."

"So, what, you think they're being framed?"

"Maybe? It'd keep us off the trail of the real culprit, wouldn't it? I mean, look how Maggie's reacting."

Gene didn't say anything, instead letting the silence sit and stretch. He was still ruminating on his theory but wasn't sure he should say anything. He was so out of depth in this area, he didn't want to get laughed at. Though surely, Jack wouldn't laugh him off…would he?

"So those things you mentioned earlier, they don't appear on camera because…?"

"Well, as I said, goblins are usually too small and quick that the cameras don't pick them up. Ghosts don't have a physical form, so there's nothing for the light to reflect off of and produce a picture. And as for vampires, you've heard about them not having a reflection, I'm sure. No idea what causes that, but it's true all the same."

Gene could feel Jack's stare.

"Why do you ask?" Jack said.

"All those things don't show up on camera for specific physiological reasons, right?"

"Yeah…"

"What if this thing, whatever it is, what if it chose not to show up?

What if it was deliberate, a way to hide itself?" Gene asked.

"What, like it can turn invisible?"

"I was thinking more of a spell of some kind."

It was quiet for long time after that. Gene figured Jack was thinking of a way to break it to him that his idea was ludicrous.

When Jack finally spoke, he said, "I never would have thought of that."

Gene released a breath he hadn't realized he was holding. "Are witches not a thing?"

Jack tilted his head from side to side. "Yes and no. They're basically extinct."

"Extinct? Aren't they human?"

"Yes, but...no? We have evidence of their legitimate existence from hundreds of years ago. Actual humans wielding magic. But witch trials—the ones you've heard of and the ones you haven't—wiped them out. And witches now—they're nothing more than your local Wiccans. I haven't heard of a human wielding actual magic in this century."

"So, it's not as simple as reading spells and boom," Gene said.

Jack chuckled. "No. It's not that simple. From what I've read, it requires years of learning and practice. And a bloodline, which is why they're mostly extinct."

"I don't get it," Gene said. "You say that witch trials wiped them out, that you don't have record of anyone using magic in the last hundred years, but they're 'mostly' extinct? What does that mean?"

Jack went quiet, and then, "Some theorize that the witch bloodlines survived, but they're broken. That the power, the heritage, has been corrupted, so it expresses itself in the form of pure chaos. Modern-day, actual witches can't wield magic. Magic wields them."

Gene tried to process that.

"Like my mom."

Oh.

"All that aside, your theory's not bad. Though it probably wasn't a spell. Maybe it was something the creature can do—" Jack said, not-so-subtly shifting the conversation to more pressing matters. "Maybe it's not so much invisibility as it is camouflage."

"Like a chameleon?"

"Exactly— Hey, she's exiting." Jack pointed toward the exit coming up in less than a quarter of a mile.

Shit. Gene had gotten so caught up in their conversation, he hadn't been paying attention to Maggie. Cutting across multiple lanes of traffic and earning a myriad of middle fingers and angry honks, he barely managed to make it.

"Nice driving there," Jack said.

"Shut up."

Chapter Thirty-One

They pulled into the driveway right as Maggie got out of her car and charged up to the house. Jack didn't wait for Gene to come to a full stop before he flung the door open and jumped out after her.

Catching up to her, he blocked her way. "Hey, hey. Slow down."

Maggie tried to step around him, but he caught hold of her wrists. She grunted in frustration. "Ugh, let me go!"

"Whoa, what's going on here?" Dana said from behind them.

Maggie wrenched her wrists away from Jack and tried to launch herself at Dana. Jack barely managed to hold her back.

"Where is she?" Maggie screamed. Jack struggled to hold her.

Dana said, utterly confused, "Who?"

"My mother. I know you—"

"Maggie!" Jack cut her off. "Think for one goddamn minute, will you?"

"You heard Gene! He said—"

"It was a car!" he yelled. In his periphery, he saw Gene approaching, but he stopped a few feet back. "Let's not jump to any conclusions yet."

Maggie looked at him, her angry eyes brimming with tears.

"Let's talk to them, okay?"

Maggie closed her eyes and lost all her fight, leaning forward as Jack wrapped her in a hug.

"Somebody want to clue us in?"

Maggie tensed at the sound of Dana's voice, and she pulled away from Jack.

Jack turned. Dana, and now Kurt, stood on the steps of the garage, leading up to the back door. In an attempt to lighten the mood, Jack cracked a smile. "What, you didn't catch all that?"

Dana only shook their head.

Gene came up and stood beside Jack and Maggie. He gave Maggie's elbow a squeeze. A beat passed. Gene cast a glance at the rest of them, and then, edging toward the house, he said, "Come on. It's time we catch you all up."

*

"The car was registered to me?" Dana said. "That's just weird. My car isn't even registered under Dana Martin."

"Huh?" Kurt said.

"It's registered under an alias. I'd never be so stupid to drive a car registered under my legal name, especially if I'm about to go commit a crime. Who do you think I am?"

Jack laughed when Gene pinched the bridge of his nose.

"I'm going to pretend I didn't hear that," Gene said.

"So what now?" Kurt asked.

"Well, it's as Maggie said earlier," Gene said. "It's time to hunt them down."

Jack looked at him and almost didn't recognize him. He'd only been gone for a few days, and Gene had already jumped headfirst into this life. It made him smile, but it also broke his heart a bit. This wasn't an easy life. And he'd dragged him into it.

Gene met his gaze and winked.

Jack cleared his throat. "Okay, where's mom's 1998–2001

journal?"

And they got to work. Jack combed through their mom's old journal. He highlighted any lines mentioning lack of animal or insect activity on dead bodies, anything mentioning lavender. He found a few lines here and there, but they were a little difficult to understand and put it all together. These were the years their mom had started to lose herself a little, and it showed in her writing. He decoded the few lines he found and passed them over to Maggie for her to make sense of.

Then, Jack started working through Gene's case files, including the ones he'd put together on the murders out of state. The Ohio and Kansas cases appeared nearly identical to the Moab kills but with one notable difference: the bodies had definitely not been moved. The pictures at those scenes were *bloody*. When he switched over to the cold case files, Jack was impressed by all the work Gene had done on it over the years.

"It's interesting. Lavender was actually left at these scenes," he said.

Gene hummed contemplatively, bending closer to him. "And why did they only kill animals and not humans?"

"Okay, assuming this religion angle, maybe it's a ritual."

"Not a bad idea," Gene said. "Hey, Mags, did you ever finish going through the journals from back then?"

"We did... No joy," she said. "But didn't you say they were active sometime in the early history of the LDS?"

Gene nodded.

"Well, we have tons of journals from then too... Let's see." She pulled a couple of books off the shelf and tossed them to Gene. "Maybe there's something in one of these."

As they started in on those, Jack went through his mom's journals again, this time searching for anything related to rituals. He decoded a few things, but none of it seemed all that promising. His eyes growing tired, Jack paused to stretch. Ambling over to the kitchen, he poured himself a glass of water. He leaned against the counter, his gaze going fuzzy as his thoughts wandered. They felt so close. As though they were on the cusp of figuring it all out, and yet, he wondered if they ever would. The answer seemed as if it was barely out of reach, like he could see the outline and yet, it felt totally unreachable at the same time.

Jack took another sip of water before making his way back to the study. He sat down and paged through his mom's journals from the late nineties to early 2000s again. He'd started decoding when he felt someone staring at him and turned his head to Gene regarding him with intense concentration—that is, not *him*, but the journal resting on the table before him.

"Hey," Gene said, reaching for the journal, "can I see that for a sec?"

Jack passed it to him. "You probably can't read it, but have at it."

Gene held the journal up close to his face. "I'm not exactly trying to read it. I…I think I see something."

Gene stood and walked over to the lamp in the corner. Curious, Jack followed him. Squinting at the page, Gene held the journal up to the light.

Then, his eyes widened, and he offered the book to Jack. "Look at this."

Jack stepped closer. "What am I looking at?"

"Between the lines, above the writing, what do you see?"

Jack didn't see anything, only his mom's scribbles, haphazard notes in an intricate code that—

"Holy shit." Jack swiped the journal from Gene to inspect it more closely.

Faint and barely visible—writing appeared between the lines, so faded Jack couldn't tell if it was invisible ink or not.

"Can you read it?" Gene asked.

At this point, Maggie had joined them. She peered over Jack's shoulder.

"It's pretty faded," she said.

"I don't know…" Jack muttered. "Hold on; I have an idea." He took a seat at the desk and turned on the LED lamp as he did. Using a pen, he tried to trace the faded writing, giving his best guess to the partials as he went along. When he finished, he decoded it before reading aloud.

"They promised to leave if I didn't track them. Told me they'd leave Utah alone. I think they're lying. Not telling me something. Argus involved. Nothing can be trusted. Need to wipe them out while I have the chance. Silver doesn't work on them, must use..."

Jack paused. The next translation wasn't perfect...*methods*? He continued aloud.

"Must try methods used to kill immortals."

He huffed. "She says it as if it's obvious."

"Well," Kurt said, "if silver don't work on them, our options are a little limited. Killing immortals usually involves a process. Got to go for the head or the heart or both."

"Both is probably the safest bet," Jack said.

"Hang on," Gene said. "I think I got something..." He'd apparently continued searching through the journal from the 1890s while Jack had been decoding.

He turned a few pages back and forth before reading aloud.

"July 18, 1846. On their journey West, Young and his followers, 'Latter Day Saints,' as they call themselves, have acquired practices which are of great concern. One who calls herself Lou Ann Everett divides the Church. She leads a group of disciples who want more from life than is natural to receive. She promises them salvation, a life elevated from others.

"It is a lie.

"She is not one of them. Rather, she, along with a handful of others who have infiltrated this Faith, is a devil feeding off the naïve disciples she has recruited to her 'Collective.'

"I first encountered one in the southeastern tip of Oregon Country. He approached me in a tavern, and I hate to say that he seemed harmless, human. He was alluring, something about him drawing me to him. By the time I realized my mistake, it was nearly too late, but luckily, I always carry a knife. I stuck it in his gut and shoved him away from me. It seemed to affect him little. So, I ran.

"I became obsessed. I tracked him to a commune farther west in the middle of nowhere. That was when I saw his group. They looked human enough, but now, seeing them together, I could tell they were devils. Not humans. Devils are deceivers, and they were no different.

"I followed them, studied them. They needed sleep as we do, so I waited until one of them drifted off by himself, and I captured him. I held him for days, experimenting. Silver was harmless to him. As were many of the usual methods we use to kill others like him. He did not seem to experience pain in the same way.

"I found there was only one sure way to kill him and others of his kind. The eyes are key. That is where they store their power. To extinguish the Light, you must first flood them with it. Only then will you submerge them in an eternal Darkness."

The voice of Jack and Maggie's ancestor lingered in the air for a few heavy moments after Gene stopped reading.

Gene released a breath. "Well, what the fuck does that mean?"

"It means you were right," Jack said. "At least, partially. It's some kind of religion of monsters."

"But how do we kill them? Why are your relatives almost intentionally vague about that?"

"Okay, hold on. Before we can even get into this, we need to figure out a way to find Mom," Maggie said. "My bet is, we find her, we find

Argus. Or maybe the one who took Jack."

"Agreed," Jack and Gene said at the same time.

"So, what's the plan, then?" Kurt asked.

They started hashing out logistics for a plan, but Jack found himself zoning out, their voices growing distant until they faded away completely. And then a very familiar feeling washed over him, like a current, wrapping itself around each and every bone in his body, from his distal phalanges to his parietal bone. Peace enveloped him—a breath of time, liminal, ethereal; he floated above it all, light as air.

And he fell to the floor, his body seizing, tight with pain. Unlike in the past, the pain never subsided, but it did change. It shifted, centered over his chest. He gasped for breath. Suddenly, he couldn't see, his vision nothing but darkness.

In the blink of an eye, his sight returned, everything gray except for a bright purple light stream emanating from his sternum. It looked like a path, stretching up into the air and winding its way out of the study and into the house, going on indefinitely, almost as if leading him somewhere, and he was compelled to follow. And then he heard her voice in his mind.

Come and see me, Jack. Bring your friends.

Chapter Thirty-Two

A thud sounded behind him, and Gene turned to see Jack, having fallen from his chair, seizing on the floor in pain.

Shouldn't have taken him out of the hospital.

Gene rushed to his side and knelt beside him. "Jack?" he said, unsure if he should try to touch him.

Jack's eyes flashed open, now a pale yellow instead of green—iris, pupil, whites and all. Gene met and held Maggie's gaze, and then Jack gasped, clutched at his chest. He blinked and tried to sit up but fell, his spine arching off the floor, his whole body tense. The fit seemed to last for an eternity, but in a heartbeat, Jack lay prone, flat on the floor, breathing heavily.

The room was silent, save for Jack's ragged breaths. Then, he sat up slowly, taking hold of Gene's hand as he did.

"You okay?" Gene asked. Jack's eyes were still yellow. *Why are they yellow?*

Jack released a sound that failed at being a laugh. "No." He gently put a hand to Gene's cheek. "I can't see your face. Only...the distant outline of it." He continued, softer, barely audibly, "Knew it was you though."

Gene squeezed his fingers. Jack squeezed back.

"What happened?" Maggie asked.

"Help me up," Jack said, bypassing Maggie's question.

Gene and Maggie supported him as he pushed himself to standing. Dana and Kurt hovered nearby. Once on his feet, Jack took a step forward and sighed in what sounded like relief. When he stepped backward three steps, however, he fell again, convulsing in pain. It only lasted a minute, but when it was over, Jack's eyes were wide, his forehead dotted with sweat, his skin flushed.

"What the fuck?" Dana muttered.

Jack turned onto his front and crawled back to Gene and Maggie. Gene could only stare. Once he reached them, Jack stood on his own. He still breathed heavily when he said, "I think I know how to find her."

"Mom?" Maggie asked.

"Maybe. If she's with *her*..."

"Jack, what happened?" Gene asked, echoing Maggie's unanswered question.

"She spoke to me. And I can feel..." He reached a hand out, his fingers dancing around.

"You're not Mom," Maggie said. "You can't—"

"I can. It's not me. It's her. She's pulling me to her. When I follow it, the pain lessens. When I don't, well..."

Gene locked eyes with Maggie. "It could be a trap," he said, more to her than Jack.

She grimaced, an odd gleam in her eyes—half desperate, half awed. A little worried. It wasn't all that dissimilar to how she had regarded her mother when they'd visited her. Only now, they held a mix of uncertainty that hadn't been there before.

"I've done stupider for less," she said finally.

"All right-y then," Kurt said. "Let's get packing. Where I'm from, you don't go walking into traps unarmed."

"Well, you would know," Dana said.

"Hey!"

Dana chuckled and left the room, an indignant Kurt on their tail.

Gene faced Jack again, aware of Maggie watching them. She didn't say anything, then inched out of the room after her companions.

"You can't see anything?" Gene asked.

Jack smiled sadly. "Everything is gray like a black-and-white movie. I can see objects, but people… They're chalk outlines at a crime scene. Only shapes, no features."

Jack cradled Gene's face with both hands this time and pressed his forehead against Gene's, and Gene closed his eyes. "But like I said, I knew it was you."

"You're sure about this?"

Jack took a shaky breath. "No. But I think it's our only option. I can only endure this for so long."

"What's it feel like?"

"It's hard to describe." Jack paused. "You remember when we did that nonlethal weapons training, and we had to taze each other?"

"Yes…"

"It's kinda like that, except this never subsides? It may be a little subtler, but it's pretty similar."

"Jesus."

Jack smirked. "You better be careful, or I'll tell your mom you used the Lord's name in vain."

Gene had the urge to swat him upside the head—good to know that impulse would never go away. "This is serious, Jack."

His smile dimmed. "I know…The rest has finally come back to me."

"You mean your memories from when you were gone?"

"Yeah. This seems to have finally flipped the switch."

"Well, what do you remember?"

"Darkness. Endless darkness," he said, his voice low. "And then light. Bright, all-consuming light. And a hand reaching through to pull me out. Her hand."

"Like in the security camera."

"Appears so." Jack scrunched up his face. "She told me, *'I brought you out of the darkness, I can throw you back in.'*" He heaved a breath.

"I don't want to know what will happen if I ignore her call."

Gene swallowed. He didn't want to know either. He took Jack's hand. "Let's not find out."

"You're good at this, you know."

"What, hunting?"

"Yeah."

Gene scoffed.

"You are. You seem to like it too."

Gene considered that. It was hard to say he enjoyed this work. He certainly didn't feel good at it; in fact, he couldn't remember ever feeling so incompetent. He didn't have the same knowledge base as Kurt or Dana, certainly not the same as Maggie or Jack. Though, at the same time, none of them had the level of experience he did tracking and interrogating suspects. It was also hard to deny that he felt invigorated in a way he hadn't in years.

Gene pushed the thoughts aside. They had more pressing matters. "Jack, what are we going to do?"

Jack sobered. "Dana's right. We try to use the immortal methods first. Theoretically, that should do it."

"And if it doesn't?"

"Then, we follow in my great-great grandfather's footsteps. We run."

*

Gene observed as Kurt loaded weapons onto his truck. He wasn't sure about some of them. Most were illegal, and the ones that weren't seemed excessive.

"Hey, don't go getting your panties in a twist now," Kurt said, catching Gene's uncertainty, as he lifted a chest of grenades into the bed of his truck. "We probably won't use most of this stuff."

As if that makes it better. "I'm technically still an officer of the law, you know."

Kurt continued lifting boxes into the truck. "Eh, are you though?"

Gene didn't answer, and before he could think of one, Dana and

Maggie joined them, carrying the last of the supplies.

"So we'll follow along in Kurt's truck." Maggie said, then glanced around. "Where's Jack?"

Gene gestured to his SUV on the street. "Waiting patiently for us to get going."

Having finished loading up the truck, Kurt moved to get into the cab, but Dana paused to extend a hand to Gene. When he reached out to take it, they gripped his forearm.

"Good hunting," they said.

Gene could only nod as they turned to join Kurt, leaving him alone with Maggie.

"This is a bad plan," he said to her.

"We don't really have a plan."

"That's exactly my point."

"Even if we had all the time in the world, there's still not much we can prepare for. All that stuff we found earlier? It was helpful, gave us insight into what this thing is—or might be. But...we still don't know what she wants, what she's planning. We can only stay inside studying for so long before we go out there and hunt. Besides, if we don't come to her, who knows what she'll do?"

To Jack.

She ran her hands through her unruly hair and pulled it into a loose ponytail.

"I know, it's— I guess it's just happening pretty fast."

"That's how this life is." Maggie gave him a pat on the shoulder before turning to the truck. "Better get used to it."

Her words sat with Gene as he made it to his car and strapped in next to Jack, sitting in the passenger seat with his eyes closed. "Ready?"

"Go straight. I'll tell you when to turn."

*

They drove for hours, the tension palpable. If Gene veered off the right path for barely a second, Jack tensed in pain. But the farther they drove, the more the pain seemed to lessen. All the while, Gene ruminated on Jack's ancestor's journal entry.

To extinguish the Light, you must first flood them with it.

Gene thought of it as a riddle and considered possible ways to accomplish such a feat. His brain went to the most obvious places first—sunlight, fire. When he contemplated the actual act of "flooding" someone with light, nausea rose within him. None of it seemed pleasant. And he wondered about the second part: *Only then can you submerge them in eternal Darkness.* The wording was antiquated, yet something told him there was more to it. The journal entry wasn't only referencing death. There was more to this. Somehow.

"There," Jack said, pointing to a turn ahead.

By this point, night had descended, and they were in the thick of the desert, away from any of the major parks. The closest one was almost two hours north, which meant they were that far from any civilization too. His and Kurt's truck were the only two cars on the road, winding through dirt paths, surrounded by endless open space, broken only by random rock formations climbing out of the earth. Their shadows cast from the waning quarter moon only made the darkness darker.

Gene made the turn, and Jack let out a shaky breath. "You okay?"

"Yeah. I think we're close. I almost don't feel it anymore."

They drove straight for about fifteen more miles, and then Jack said, "Stop."

Gene brought the car to an abrupt halt.

"This is where the trail ends."

Gene swallowed. The others were a few miles behind them, so for now, he and Jack sat in the silence. Waiting.

He felt Jack's fingers wrap around his own. Gene took a deep breath before turning toward him.

His eyes had returned to normal, and Jack offered him a brilliant smile. "There's that face."

Gene laughed, relieved.

"You ready for this?" Jack asked.

"Nope."

"I'm not a fan of the dark," Jack said. "Mags always teases me about it, but what can I say? Knowing what's out there certainly doesn't make the dark any more welcoming."

Gene could imagine.

"Hey. I know you're not totally on board with this scrappy plan."

"I never said that."

"Not to me, maybe, but…" He gave Gene a knowing look. "I'd like to think I know you well enough by now to have an idea how you think, how you work. I've been on takedowns with you, and you don't go breaking down doors without an ironclad warrant. So come on; don't bullshit me."

"Yeah, well. I've been told that's how this life works."

Jack faced the windshield. "This is our chance, Gene," he said, his voice quiet, different. His fingers tightened around Gene's. "She opened this…this connection between us, and my guess is she thinks it's one-way. That only she can feel me, but—I can feel her, what she's doing, how much power she's using… It's—it's tearing her apart. She's spread too thin."

"So, what, she's weak?"

"No. I'm saying she's vulnerable. I'm saying if we don't strike now, we may never get another chance."

The full weight of that hit Gene, and they sat in it until Kurt's headlights emerged from around a corner, illuminating the front seats, effectively breaking the spell.

"This it?" Maggie's voice came through the walkie-talkie in the cupholder when the truck stopped beside them.

Gene picked it up. "This is it."

"Roger that."

Kurt cut his engine and lights, and Gene did the same. The previously illuminated road stretched into the night.

What now, he wanted to ask. But deep down, Gene knew.

He heard the others get out of the truck next to them. He assumed they attempted to do so quietly, but this deep in the desert, it didn't matter how quiet they were; the sounds seemed louder than if they had been in the bustle of the city.

"Well, come on. We can't let them show us up." Jack unbuckled and climbed out of the SUV.

Gene sat alone for a second or two longer, then followed after Jack. *Okay. Let's do this.*

He approached the others as they silently strapped weapons to their bodies. Dana brandished a fancy hunting crossbow, complete with a scope and a flashlight strapped to the top. Kurt hooked a standard hunting rifle over one of his shoulders and holstered two sidearms to either side of his hips. *"Silver bullets,"* Kurt had said, *"supposedly don't hurt the damn thing, but, well. Worth a shot anyway. Maybe we distract 'em, huh?"*

Maggie and Jack both went for an assortment of knives in addition to a larger weapon. Maggie pulled out an aluminum baseball bat, and Jack unsheathed a machete, its blade's edge catching on the moonlight, reflecting its sharpness. Gene felt wholly unprepared with his standard-issue Glock with normal ammo, his taser with only a few clips, and plain old handcuffs. What use would they be against a monster?

Jack passed him a machete and a knife. The machete had a heavy blade, wide at the hilt and curved to a dangerously sharp edge at the tip. Gene wasn't confident he'd be able to use it very well, but he hooked it onto his belt anyway.

They all nodded at each other, a silent understanding, as trust passed among them. Dana tapped Jack's and Maggie's shoulders and gestured forward with their left hand before moving stealthily in that direction. Maggie and Jack followed after them. Kurt did the same to Gene but headed on a different path forward, swooping down and around the open land before them. Gene drew his sidearm and kept close to Kurt, unsure of what else to do.

Kurt moved quickly and quietly, crouched low, his rifle at the ready. Gene stayed upright and swept his eyes around the area as if about to raid a suspect's house. Kurt led him to a tall pinnacle that Gene hadn't noticed. They ducked behind it for a few long minutes. Across the desert, he barely heard the others' footfalls over the sandy dirt—until his hearing suddenly cut out.

A bright, blinding white light inundated the area, the scent of lavender dancing on the wind. Gene squeezed his eyes shut, then cautiously opened one and the other. Behind the pinnacle, there was enough of a shadow to make it bearable. He worried for the others, though. Had they made it to cover?

He turned to Kurt, who pointed at him, put two fingers up to his eyes, and gestured for Gene to look around. Gene signaled with an OK, then peered around the side of the rock formation.

He waited for his eyes to adjust, but once they had, he knew they'd made a mistake.

Across the way, Jack, Maggie, and Dana were all on their knees, their bodies tense, backs perfectly straight. A woman stood before them, tall and ethereal. Her long, dark hair, contrasted by her pale skin, rippled in the gentle breeze. She reminded Gene of the earlier journal entry. She had an alluring air about her that called him to her, made him want to join his companions on his knees before her. But he resisted. He caught a movement next to her.

Oh no.

An older, smaller woman, a little shrunken in on herself, crouched next to her. Ilka.

The younger woman's mouth moved, and Gene's hearing returned as suddenly as it had gone, but he still couldn't make out what she was saying. She raised her arms out wide and beckoned Ilka closer. Ilka went to her without a fight. The woman placed a hand on Ilka's shoulder, and the woman's eyes flashed a bright purple.

Ilka's head fell back, her mouth opening wide. And the ground beneath him started to shake.

Well, shit.

Chapter Thirty-Three

EMERY COUNTY, UTAH
About 70 miles west of Moab

Flipping down the driver's side visor, I opened the car mirror and inspected my reflection. A small wrinkle had sprouted up between my eyebrows. I'd noticed it this morning, but I hadn't done anything about it. But now? Well, now, I needed my strength back. I could feel it throughout my body. It wasn't just the wrinkle.

My muscles ached, my bones creaking. As I moved, I felt weaker, more tired. That wouldn't do.

Without looking at her, I placed a hand on Ilka's shoulder. I took a deep breath, and my vision went purple, blurry, as a familiar sensation worked its way through me. It moved upward from the heels of my feet to my chest and down into my arm, all the way to my hand resting on Ilka's shoulder. As I breathed out, her energy began to seep into me. A subtler sensation, it tickled a bit, the same way it always did as it swam through my veins. The wrinkle between my brows vanished. I turned to Ilka, and as her skin began to shrink in on itself, I released her.

Now, feeling more myself, I could complete the ritual. I exited the vehicle. Inside the trunk lay a collection of items to build an altar: a small, handcrafted table; a cloth about the size of a baby blanket made of cotton and human hair; a clean, shallow sterling silver bowl; and an old leather-bound Holy Book.

Gathering the items, I carried them about fifteen feet from the car and set up the altar: the white, lacy cloth laid over the table, the silver bowl set in the middle, and the Holy Book off to the side. When I was done, I returned to Ilka. I needed one more thing from her before the others arrived. She was fast asleep now, no chance of her waking, which made what I was about to do that much easier. Using a simple needle and tourniquet, I drew blood from her left arm—about three vials worth. Now, I was ready.

I reviewed the steps in the Holy Book before beginning. I'd never completed this ritual; in fact, until recently, I hadn't known it existed. It was quite useful, though, and I had already initiated it when I'd had Jack in my custody. That had been the simple part—binding him to me. Now came the difficult bit—summoning him here.

What we did... It wasn't right to call it magic. It wasn't magic but an innate ability we were born with and forced to nurture should we plan to survive.

This ritual was the closest we got to dealing in magic, in something akin to spell work. Of course, our...faith included many rituals and rites. After all, what was a religion without a bit of pointless, drawn-out practices? But none of them produced magic. Instead, they were only placations, a façade meant to distract us from the truth.

When I first discovered this ancient Holy Book, I thought it was blasphemy, fiction. How naive I was. It only took trying one of the rituals—one of the spells—to find out they'd lied to us our entire lives. They'd always told us magic was forbidden, that nourishing our innate power was all we needed. We were taught that witches had stolen power from us to use for their own gain, that we had more power than they could dream of, so we had no need to sully ourselves with *human magic*. If we followed the Founder's teachings and stayed with the Collective, we would become more powerful than ever imagined. We would be invincible. And the tenets were quite simple to follow.

> *Kill the young; feed on them, as their youth provides the most nourishment. Be merciful; do not toy with those off whom you feed, as this will keep your soul intact. Stay faithful to the Collective, for as One, we persevere; alone, we perish.*

What they didn't teach us was how much of our potential was *wasted* by simply not using it. By focusing on youth, we were absorbing only a fraction of what we could from someone three or four times their age. By being merciful, we forewent the benefits of feeding after a fight, again affecting how much we absorbed. And the Collective? Alone, we *thrived*. The Collective hindered our absorption because we were forced to share it with others.

Learning to let go of these myths made us unstoppable. At least, according to this rogue Holy Book.

I added Ilka's blood to the silver bowl on the altar and, giving it a stir with my index finger, chanted the words. "My bonded, I call to thee." I repeated the phrase three times and waited. At first, nothing happened, and my newfound faith wavered. And then I felt it.

An electric pulse radiated from my body, reaching far and wide. It clicked into place and stabilized in me. *There you are.* Testing the strength of the connection, I wound myself around him and *squeezed*.

I felt him writhe on the other end and knew contact had been made.

"Come and see me, Jack. Bring your friends," I said, releasing my hold on him. The spell would do the rest.

*

I could feel it when Jack arrived. He and his two companions approached from the north, and I waited until they were close before opening my arms wide and releasing my absorptions into the air. Light surrounded us, a brilliant display of energy returned to the world. As the three hunters shielded their eyes, I took the opportunity to subdue them and bring them under my control. It was easy enough, as I already had Jack, and I only had to extend past him to the others nearby. I brought them to their knees.

"So nice of you to come," I said, approaching them.

The woman—Jack's twin by the look of it—caught sight of Ilka trailing behind me. Her eyes went wide, and she opened her mouth to speak. But I tightened my grip on her, and a scream ripped out of her instead.

I returned my focus to Jack. "I have to say, you had me worried there. Started thinking you wouldn't fall for it." I smiled. "I should have known better than to overestimate your intelligence."

His face twitched, but he was smart enough not to speak.

"You've exceeded expectations, Hunter. By far. It tells me I made the right choice in bringing you into the Light." I turned to Ilka, opening my arms. "Ilka, come."

The old Cartwright matriarch trudged over to me.

"Now, this may sting a bit." I placed a hand on her shoulder.

Instead of pulling energy from her, this time, I channeled it into her. As I did, her head fell back, and her mouth opened in a silent scream, sending wave upon wave of energy into the air. The ground began to shake, and my power began to wane. Pulling on the energy I had released, I drew it back into me—slowly, biding my time until Ilka was done. Finally, Ilka's mouth closed, and her chin fell to her chest. I drew the rest of the light into me, and we were plunged into the darkness once again.

I removed my hand from Ilka's shoulder, and she collapsed to the ground.

Pulling on the energy from the three hunters before me, I restored myself enough to cast light above us once again. I wasn't sure how long this part of the ritual would take. Using Ilka as a kind of antenna, I'd summoned the remaining Elders of the Collective to me, but I had no idea how long it would be until they started showing up.

I took the few minutes we had to assess the others. Jack and his sister, still on their knees, stared at their mother's unmoving body; the other one glared at me defiantly, calculated rage in their eyes. I smiled at them.

"A crossbow." I walked over and pried it from their grasp. It was heavy, and I certainly didn't know how to use it, but they had no use for it now. "Tell me, did you plan to use this on me? Did you think it'd kill me?"

The hunter seemed at a loss for words because when they finally spoke, all they managed to come up with was "Maybe."

I laughed. Holding up the crossbow, I inspected it further. They had it locked and loaded, ready to fire. I lowered it and aimed at them. The hunter lost a bit of their fight as fear seeped into their eyes.

"Please," they said.

I smiled again. "I've never used one of these before. Not that I have much use for one." I put my finger on the trigger. "Does it have much of a recoil?"

The hunter let out a scream as they attempted to move. When they were done, kneeling before me with their back straight, they repeated, "Please."

I raised the crossbow half an inch and pulled the trigger. The arrow lodged itself in the hunter's left shoulder, going almost all the way through. The hunter screamed again and let out a string of curses.

"Hmm, it definitely has a bit of a kick, but it's easier to handle than I expected." I tossed the weapon aside, sending it clattering to the ground.

I shifted my focus to the twins and wandered over to them. Taking the woman's chin in my hand, I tilted it up. "Maggie, isn't it?"

She held such contempt in her eyes it was difficult to keep that contact with her. Though, truthfully, I'd faced far scarier than her.

"I'll kill you," she spat.

"*Ooh*, shocking." I laughed, then dropped her chin and turned to Jack. "It really is such a pity neither of you inherited your mother's gift."

Jack's eyes cut to me, and I smiled.

"It doesn't matter though. Your blood will do just the same. Ilka's was so useful earlier."

Maggie twitched as if she were trying to jump at me, but as Jack knew too well, that would only cause her pain. Sure enough, she seized and shrieked so eerily similar to her mother's, it was almost as if Ilka was back amongst the living.

I *tsk*ed. "I see Jack didn't let you in on the secret. Don't worry. He was a quick study. I'm sure you will be too."

Maggie's eyes shot daggers my way.

"Anna Marie."

That voice. I spun around to find Argus, bewilderment etched on his face, standing a few paces from me.

"Ah. So glad you could make it."

Before he had a chance to respond, another Elder wandered in from the darkness, followed by another and another and another...until all nine Elders of the Collective stood under my little umbrella of Light. They gazed at one another, faces clouded in confusion, and I reveled in the pleasure of having surprised them. Argus was the first to recover.

"Whatever this is, Anna, remember our words—as One, we persevere; alone, we perish," he said in that annoyingly fake Scottish accent.

The others sounded their agreement, casting me looks ranging from contemptuous to condescending. None of them seemed frightened. None of them thought to plead for their lives. Fools.

I took a deep breath, drawing as much energy as possible from the hunters behind me, before throwing my hands forward and then tossing it to the nine Elders. Wrapping the energy around them as a lasso, I pulled them together and brought them under my will. Some of them yelled out.

"Impossible!"

"You cannot!"

"*Witch!*"

I chuckled. "Witch, huh? Is that what you think of me? As if a *witch* could do this." I stretched my hold on them all, and one by one, they screeched. Even Argus, who held out until the pain became too much. It always did. "Shall I demonstrate my skills? For old times' sake?"

I didn't wait for an answer and pulled one of the closest members to me. She was one of the teachers who had "guided" me through my youth. I gripped her head in both hands and began drawing on her power. It was a rush, a thrill. Nothing like feeding on a human. She was hundreds of years old. All the energy she'd consumed, all the power she'd absorbed and nourished over that time, coursed into me now, filling me with strength and resilience. As I fed, she withered. Her skin slowly shrank in on itself like clean film. Her eyes lost their color, and her hair thinned until there was practically nothing left. I dropped her lifeless body to the ground.

"See?" I ran my thumb and middle finger along my lips as if tidying lipstick. "Show me a witch that can do that."

"What do you want, girl?" Argus spat at me.

I flicked my attention to him and contemplated killing him too. But eight was already on the low end of what I needed to make this little spell work. So instead, I closed my fist, and he doubled over in pain, yelling out into the night.

"Any other questions?" I asked the others. No one dared speak. "Good."

I approached the twins, took hold of Maggie's hair, and dragged her over to the altar I'd built earlier. I left her there and went to retrieve her brother. With both of them kneeling before the altar, I pulled out a knife.

"I am sorry about this," I said with little inflection of guilt. "I'd grown fond of you, Jack." I put the knife to his throat.

A booming sound echoed off the rock formations around us. Then, pain wormed through me, dull and barely noticeable, but there all the same. I stared down at a hole in the left of my chest, blood staining my shirt red. Before I had a chance to react, another shot rang out, entering my body an inch below the first one. And then another struck me in the shoulder, hitting a nerve. I let out a grunt, more out of frustration than pain. I abandoned my plans for the twins for now and faced the direction of the shots, searching for the exact location from where they came.

There, peeking around the pinnacle on the far south side of the area, the tip of a hunting rifle smoked slightly. Apparently, I'd miscounted the hunters. The cocking of a gun *clicked* before another shot rang out. I dodged to the left, and the bullet only grazed me. I reached out and tried to pull on the hunter's energy, but as I did, my connection to all the others splintered like frayed wire. No. If I wanted to deal with him, I'd have to get my hands dirty. *Well...*

I charged the pinnacle.

The man wielding the weapon stepped out and kept firing, walking backward as he did. I dodged his bullets easily; although, I'd have to admit, he was a good shot, and some of them came dangerously close to me. As I neared him, I grew angrier and angrier. *Seriously, what are these hunters thinking?*

As I passed the pinnacle, I barely caught the blur of motion in my periphery before another one was on me. I had miscounted. Again. *Dammit.*

He tackled me to the ground and struggled to get the upper hand. But I wasn't going down without a fight. I kicked him, thrashed under him, hit him with open hands. He had a knife ready, and he was trying to use it but failing, his movements uncoordinated and clumsy. I managed to knock the weapon away from him and, in the skirmish, kneed him in the back. That got him off me.

I rolled away and tried to stand, but the other hunter was on me again, shooting at me. Growling in rage, I'd only made it to all fours when the man who had tackled me grabbed my ankle and pulled me to him again. My knees scraped against the ground. He kept me on my stomach and pulled my hands behind my back. Something cool and metallic clicked in place around my wrists. *Handcuffs.*

He hauled me up. But I wasn't done.

I turned and headbutted him. He stumbled back, and I broke the handcuffs, snapping the chain holding them together. As I began advancing on him, a bullet hit my spleen. *Fuck.* A damaged spleen was never pleasant.

I spun around and charged at the shorter one. He pulled the rifle's trigger again, but nothing happened. He was out. I sneered as he scrambled for another solution and was on him before he could reload or switch weapons. Unfortunately, his reflexes were far better than any human's had any right to be, and he quickly made use of his rifle as a blunt instrument. The butt hit me in the nose with a powerful thrust, sending me backward.

The other hunter caught hold of me and put me in a headlock with one arm. I elbowed him hard in the belly, but it wasn't until I hit him in the nuts that he released me. I stepped forward and punched him in the jaw. He fell to his hands and knees. I kicked him in the ribs, and he collapsed. I spat blood on him.

By this point, the short one had pulled out another gun and began firing again. I'd had about enough of that.

Reaching a hand toward him, I drew on his energy again—*fuck it.* It took too long. Trying to bring another person under my control without losing what little I had left over the others took far too much attention and concentration. But I almost had him. Almost, *almost*—

Suddenly, I lost it as light clouded my sight. An electric current pulsed through me. It wasn't painful, but it did render me useless. I fell to my knees, suddenly paralyzed.

"Gene," the gunner said, a note of urgency in his voice.

"I know," the other one answered. Unable to see, I heard him walk a few paces away, and as he stalked over to me, he muttered, "This better work."

And then my right eye went dark.

He was quick, plunging the knife deep into my right and then left eye, leaving no room for a fight, no time for defense, before I regained any movement from the taser. He did it mercilessly, smoothly, cleanly. And as he drew the knife from my left eye, my hold on the others dissipated, dissolving altogether.

Slowly, my power drained out of me. Darkness encompassed me, surrounding me in its cool embrace. And eventually, I fell to my side, where I lay panting. There was nothing to be done now. I'd failed. And all of this had been for naught. I heard someone approach. I sensed the swing of a blade before it collided with my neck.

As it sliced through me, Darkness took hold, once and for all. And for an instant, there was peace before there was nothing.

Chapter Thirty-Four

Jack stared at the head rolling away, the once beautiful woman's features distorted. Her skin had gone from pale white to gray, become wrinkled and aged. Her body stilled. Jack shifted his gaze to the man wielding the weapon that had done the deed.

If Jack thought he hadn't recognized Gene earlier, he certainly didn't recognize him now. Blood covered his face, his nose bleeding, bruises already starting to color his skin—but it wasn't all his blood. Some of the creature's had splattered on him, giving him a rugged, dangerous look. What had Gene called him at the beginning of this case? A bad boy—a description better fitting Gene now, it would seem.

Gene stood, tensed, only relaxing when the woman on the ground didn't move. He locked eyes with Jack fleetingly before shifting to something behind him. Jack turned.

Eight people—at least they appeared to be people—stood there in the desert, all recently released from the monster's hold, Argus among them. Jack adjusted his grip on his own weapon.

He wasn't sure who moved first, who fired first, but it all happened so fast, it didn't matter. Kurt was shooting again, aiming to distract more than anything else, it seemed. Dana, despite having an arrow stuck in their shoulder, had gotten hold of their crossbow, and arrows started flying, some hitting a few of the people square in the eyes. Gene barreled forward, taser in one hand, knife in the other. He tasered one of the men, bringing him to his knees, and then shoved the knife into his eyes, one by one. Jack charged in, entering the fray.

The others were different from the monsters Jack was used to fighting. They moved as humans did but had the strength of Weres and vampires. They'd clearly been surprised at the hunters' rush to attack, making the first two or three kills, dare Jack say it, "easy." But that didn't last long.

Dana was the first to yell out. Jack paused midswing to glance over at them, caught in Argus's deathly grasp. He had one hand on the arrow sticking out of Dana's shoulder, the other around their throat.

Jack's brief distraction opened him up to an attack, and someone hit him in the abdomen—hard. He flew back about ten feet and crumpled to the ground. The one he'd been fighting pursued him, and before Jack had a chance to react, it placed a hand on his shoulder. As its eyes flashed a bright purple, Jack awaited the usual sensation of pain to wash over him...

Only, it never came.

Instead, his energy slowly drained out of him as if he were running on an hour's sleep. He was tired; perhaps a nap would help. Maybe if he closed his eyes—

Suddenly, a hot spray of blood rained down on Jack as the creature's neck was cut clean through. It was as if he'd had a bucket of water dumped over him. He jolted up. And spat blood out of his mouth. Gene knelt next to the head, gouging out its eyes. When he stood, he cracked a small smile at Jack.

"I'd say sorry, but that's twice now that I've saved your skin."

And then he charged back into the fight. Jack could only watch, completely transfixed by Gene the killing machine.

Dana was still caught in Argus's grip, but Gene and Kurt seemed to be holding their own. The numbers were dwindling, down to three now. So many bodies were strewn across the rocky desert floor that Jack wondered how they'd clean it all up. But that was—

Maggie. Where the fuck is Maggie?

Jack panicked, searching the strewn bodies. *No, no, no...* He turned frantically, this way and that, and then he saw her.

She knelt next to one of the bodies. Jack swallowed and started toward her when a nearby scream pierced the air and drew him back. Later, he thought, and turned to Argus, charging him.

Jack was almost to him when Argus held up a hand and stopped him in his tracks. He tried to move, tried to take a step forward, but his feet wouldn't obey. Jack wondered how he'd ever thought Argus was human. His eyes hadn't turned purple like the others. Instead, they were a blazing red.

Argus grinned. "I told you I'd enjoy killing you. But maybe I'll kill your friends first. Anna Marie may have been on to something—toying with her food before eating it. Something about it gets the blood pumping. Especially in you. And that—" He strode over to Jack, dragging Dana by the arrow, leaned into his space, and took a deep sniff of his neck. "—well that only makes you more delectable."

Jack couldn't help but look worriedly at Gene, something Argus didn't miss. He laughed.

"Don't worry. I'll save him for last. And I'll kill him nice and slow. Just for you."

A shot rang out, and Argus dodged to the right, pulling Dana in front of him as a shield. The bullet grazed their arm.

"Fucking hell, Kurt, *shit*," Dana grunted.

"Go on, Mr. Taupin. Keep shooting and see what happens," Argus called out.

Jack surveyed the scene. Kurt and Gene had taken out the other two. Argus was the only one left. Kurt didn't lower his weapon, but he didn't fire again. Gene stood near him, eyes hard, assessing the situation in the way only a cop could. He adjusted his grip on his machete and rolled his shoulders, taking a stance that said he'd be ready to go whenever the opportune moment presented itself.

"Smart boy," Argus said. "Now, now, I don't want to do this; I promise. But I'm afraid she's left me no choice. You truly have her to thank. So, when you go to blame someone, please leave my name out of it—" His ridiculous speech was cut off as a knife flew through the air and entered his skull from behind, the tip poking through his left eye.

And that was the moment.

Dana and Jack were released, and Jack scurried to Dana to help them away from the excitement. Meanwhile, Gene ran toward Argus. Maggie threw another knife and, with impeccable aim, hit his other eye. Gene tazed him in the neck and claimed the killing blow by chopping off Argus's head in one clean swing.

And like that, it was over. They could breathe again.

The rising sun had started to turn the eastern sky orange at the horizon, the various rock formations casting short shadows along the ground and the bodies littering it. Jack watched numbly as Kurt and Dana—clutching their bleeding bicep—started dragging them into a pile. *Yes, that's one way to ensure they don't come back.*

He joined Maggie on his knees next to their mother's unmoving form. For what it was worth, she seemed at peace. He placed a hand on his sister's shoulder, and she fell into him. Jack sensed Gene's presence near them, but he didn't intrude and let them grieve together.

Jack wasn't sure how long it was before he heard the crackling of a fire behind him, felt its heat, smelled the ghastly scent of burning flesh. Pulling Maggie closer, he gazed upward as the smoke danced into the early morning sky.

Chapter Thirty-Five

Maggie lay, staring blankly up at the ceiling. She supposed she could get up and start her day now that it was a socially acceptable hour to do so. She'd been awake for a while, unable to get more than about an hour of sleep. That was how it had been for the past week or so. Since they'd returned from the desert, she couldn't stay asleep, her mother's face haunting her dreams.

She threw the covers aside and got up.

Downstairs, she found the house still and quiet. Cold. The heat didn't run down here during the night and wasn't set to kick on for another hour or two at least. She pulled an Afghan off the couch and wrapped it around her shoulders as she shuffled into the breakfast area. She pulled a chair out and turned its back against the table, facing the window to the backyard.

The sun rose beyond the fence, lighting up the sky. The rear gate stood open, and tracks of footprints and pawprints led through the frosty grass to the easement behind the house. Elliot had taken the dog for a run, leaving their bed cold and empty. She wrapped the blanket tighter around her shoulders.

An hour later, Elliot returned, a sheen of sweat glistening on his dark skin, puffs of breath visible in the cool morning air. Their dog trotted in behind him and ran past him onto the deck as Elliot paused and closed the gate. He turned and dodged left, then right, and the dog got down low, her tail high in the air, wagging wildly. Elliot charged at her, and she jumped and ran around the yard before leaping onto the deck and waiting for him to let her in the door. His face was bright and happy as he made his way up.

Maggie's chest tightened. She wished she had the courage to tell him. She wished, not for the first time, that she had a normal life.

He came into the house, and the dog bounded up to her. Maggie gave her some scratches behind her ears.

"Oh, you're up," Elliot said.

"Yeah."

He took a seat at the head of the table.

She didn't look at him.

"Still can't sleep?" he asked.

She shook her head.

"Maggie—"

"I can't talk about it," she said.

"You can't talk about it to *me*."

She remained silent and kept her eyes trained out the window.

Elliot unzipped his jacket, the sound echoing through the silence of the room. His gloves went next, then his shoes, a quiet *thump-thump* under the table as he slid them off his feet without untying them. She always chided him about that, telling him the back of the shoe would wear out quicker that way, but he never untied them before taking them off. Never.

"I'm sorry," she said finally.

"I know this is a difficult time. But if you don't tell me anything, how am I supposed to— I'm just...I'm worried."

She finally turned to him. His face conveyed that and more. And she wanted to spill it all to him, every last thing. Tell him about the realities of the world, about the monsters in his closet and under his bed.

Tell him she knew how to kill them, that her brother did too. That her mother died caught up in the middle of it all. And that one day, she could too.

She didn't say any of that. Instead, she lashed out. "You don't miss a beat, do you? You can't let it go. How many times do I need to apologize for not telling you about Jack?"

He stayed quiet as her angry words hit him, but to Maggie's annoyance, he didn't rise to it. "Maggie. Please. That's not what this is about, and you know it."

When she didn't respond, he continued.

"You know—*you know* you can trust me, and yet you won't open up."

"You never cared before. Why now?" Her voice came out raspy.

"Yeah, well...maybe I should have. I never thought you were..." His eyes danced down to the space between them and then up to meet hers. "Look. It doesn't matter right now. You don't have to tell me anything, Maggie. You can trust me, but you don't have to tell me anything."

Why not? Why don't you want to know?

"I love you," he said, as if sensing her need to hear it. "But you don't owe me anything."

Something broke in her, and she started crying.

In an instant, he crouched in front of her and pulled her to him. She buried her face in his sweaty neck and let it all out. Sobs wracked her body, and he ran soothing hands down her shoulders until eventually, her breathing slowed, and her tears began to dry. She pulled away.

"I'm sorry," she said again. "I didn't mean to—" She couldn't face him.

Elliot tilted her chin up, forcing her gaze to his. "Losing a parent isn't easy. But it gets better. I promise."

She took in a shaky breath. She'd lost her mother, but in a lot of ways, she'd lost two parental figures this week. And she'd killed one of them. Maggie closed her eyes, the image of Gene cutting through Argus's neck flashing behind her eyelids.

"But it will suck for a while," he continued.

A small laugh ripped out of her.

"And I'll be here. Whether you want to talk or not. Okay?"

She leaned forward and gave him a brief kiss. Breaking it, she rested her forehead against his. "Thank you."

He gave her a smile before rocking on his heels and standing. "Come on." He lent her a hand. "I'm making you some breakfast, and then you're going to take a nice long overdue nap."

She took his hand. "Deal."

*

Elliot was gone three days later. Called away on business. Maggie had managed to sleep the past few nights, though, whether from exhaustion or grief or some mixture of the two, she didn't know. Her head felt lighter, clearer.

So now it was time to get to work.

She called Gene first. The decision oddly came to her naturally. Dana and Kurt wouldn't be able to hide the pity in their voices, neither of them very good at keeping their emotions at bay. And Jack...well, they'd talked over the past week, of course, but neither of them had said much. They'd agreed to let her take the reins of arranging the funeral since she was still more connected to the hunter network than he was. But other than that, their phone calls had been full of dead air and small talk, each of them processing their grief separately. The same way they had when Granddaddy had died. Yet this time, when they called each other and the conversation lulled, neither hung up, instead choosing to listen to the other breathe through the line, the simple sound comforting enough.

Gene seemed surprised she was calling. "Hey, Maggie?"

"What, am I not allowed to call you anymore?"

He didn't say anything, his silence speaking for him.

"What are you doing?"

"Um, I'm at the office. Trying to...well, I guess the only way to put it is...well—"

"To cover it all up?" Maggie offered.

"Yeah." He paused, and she heard the sound of his chair squeaking. "Hey, I realize I never reached out to you after—"

"It's okay," she said, her throat getting thick.

"Right." It sounded as if he'd been hearing that a lot lately. He didn't push though. "Well, I'm sorry anyway, okay?" He paused again. "You need anything?"

She swallowed the lump in her throat and continued on business as usual. "I need you to help me write up a journal entry for everything that went down in the desert."

"Oh? I've, uh, actually been working on that."

"Really?"

"Yeah... Yeah, I found this book that Anna Marie was using. It's a spell book or bible or something—"

She heard the sound of the phone being shuffled around as if he was rifling through papers on his desk.

"It's interesting," he continued. "I've become a little obsessed with it. Do you...do you want me to come by later? We can go over it?"

She blinked. Gene was no longer very green about this, was he? "Uh, sure. Yeah. Come over whenever."

"Great, I'll be by in about half an hour."

She laughed. "Careful, now, Gene, or you'll start to make my brother look good."

He chuckled. "I don't think that's possible."

Grinning when she hung up the phone, Maggie felt lighter than she had in a long time.

Chapter Thirty-Six

When Gene got to Maggie's house, he noticed hers was the only other car in the driveway, which he thought was a little weird, but he didn't read too much into it. He didn't bother knocking and let himself through the unlocked door. It was warm inside, if a little too warm, and it smelled of vanilla and cinnamon.

"Mags?" he called.

"In the kitchen!"

He made his way there and found her wiping down the counters, a "snickerdoodle" candle lit on the bar. She smiled at him when he approached.

"Hey," she said.

"Been keeping yourself busy?"

"Honestly, I haven't been doing much since— Elliot left three days ago, and already, the kitchen is a disaster." She filled the sink with hot water and soap. Gene noticed a stack of dirty dishes nearby that were certainly planned sacrifices to the sink gods.

He took out the old leather book and set it on the bar carefully before he took a seat. Maggie shut off the water, shoved the dishes unceremoniously into the sink, and joined him at the bar, wiping her hands on a dish towel tucked into her pants.

"This it?" she asked.

He nodded. It was nothing special. The book was sewn together, the front and back covers made of wood and bound by leather. Rusted metal pieces garnished each corner, and two metal clasps adorned the fore edge of the front cover to keep the book closed. The cover itself was blank, no decoration at all. Inside, pages and pages of parchment were covered with writing and illuminations in varying states of fading. The book had clearly gone through numerous edits, and countless authors had contributed to it over time. Gene had also found evidence that the book had been unsewn and resewn to add new pages or change the binding. Based on the style of lettering, it was obvious later pages had been added several years later.

Gene might have gone down the rabbit hole researching ancient manuscripts...

"This is amazing," Maggie said, leafing through the pages gently. "So, give me the scoop. What were these guys?"

"Well." Gene told her everything he'd been able to figure out so far.

They were some species evolved monster. Not quite witches, not quite human, not quite succubae. They fed off energy, more specifically *light* and years. The older a person was, the more they could consume. They believed that sharing the power amongst a united Collective would help them tame it, prevent it from consuming *them*. However, this book argued the opposite. That by sharing power, they would spread it too thin, forcing them to feed more often than necessary. This book referenced "the Collective" as a group its authors had split from, though some authors still seemed to believe various tenets from the Collective's ideals.

The most recent entries were the most interesting. They included spells and rituals that could be used to destroy the Collective.

Pointing at this section, Gene said, "This is the page it was opened to when I found it. Check it out."

He pushed the book closer to Maggie, who peered at it, trying to read the top of the page. "Binding ritual?"

"Yeah. I think that's what she used on Jack. The ritual binds the caster to the subject and allows them to create a—a pathway, I guess, to find them." He turned the page. "And look—this is the altar she'd set up." He indicated a diagram of an altar with its various components labeled. "She didn't get to finish this spell. She started it though. She needed—"

"What?"

"She needed a witch's blood to complete the ritual. Preferably from an old bloodline."

Maggie's face shifted and closed off. "That...explains some things."

"It does. Part of this spell entailed using one of you as a conduit of sorts..." He trailed off, unsure if he should go into all the details.

"A conduit," Maggie repeated, her voice blank. "What does that mean?"

"From what I can tell, these creatures can't perform magic themselves; they have to have something for the magic to pass through. In this case, she needed a witch to summon others of her kind to where we were."

"A witch." Maggie closed her eyes. "My mom wasn't—she couldn't—"

Gene pressed on gently. "She couldn't wield magic, but...magic could wield her. And that was all Anna Marie needed. You and Jack...neither of you could have done it."

"So why bother with us at all?"

"Part two." He turned the page again.

She read the first step out loud. "Drain two witches—or witches' kin—of their blood." She stared at the page and said quietly, a little defeated even, "What was the point of all this?"

Gene wasn't sure if she was asking a rhetorical question, so he answered softly, "She wanted to destroy them. This ritual would have consolidated power from the entire Collective, and she would have absorbed it all."

Maggie didn't say anything, so he kept going.

"If she'd have done that, the Collective would have died instantly, their bones, skin, and flesh turning to dust. And she'd have become 'all-powerful.'"

Gene paused, pulling the book closer to him. He turned to a page in the middle from one of the authors who was more of a centrist on the issue. "One author argues that the Collective is correct in that they cannot survive on their own. That if they did not share power, and it was all consolidated, the one to hold the power would, essentially, explode."

He had no idea if they were right though. All he knew was what Jack had told him before they headed into Anna Marie's trap—that she was vulnerable. The more power she drew, the more vulnerable to an attack she was. And *that* had proven to be true. So, who knew what would have happened if she had killed Jack and Maggie and completed her ritual? Maybe she would have become God. Maybe she would have exploded into a brilliant sun, light raining down upon them.

Maggie stood abruptly and left the room, disappearing in the direction of the office at the front of the house. Gene didn't try to follow her, suspecting she needed space to process it all. Only, she returned a minute later, carrying a leather notebook.

She handed it to him. "I thought I'd get you something."

He opened it and leafed through the pages, every one of them blank. He glanced up at her, skeptical.

She smiled. "Welcome to the team." She handed him a pen too. "Now, time to write it all up."

He accepted the pen and laughed a little, then scribbled his name in the inside cover with the month and year below it. "Is there a reason this stuff isn't all digitized by this point?"

"Okay, Mr. Flip-Phone, I thought you'd be more open to old school."

"I mean, come on. I'd take typing over handwriting any day."

"That's not how we do things," she said, returning to the sink and pushing up her sleeves. She stuck her hands into the soapy water. "Get to it."

He stared down at the first blank page. *Okay, so where to begin?*

*

Gene didn't make it to the office again that night. The next day, he was surprised to see Jack at work, but he didn't tease him about it. Not that he didn't want to, but Jack already looked like a kicked puppy.

Instead, Gene took a seat at his desk and said, "What's up?"

"Oh, nothing. Got an earful from the captain this morning."

"Why, exactly?"

"Apparently, my stint in the hospital isn't enough to excuse my absence from work. It's okay, honestly. He didn't suspend me or any-thing, only gave me a lecture and said next time I screw up, I'm gone." Some of Jack's usual confidence seemed to return to him. "He can't af-ford to lose his best detective, though, so we'll see if he keeps to his word."

Gene snorted. "Well, you're already showing up earlier than me, that's gotta count for something."

Jack grinned. "Hey, it's briefing day, I never miss briefing day."

Gene could list on one hand the number of times Jack had been on time for briefing days. "Speaking of which...I left the files for our two closed cases for your review." He placed special emphasis on "closed."

"Oh?" Jack reached for the folder and opened it. "Animal attack, huh?"

"What else could have done it?"

"You're gonna have to work on that. You sound too sarcastic."

"Do I?"

Jack had an amused smile on his face as he continued perusing the case file. "Did you talk to the ME?"

"Yep. He agreed."

"Wow, you two agreed on something for once? Damn, things have changed."

Gene swatted him on the arm.

The briefing went smoothly enough. They fielded a few questions about how they could tell it was an animal and why it had taken them so long to come to this conclusion. Gene lied through his teeth and bull-shitted something about animal hair they'd found on the bodies—

something that had gone unnoticed by the medical examiner at first look. He did feel a little bad about passing the nonexistent blame to the ME, but it was something no one would ever follow up on, seeing as this case would never be prosecuted.

When he was done and had taken his seat next to Jack again, Jack nudged him under the table with his knee. Gene looked over at him, and Jack gave him a wink as if to say, *good job.*

Chapter Thirty-Seven

About two weeks later, Maggie arranged a funeral for their mother, and Jack was oddly excited for it, hoping it'd help him and his sister move on. It was a traditional hunter affair. Dana, Kurt, and some members of other families traveled to Salt Lake to attend. And Gene came along as well, though it became clear he didn't know what he was walking into.

When he showed up at their mother's house, dressed in a black suit and carrying a casserole dish, Jack realized he should have filled him in.

"Um, what is this?" Gene asked when Jack ushered him inside.

"Yeah, I, uh, realize I didn't exactly tell you what our funerals are like."

Gene took in the scene, and Jack wondered what he was thinking. All around them, the house had been decorated in bright lights, all different colors, like Christmas lights. Lit candles sat on nearly every table in the place, along with framed photographs of his mother from all walks of her life. Her first journal rested on one of the tables for all to read—though because of the code, not many did. Upbeat music drummed in the background, playing throughout the house, filling it with a happy sound. And the milling people all wore varying shades of green and yellow—his mother's favorite colors.

"No," Gene said finally. "It's beautiful. It's a celebration of life. Which is what it should be."

Jack smiled at him, turning it into a teasing smirk as he pried the dish from Gene's hands. "Thanks for the food though. I'm sure someone will want to eat whatever this is."

"I'll have you know those are my mother's famous funeral potatoes."

Jack quirked an eyebrow.

"We are in Utah, aren't we?" Gene's fake innocence wouldn't work on him. He took off his suit jacket and undid the top few buttons of his shirt in an apparent effort to appear more relaxed. A flirtatious glint appeared in his eyes. "What, you don't have a buffet and punch for your guests?"

Not bothering to respond, Jack dropped the dish on the table near the door and led him into the house. He felt more than heard Gene follow him.

The house opened up into the living room. There, they found most of the guests, sitting around the coffee table, passing around a bottle of Unicum—a bitter, fruity liqueur from their mother's native country, Hungary. Joining them, Jack was sure it wasn't their first round, though how anyone could drink more than one or two shots of it, he had no idea. He liked the taste of it, but it was strong and bitter, and any more than two shots would risk alcohol poisoning.

"Detectives!" Dana yelled. "So nice of you to join us!"

Maggie poured each of them a shot of the dark liquor. Jack grabbed the glasses and passed one to Gene.

At Gene's uncertainty, Maggie clarified, "Hunter tradition. You always have at least one drink in honor of the fallen. Even if it's a nasty-ass Hungarian liqueur that tastes like burnt tar."

Jack swirled the liquid and gave it a sniff. "I think it's good."

"Me too!" Dana added helpfully.

Maggie raised her glass. "To Ilka."

Everyone lifted theirs.

"*Egészségedre*," Maggie said—Hungarian for *cheers*—and downed it.

"*Egészségedre!*" came the reply from the crowd—who could pronounce it anyway.

Jack downed the bitter drink and immediately felt its affects. He looked over at Gene and couldn't help but feel sorry for him. Unicum was definitely an acquired taste, and if Gene's rapid blinking and almost cartoonish scowl were anything to go by, it was certainly *not* to his taste. He caught Jack's gaze and coughed.

"I agree with Maggie," he rasped.

"Come on," Jack said, grinning. "I can't have you two ganging up on me."

Gene was still grimacing. "That is the worst thing I've ever had. And I once had a margarita made with peach schnapps and lime Gatorade."

"I'm sorry—what? That's not a margarita. Why the hell would you drink that?"

"Do you think soon-to-be lapsed Mormons know how to make good drinks?"

Jack laughed. "No, but I thought you'd at least have brains."

Gene stepped closer, hooked a finger into one of Jack's belt loops, and drew him nearer. "I was barely eighteen," he said, his voice neutral, as if he wasn't invading Jack's space, as if he wasn't staring at him like he wanted to devour him.

Jack didn't say anything. He'd forgotten what they were talking about.

Gene smirked. "Cat got your tongue?"

"Oh, shut up," Jack said and kissed him. Gene's lips were soft and gentle. Warmth radiated from him and surrounded Jack in a sweet embrace. He'd be content to stay like this for a while. That was at least until his friends started heckling them.

"Get a room!" Dana yelled.

"Y'all this is *not* the time!" Kurt said.

"Really? In front of my liquor?" Maggie quipped.

Jack and Gene pulled apart, laughing. The tips of Jack's ears burned. But he hadn't felt such a lightness since they'd returned from the desert. Since his mom had died. And now, surrounded by friends and family, being teased about something so trivial, he knew all was going to be okay, that all was right with the world.

At least for now.

Epilogue

ONE MONTH LATER

Gene was running late. Leave it to government administration to slow things down. He was on the last form, but it was taking forever to fill out. What governmental form had free-response questions? What was this, the SAT?

Finally, he finished. After checking to make sure he hadn't missed a spot to initial or sign, he stapled it and dropped it off at the front desk on his way out of the office.

He got into his car and headed over to the diner down the street—where he was supposed to be fifteen minutes ago. Jack flashed him a smile as Gene slid into the booth across from him.

"Since when do I beat you somewhere?" Jack asked.

"If I remember correctly, I was out of bed before you this morning."

Jack just leaned back in his seat, throwing an arm across the top of it.

"You order already?"

"Yep." A comfortable silence settled over them until the waitress dropped off two coffees.

Jack reached for the cream and sugar. "So why the early call time?"

Gene took a sip of his coffee. "I wanted to talk to you about something."

"Okay…" Jack sounded unsure.

"Don't worry. I'm not firing you or anything." Gene paused. "Kind of the opposite."

"What?"

"I'm quitting the force."

Jack blinked at him, seemingly at a loss for words.

In the silence, Gene grew nervous. "That's why I was running late. Had to fill out, like, five different forms before anything was official. And they were all twelve pages long. It was a lot. I had a major hand cramp by the end of it because, of course, everything had to be done by hand. The government is allergic to computers, so—"

"Gene," Jack said. "Why didn't you tell me?"

"I wanted to, but…" He'd asked himself that same question as he'd wrestled with the decision over the past few weeks. Finally, he said, "It was a decision I needed to make on my own. And I only made up my mind last week."

"Okay. So, what are you going to do, then?"

Gene didn't say anything. But he didn't have to. Jack figured it out.

"No way," he said. "You're turning full hunter, aren't you?"

"You were right. I did enjoy it. And I feel useful, you know? Like I'm doing good. Not that I didn't feel that way during my time on the force, but…it's different somehow. I'm reaching somewhere the police can't."

Again, he was met with silence. He didn't like that. He wanted Jack's snarky commentary. He wanted him to say something that made him feel he hadn't made a huge mistake.

Eventually, Jack spoke. "Maggie said something to me after we got back. She said you'd taken to it. Quicker than anyone she'd ever seen that hadn't grown up in the life, anyway. She said you were a natural."

Gene waited for a "but."

"And I saw it too."

Gene released a breath.

"I was only gone for a few days," Jack continued, "but in that time, you'd become a different person. And when I saw you out there, in the fight... I gotta admit, you rivaled Dana."

Gene huffed a small laugh. "Thanks. To be honest, I don't know what came over me. I think I was so focused on staying alive and keeping you alive I didn't stop to think. I simply acted."

"That's what good hunters do." Jack paused, and then he said, "So, what, you're leaving me all alone on the force?"

"You'll be fine," Gene said. "We need at least one person on the inside. It'll help us access autopsies and stuff more easily."

Jack laughed. "That was exactly my argument all those years ago. It's only now paying off. But I don't know if Maggie would agree."

"Actually, Maggie and I talked about it yesterday. She was very adamant one of us stay on the force."

Jack's eyes bulged. "You told Maggie but not me?"

Gene shook his head, a smile on his face. "What can I say? She's more approachable."

Jack's response was to kick him under the table.

"Ow!" It didn't hurt.

"Oh, come on. I barely touched you."

Before Gene had a chance to respond, the waitress came by and placed a big plate of pancakes between them, along with a bottle of syrup. Jack took the liberty of drenching them with it, and as he set the bottle down on the table, Gene snagged the plate and cut the first bite.

"Thanks for breakfast," he said around his mouthful.

"Hey! My pancakes!"

"Truce?" Gene said, nudging the plate toward the center of the table again.

Jack narrowed his eyes at him, but then they softened into puddles of affection. "Fine."

Picking up his own fork, he cut himself a bite and held it up. They clinked forks and dug in.

Acknowledgements

First and foremost, I'd like to thank my family: my parents, John and Karren, and my brother, Jacob, for always supporting me and my dreams, for being my cheerleaders and my rocks. To my friends, Micaela, Jackie, Braden, and Ryan for letting me info dump on them about my characters, for putting up with random phone calls just to ask, "What word am I thinking of?" For being my best friends.

This work would not be what it is without my peers in my writing groups. Each one of you inspires me. To the LA folks—Jacob, Gareth, Jack, Sean, Megan, Jil—y'all gave me ideas, helped me think through the plot, and read every last word of the first draft. Thank you for sharing your insights and your enthusiasm for this book. To my locals—Morgan, Brian, Cassie—thank you for being my second sets of eyes and for picking apart my sentences. You are awesome.

Thanks to the entire NineStar Press team. A special shoutout to my editor, Elizabetta, who was a great collaborator and who took a chance on me and my writing. You helped bring Jack and Gene's story to life, and for that, I'm eternally grateful.

Finally, thank you, dear reader for taking the time to read this book. I hope you enjoyed it. Until next time!

About the Author

L. Alyse likes stories that push against and break genre norms. She likes to crack genres open and write about what's most interesting. She's fascinated by characters who are different, unapologetically themselves, and morally complex. Her stories are filled with dark, twisty plots that let the characters breathe.

When she's not working or writing, L. loves to crochet, watch TV, cuddle her dog, and spend as much time outside as she can.

Email
lalysewriter@gmail.com

Website
www.lalysewriter.com

Instagram
www.instagram.com/l.alyse_writer

Connect with NineStar Press

Website: NineStarPress.com

Facebook: NineStarPress

X: @ninestarpress

Instagram: NineStarPress

BlueSky: NineStarPress

Threads: @ninestarpress

* 9 7 8 1 6 4 8 9 0 8 5 8 3 *